TATTOO BLUES

MICHAEL McCLELLAND

POCKET BOOKS
New York   London   Toronto   Sydney

POCKET BOOKS, a division of Simon & Schuster, Inc.
1230 Avenue of the Americas, New York, NY 10020

Copyright © 2004 by Michael McClelland

Published by arrangement with ibooks, inc.

ISBN: 0-7434-7732-4

First Pocket Books printing February 2005

10 9 8 7 6 5 4 3 2 1

POCKET and colophon are registered trademarks
of Simon & Schuster, Inc.

Cover design by Rod Hernandez
Cover art by Marc Gerber

Manufactured in the United States of America

For information regarding special discounts for bulk
purchases, please contact Simon & Schuster Special Sales
at 1-800-456-6798 or business@simonandschuster.com

Also Available

Oyster Blues

This book is for my mother,
Betty Moon Swofford

Acknowledgments

The Cedar Key history and the ecology I have presented in *Tattoo Blues* are entirely factual. So is most of the geography, though I did invent a state park and move a few buildings to make room for Mamasan's and the Pinprick Palace. The characters are all fictional, though in several cases inspired by the inhabitants of that enchanted village.

Thanks to the people of Cedar Key, who kindly tolerated my nosy questions whenever I visited their island home. I am grateful to Wittenberg University, whose financial support made my research possible, and to Barbie Ryals, who introduced me to Cedar Key. Thanks, too, to Aly Birt, who gave Amelia the emu her name and kept me from putting old expressions into the mouths of young characters.

Most of all, I am passionately grateful to Patti Birt, who loves me and pampers me and keeps me inspired in so many ways. Patti dear, you are my muse.

What dreams and speculative matter for thought arose as I stood on the strand, gazing out on the burnished, treeless plain!

—John Muir,
on his arrival at the Cedar Keys
October 23, 1867

Prologue

"Says here there's a fire-breathing sea monster killing people in Seedy Key," Maxmillian J. Pire said, tossing a folded-over copy of the *St. Petersburg Times* on the desk of his best reporter. "Go check it out. And quit drinking on the job, too."

Robin Chanterelles reluctantly looked up from her half-finished crossword and blinked her boss into focus. "I can drink anything I want on my lunch hour. Besides, it's a soft drink. What's a Seedy Key?"

"I dunno. Island somewhere, I guess, down in the Keys. And it's not your lunch hour, it's 10:30 in the morning." Pire hoisted the Mountain Dew can off of Chanterelles' desk and sniffed it suspiciously, dropped it into a trashcan and glared down at the slender slip of a girl before him. Hard to get aggravated at somebody who looked like she belonged in junior high, but he gave it his best effort. "Have I fired you yet this week?" he asked.

"No, but it's only Tuesday. This says there's only one person unaccounted for, and that she was wearing a dragon costume when last seen."

"Right, even better. The sea monster mistook her for a mate and kidnapped her. And it's Thursday."

"And it's Cedar Key, not Seedy."

"Cedar Key, right. Where's that?'

"Gulf Coast, west of Gainesville."

"Too bad, there goes the monster-moving-on-Miami headline. Love that alliteration," Pire said. "Any decent-size cities on the Gulf Coast?"

"Tampa, St. Pete, Pensacola, Panama City." Apalachicola, she thought, but didn't say. "Why me?"

"Because some fresh sea air might do you some good. Because I'm tired of seeing your lazy ass here in the newsroom. Because nobody else is free."

"Thanks boss. I love you too."

Don't I wish, Pire thought. Maybe ten years ago, when he had less belly and more hair. And more ethics. Something about ethics impressed the young ones. So okay, maybe twenty years ago. Pire shifted the wet cigar stub from one side of his mouth to the other and leaned in close, his voice low so none of the other half-dozen or so reporters in the room could hear him. "Because you did such a kick-ass job on the man-eating emus."

Chanterelles groaned. "I didn't do that. You did that."

"Had your by-line on it."

"It also had the startling news that six people were attacked by a rampaging giant bird intent on carrying them off in bloody chunks."

"So?"

"So there were three of them, and they weren't attacked, they were startled. And the emu wasn't rampaging, it was rummaging through a trash dumpster."

"Rummaging, rampaging, what's the difference?" Pire pulled the cigar butt from his jaw and leaned in close to Robin, knowing full well that his breath reeked of tobacco and last night's garlic. "Like I keep telling ya, kid, this ain't the fucking *New York Times.*"

"You got that right, Max. This sure as shit ain't the *New York Times.*" Or the *St. Pete Times*, or the *Podunk Times*, or even the *Destin Daily Diary*. This is *The Weekly Alarm*, a two-bit scandal sheet with no integrity, no respect and no ethics. Also, 29 million fanatically dedicated readers, an annual budget larger than many countries, and the third-largest circulation in the Free World. Chanterelles scowled and thought longingly of the gin-laced Mountain Dew dripping its life away at the bottom of her trash can.

"Get a car from the motor pool, something small with good mileage. Tell Eddie to assign you a photographer. Anybody but Pincushion; don't want him scaring the locals. Play up the abducted waitress angle. Sex and sea monsters, terrified townsfolk, you know the drill. Six hundred words, by Sunday." Max straightened and headed off towards his office, mumbling and scratching his side. Robin waited till he had rounded the corner before she retrieved the Mountain Dew.

Damn near empty, she thought. Bummer. She slid her big floppy purse into her lap and searched around among the pens, pads and spare tampons till she felt the familiar smooth coolness of a Boodles minibottle.

She cracked it open, poured it surreptitiously into the Dew can, and allowed herself one long sip before picking up the phone and dialing the photo desk.

"Hey Eddie," she said when the editor picked up. "Pincushion there?"

"So. Hey, okay, right, tell me again, why is it you won't let me drive?"

"Because you make me nervous, Pincushion," Robin said. She snapped off the CD player the multi-colored young man squirming in the seat beside her had just turned on. "Can't you take a chill pill or something?"

"Nervous? What, me, no shit? Wow, didn't know that, didn't know that. So, okay, Cedar Key, that's like way south of Miami, right? That's like a eight, ten-hour drive."

"Right. You just relax, and I'll tell you when we get there. Take a nap or something."

Pincushion nodded enthusiastically, popped open the glove compartment and began rifling through the contents. Robin caught a glimpse of something ten-drilly etched in red and blue ink emerging from the top of Pincushion's neckline. "That a new one, P?"

"What? Where?" Pincushion stopped trying to pry open the vial of replacement car fuses in his slender fingers and looked frantically out the car windows.

"On your neck, Cushion. The thing with the ten-tacle."

"On my neck? Oh, yeah, right right right! That's

Lorelie. She's a mermaid, mostly, but with teeth and shit. Wanna see?" Pincushion sat up and tried to yank his Offspring T-shirt over his head. Robin and the seatbelt he was wearing stopped him. "Maybe later, P. Couldn't really appreciate it right now."

"You couldn't?" Pincushion voice sounded hurt, even muffled as it was under his half-off shirt.

"Because I'm, you know, driving."

"Oh. Oh right." Pincushion pulled the shirt back down, grinning like a happy turtle. "Later then, right?"

"Right, P. Later." Chanterelles was actually mildly interested. Not in the monster mermaid herself, but rather in seeing where Pincushion's artist had found a place to put it. Pincushion's hands, neck and face were as pristine as the day he was born, but every other inch of him sported some sort of tattoo. Fantasy creatures mostly, unicorns and dragons and such. He had "left" and "right" tattooed on each corresponding foot, a single snake that wound its way from his left ankle to his right shoulder, and a map of Middle Earth embossed on his back. Newsroom lore held that he had the name of the woman who'd taken his virginity stenciled on his prick, and that it couldn't be read unless he was excited.

"So, tell me again why Maximilliman assigned me to this one? 'Cause I didn't really think he really liked me all that much."

"Nonsense, P, the man loves you. He mentioned you specifically when we were talking which shooter was right for this gig."

"Dude, that is so cool. Because the man, you know, the man is like a god to me. Or a mentor, even. The mentor-god of journalism." Pincushion nodded thoughtfully; to Robin's dismay, he was dead serious. "You know, he taught me like everything I know about journalism."

"Oh god. Everything?"

"Everything. Well, except how to shoot. I already knew that. And how to develop pix. And digital, I taught myself that. And taking notes and getting names and stuff, I guess Eddie taught me that. And libel, and open records laws and all that sorta shit, I learned that in j-school. But everything else I know about journalism, I mean *everything,* I learned from Maxmillian J. Pire."

Robin slipped her hands into a better grip on the wheel of the LTD sedan and glanced at her shooter from the corner of her eye. "You went to journalism school, Pincushion?"

"Yup. See?" Pincushion held his right arm out, tugged up his shirt-sleeve and pointed at a tattoo just below his elbow—a cartoon alligator wearing an orange sweater adorned with a bright blue "UF," flanked on one side by a hookah-smoking caterpillar and on the other by three black bands of inky barbed wire. "University of Florida, class of oh-oh. Taught me everything I know about journalism. Go Gators."

"Right, gay goaters." Robin eased the LTD into the line of traffic heading out of Orlando on Highway 408, then pulled her purse over to her and started rummaging around in it with one hand. "Pincushion, you see that cooler on the back seat?" she said. "Be a good lad and dig me out a Mountain Dew."

Five minutes later, with drink in hand, cruise control engaged and Pincushion happily playing with the LTD's automatic door and window buttons, Robin found her mind wandering back to her assignment. A fire and a couple people missing, big deal. Accident, arson, maybe insurance scam gone wrong—nothing new there.

But why in the name of Edward R. Murrow would someone in sleepy little Cedar Key be wearing a dragon suit?

Chapter One

The ornate Chinese symbol tattooed on her practically perfect left breast, Desiree Dean always planned to tell anyone who was curious enough to ask, translated to "Stop staring at my boobs!" She doubted, though, that she would actually have the nerve to say such a thing to a total stranger (or anyone else, for that matter). She was also beginning to doubt that anyone was ever going to ask, about her tattoo or her breasts. Still, the tattoo was a badge of honor for Desiree, and she took great comfort in knowing it was there, and knowing what it meant.

What the tattoo really meant, Desiree knew down in her secret heart, was "golden dragon," which she thought was sublimely sexy. She had no idea that a more precise translation would be "with hot sauce." Desiree had labored under her pleasant illusion for several weeks now, and was likely to continue doing so for quite some time. After all, how many Florida Gulf Coast fishing village topless, Chinese food waitresses—or topless, Chinese food waitresses' customers, or topless Chinese food waitresses' tattoo artists—could actually read Chinese?

Certainly not Pimlico Phil, Desiree's artist, who couldn't tell calligraphy from tire treads, or Cantonese from cat calls. But Phil did know a hot trend when he saw one, and Phil, as he so often said, was nothing if not a businessman. This was why he kept a stack of purloined Chinese restaurant menus in the back of his tattoo parlor and a handful of dramatic translations in the forefront of his opportunistic mind. This was also why the summer of 2004 saw a great many bright-eyed and bronzed beauties returning north from their summer side trips to quaint little Cedar Key sporting tattoos that proudly proclaimed "extra spicy," "with noodles," or "gratuity not included."

Pimlico Phil saw no harm in any of this; he wouldn't have done the tattoos if he had. Phil was at heart a gentle old soul, a barrel-chested, sleepy-eyed gentleman who in another life could pass as a slightly swarthy Santa Claus. But Phil had been in the business a long time, long enough to know the cyclical nature of the beast, long enough to know that he'd best strike while the fad was fresh. And he had spent quite enough time eking out a living gouging anchors, snakes and I Love Mothers into the biceps of drunken sailors and greasy bikers, always one city ordinance or a prissy new base commander away from exile and bankruptcy. That was, in fact, how he'd ended up in Cedar Key—run out of Okaloosa County and the lucrative Eglin Air Force base market by an uptight new commander with vengeance on his mind.

One little hepatitis scare, probably not even Phil's doing, and suddenly there was talk of civil fines and background checks. Phil probably could have paid the fine and maybe even passed the background check, but he knew that being on the commander's shit list meant his days in Okaloosa were limited. Best to get while the getting was good.

And that had turned out just fine. There wasn't much of a market for tattoos in Cedar Key, but costs were low. He had a little studio apartment right above his shop, and had gotten a break on the rent by agreeing to let his landlords store supplies for their busy restaurant in his back room. He liked the slower pace here, the little arts-and-crafts stores and the island-time feel to the place. And, having spent four dreadful years of his youth in the United States Navy, he liked students much more than soldiers. That was the bulk of his Cedar Key clientele—bored University of Florida students who'd driven the 60 miles from Gainesville for a weekend blowout, or snowbirds from up north seeking a low-cost alternative to the neon-lit Panama City Beach strip—and, for the most part, Phil genuinely liked his youthful customers. He didn't understand them, not one bit; it still embarrassed the bejesus out of him when a voluptuous young woman would pop open her shirt to discuss the aesthetics of a breast tattoo as if they were debating how to best dress a turkey. He wouldn't do piercings, though God knew he got plenty of requests. In tattoos, Phil could see beauty and self-expression, even if that self was expressed as a snarling Tasmanian Devil or a blood-spattered, flame-covered human skull. But piercings struck him as desecration rather than decoration. He had discussed that with some of his clients until a sweet little thing young enough to be his granddaughter explained to Phil she wanted her tongue pierced so she could give better blowjobs. Phil had blushed furiously and never asked again.

Still, Phil was a businessman. Everything he knew he'd learned from his father, and Pop had always stressed the importance of keeping up with the times. "Three things," his pop would say, "spot the trends before they get there, stay liquid, carry plenty of insurance." To that mantra, Phil had added, "Go with your strengths." In his case, that meant admitting to himself that he was a solid craftsman, that on a good day his work could rise to the level of art, but that he really did not have much imagination. So he studied the work of other artists, and he kept a close eye on what he saw on the barely dressed human canvases parading by his door every sweltering summer day. And he had placed a large placard in his window, promising that, "You bring it in, we'll put it on." That worked well; half his customers came in carrying pictures they'd ripped out of magazines or copied off a CD case. For the most part, they left satisfied.

For the other half, the impulse buyers, Phil had a dozen thick black binders packed with images and ideas to choose from. The walls of his outer shop—the backshop was where he actually did the work—he kept postered with blow-ups of his most popular designs. Leaping dolphins, leering demons, cartoon characters and big-breasted, sword-swinging women warriors—there was something there for everyone.

But even so, one night in early spring—a late night at the end of a long day, when Phil really wanted to close the shop and head upstairs for a hot-plate meal of tomato soup and beanie-weenies—an obnoxiously drunken frat boy from Memphis State had wandered in, taken up residence in front of the display case and gone through four or five of Phil's books, scornfully trashing each and every page. Phil had been right at the point of tossing him out, Pop's admonitions be damned, when the kid pushed aside a just-finished binder, stopped, and then emphatically said, "That one!"

Phil looked at the exotic design the boy was pointing at and frowned in exasperation. "You can't have that one, son," he said.

"Why not? What's it mean?"

"It means that you are fucked up beyond all recognition."

"Perfect! Fucked up beyond all recognition! Do it."

"No, I mean—"

"Do it, old man, do it! Right here, around my bicep, in big black ink. I got the money right here."

And he had, he'd produced a fine leather wallet and spread it open for Phil to see, to see all the cash his poor deluded parents had no doubt intended for textbooks and tuition. The money alone might not have convinced Phil to do it, but that "old man" crack . . . Phil shrugged, swabbed the boy's arm down good and set to work producing a perfect copy of the Oriental characters embossed on the back of the Chinese take-out menu that had been left sitting on the counter. He'd done a nice job, and did it in good time too. The boy sweated a bit and winced once or twice, but he'd strutted like a banty rooster when he left the shop, his bicep proudly proclaiming that he was a "Tasty Buffet."

Phil had felt a little bad about that. The next day, when he looked up to see that same boy striding into his shop with two muscular friends in tow, he'd felt sure he was about to receive his well-deserved punishment. He was wrong.

"My boys want 'em too," the boy said, while his two friends nodded their emphatic agreement. "Fucked up beyond all recognition, just like me."

Phil stood staring out his shop window for a long time after the freshly tattooed trio left, gazing out at the sun-drenched streets and thinking about things like artistic integrity and business ethics and his pop's thoughts on trends and times. It was a slow morning, as usual, and Phil closed up for an hour at noon, as usual. But when he left, he didn't walk down to the Gulf Side Cuisine for chicken salad and sweet tea. Instead, he got into his battered Dodge Dart and drove over the bridges and bayous of Levy County, east to Otter Creek and then south through Gulf Hammock, Lebannon and Inglis, on into Citrus County, one-and-a-half hours of slash-pine shadows and winding roadkill highway to cover the 56.2

as-the-crow-flies miles to the not-big-but-getting-there tourist town of Crystal River.

There was a new Chinese restaurant there Phil wanted to check out.

Pimlico Phil's Pinprick Palace had been transformed from a sleepy backstreet shop into a thriving business with a near-cult reputation by the time Desiree Dean tentatively stepped into the crowded store, several weeks after the boys from Memphis State strutted out. Like most of the other college-age customers packing the small shop that afternoon, Desiree had learned of Pimlico Phil by word-of-mouth. Easily half of Phil's clients told him they had specifically sought him out, that they had been told by proud former clients the only place to get one of the uniquely self-expressive, personalized character tattoos was at a hole-in-the-wall joint in an end-of-the-line town way the hell off the spring break circuit. The Memphis boys, it seemed, had stopped at every frat chapter house from Tallahassee to Tennessee to bum gas money and show off their tattoos. In Atlanta, a Georgia Tech brother with a scanner and a love for dramatics had sent the Tiger trio's tattoos, along with some cock-and-bull story about a genius artist hiding from the world in a Florida fishing village, skittering all across the internet. Now college kids from Denison to Dartmouth were showing up at Phil's doorstep, demanding a tattoo just like the one his/her girlfriend/boyfriend/sorority-fraternitymate/teammate/classmate or professor was sporting. Or better yet, a carefully calligraphied character picked out just for them, so they could be unique, just like everybody else.

At first, Phil had said no. Even if he couldn't bring himself to admit the truth, that the trio of Tigers were wearing nothing more than an advertisement, he just didn't like the idea of scamming his trusting young clients. He tried to steer people towards his more traditional offerings, toward the leaping dolphins and dancing girls. He'd actually turned several people away, despite his borderline finances and the nagging voice of his father's "Give 'em what they want" echoing through his head. But that had backfired. Somehow, word got out that it took more than money to get one of Phil's calligraphies, that you had to *deserve* one. Next thing he knew, potential customers were quoting Eastern mysticism to him, or boasting of their good works, or offering him outrageous sums of money. And suddenly, he was doing calligraphy.

Because he had an innate understanding of what his customers were really after, Phil would, in his sagely grandfatherly way, carefully study each such client, find some clue as to what that person thought of himself, and then tell that person pretty much what he or she wanted to hear. This was a talent that had served Phil quite well over the years, a talent born of long nights watching his pop play poker and longer days listening to clients tell their life stories while he drilled away stoically at an arm, leg or other appendage—and now it was paying off big-time. It all reminded Phil of a short-lived but lucrative business Pop had once started, a cosmetics and toiletries business he dubbed New Generation Ventures. Phil had spent many after-school hours emptying economy-size bottles of cheap perfume into tiny bottles bearing big price tags and the NGV label. "Remember, Phillip," Pop had said. "What you actually sell 'em doesn't matter. It's what they *think* they're getting that counts." And then Pop would tap sagely on the NGV label and wink. Phil knew what he meant, and he knew what NGV really stood for; the only three reasons anybody in America ever spent money on anything, Pop said, were need, greed and vanity.

Years later, Phil was employing exactly that philosophy, along with some flattering talk and a few stolen symbols, to give people just what they wanted. Phil felt a little guilty about it sometimes, but he was making a killing.

And Pimlico Phil was a businessman, after all.

Desiree Dean didn't know any of that, of course. All she knew was that she was in desperate need of a change, in her life in her lifestyle in her very soul. She had been in Panama City Beach for the last week, despondently watching her decidedly dull spring break dribble away in a mocking miniature of her deadly dreary life. Her sorority sisters had spent that week getting loaded and laid, but Desiree—well, Desiree had not. No matter how hard she tried, Desiree couldn't pick up a beer or glance at a well-muscled male without hearing her father's disapproving voice echoing through her mind. So, she'd spent most of her break sitting at a beachfront ice cream stand, nursing cherry slushies and dreading the day she'd have to return to Ohio and school. Not that college was that much worse than where she was. Truth is, Desiree carried her misery with her wherever she went. Desiree knew that about herself. And, like mostly everything else about herself, she hated it.

What she needed, Desiree told herself time and again, was a dramatic change. She needed a new life, a new future, a new body, a new past, a new self. She needed everything she was to become everything she was not. And she would start, she decided, with a tattoo.

Not just any tattoo. Not a fairy princess on her shoulder or a rainbow on her rear, not some generic graphic that would fit equally well on anyone's random stretch of skin. Desiree wanted—no, *needed*—something uniquely hers, uniquely special. She needed a constant reminder to herself of what she wanted to be, and what she did not want to be. She needed something that would shout to all the world, "Look out, people, there's a new Desiree in town!" Well, maybe not shout. Nothing obnoxious. Something subtle but strong, like a good perfume. She wanted something people would admire, sure, but mostly it was to be a message to herself. She didn't need a billboard, she didn't need a spotlight.

"What I need," Desiree said to the genial, white-haired gentleman smiling at her over the countertop at Pimlico Phil's Pinprick Palace, "is a symbol."

"Ah," Phil said. "A symbol. A symbol of . . . ?"

"Independence. Strength. Daring. Courage."

"Hmmmm . . ." Phil studied Desiree closely, one finger propped thoughtfully on a hairy cheek. "A lion, perhaps? Or a lioness, in your case? A brave beast, strong, free. . . ."

"An animal, yes, that's good. But I was thinking maybe about one of those Chinese characters you do. Something that would mean something to me, but not necessarily to everyone else. Mysterious and meaningful at the same time." Pimlico Phil nodded and, Desiree thought, hesitated just a bit before reaching behind the counter to produce a hefty, unmarked black folder. The famous Black Book, source of Phil's legendary designs.

Desiree caught her breath, flashing back to the hushed words of Keith Wade, a tight upperclassman from Michigan State who had spent much of the prior week in the arms and bed of Desiree's sorority sister Irene. "It's a Pimlico Phil original," Keith had said to the group of people staring reverently at the fist-sized Chinese character freshly embossed on his left shoulder. "It means, 'Thunder Lover.'" Irene had blushed furiously at that, but Keith either didn't notice or didn't care. "I drove all the way to Cedar Key," he said, "which is like practically out in the swamps, and I tracked down his shop and walked in and told him I was ready for the world to see the real me. He just looked at me and knew just who I am. It's like he's psychic or something, just like everybody says. Like he can see right into your soul."

Psychic, Desiree had thought then, *that sounds like what I need*, and a fishing village hidden at the edge of the world fit her plans too. So she spent thirty bucks and six sweaty hours on a bus ride to Cedar Key, which was not in a swamp at all, but on a lush green island separated from mainland Florida by a delightfully scenic system of inlets and bayous. But now, flipping through the Black Book Keith had praised so lavishly, she was a little disappointed. According to Keith Wade, Phil and his famous book ranked up there with Moses and the Ten Commandments. Desiree had expected something more than a stout old man wielding a black plastic business binder.

"Something wrong?" Phil said. He started to pull the book back away from Desiree. "This is your first tattoo, correct? Perhaps you'd prefer to start with something small, something simple. I do a very nice daisy, very dainty, almost painless . . ."

"A daisy?" That caught Desiree by surprise, and instantly made her reconsider her evaluation of Phil. Daisies were her favorite flower, always had been. Her room back in Dayton was covered with them, dazzling white and yellow flowers wallpapered on the walls and the ceiling, plastic daisies in plastic flowerpots, daisies on her sheets and pillowcases. Even at college, in sleepy little Springfield, Desiree's notebooks and book covers all featured the golden flowers. The thought brought with it a sudden surge of nostalgia, a sense of longing and loss and—

Desiree shook herself mentally and pulled the black book back towards her. "No," she said firmly. "No flowers. No kittens, no bunnies, no rainbows or puppies or smiley faces. Something strong, something bold. Something with teeth, metaphorically speaking."

Phil studied her again, shrugged, and flipped the book open about one-third of the way through. He turned the pages, slowly, watching her take in each of the half-dozen or so twisting black characters on each. The calligraphy was wonderful, some drawn in a strong, masculine hand, others delicate, almost feminine. There were no translations; each character held a message, a meaning known only to a few. Desiree studied each one intently, waiting for one to call out to her. Some were too massive, others twisted this way or that in spirals and curves that intrigued but did not captivate. Phil turned the pages in a slow rhythm, almost hypnotically. And then—Desiree took a sharp breath and leaned forward even closer over the book. Phil hesitated, then took his fingers away from the page he had been about to turn.

"Yes, of course," he mused. "I had thought about that one, about what you said about strength and independence. Certainly it fits. But—no, perhaps not. This is a symbol of great power, of frightful strength and raging passion. On a delicate, sweet young lady such as yourself. . . ."

Desiree tore her eyes away from the calligraphy and glared at Pimlico Phil. Was he mocking her? Could he really look at her big-boned gawkiness, her klutzy walk and coke-bottle glasses, and see delicacy? Or was it simply that this Guru of the Gulf looked at her and saw nothing but daisies?

"What's it mean?" she asked. She stared Phil right in the eyes as she said it, trying to keep her voice steady and strong.

Phil returned her gaze for a long moment before he answered. "Golden dragon," he said ominously in a voice so low it was almost a whisper. He let the words dangle in the air for a moment, evaluating the determination Desiree was forcing into her heart and her gaze. She boldly nodded her assent, lips pursed tight, fearful that Phil might not think her worthy of such a powerful symbol. She reached into her purse and dropped a fat wad of bills on the counter, not knowing or caring how much a golden dragon cost. Phil glanced down at the money and then back up at her; Desiree thought she saw a flicker of distaste dart through his eyes, and was instantly horrified that she might have just insulted him. The daring future she imagined for herself teetered on the brink. So much depended on finding this perfect symbol of what she could and would become. It was her declaration of independence, her starting place for a new life. If she lost it now . . .

But then Pimlico Phil shrugged, scooped up Desiree's dollars, and gestured for her to follow him. Desiree stood shakily and hesitated no more than a second before hurrying after Phil. *Into his parlor and into my new life*, Desiree thought, *all on the wings of a golden dragon.*

Chapter Two

Desiree Dean wiped the trickle of sweat dripping tear-like down one cheek with her right forearm, careful not to rake her eyes with her six-inch long, forest green claws. The claws were rubber and fairly flexible, but as she'd proven to herself time and time again, they still hurt when poked into the wrong spot. And right now, the one thing Desiree did not need any more of was pain.

Not that she was in any real physical distress. Certainly, she was weary. Who wouldn't be? She was well into the sixth hour of her shift, manning the front desk at Mamasan's Chicks and Chinese. Mostly that meant collecting cover charges and directing smirking businessmen to their tables in the cramped and smoky restaurant, but she'd also done her share of busing tables and taking orders when the under-dressed staff got over-occupied with the clientele. And unlike the other women flitting and flirting half-naked around the place, Desiree had done it all while wearing a 20-pound rubber suit.

And yes, her left shin still throbbed from smacking

it into the plaster Chinese temple dog by the cash register for at least the tenth time in the three weeks she'd been working here, and yes, she'd scorched her left pinkie a little—and some unhappy customer a lot—delivering microwaved egg drop soup to a table so Chipmunk could slip out onto the back deck for a cigarette. So, okay, she was a bit uncomfortable. But none of that was what really hurt.

What really hurt was that people were laughing at her. Well, maybe not at her directly. But there was no doubt in Desiree's mind that the two red-faced tourists at table 12 were laughing at her ridiculous dragon suit, and that pretty much amounted to the same thing. They were trying to be polite about it, turning their heads whenever she glanced their way, but they were too far into their drinks to be even passably discrete. They were trying not to be cruel—but they were not succeeding.

The darned dragon suit, Desiree knew, was definitely worth a laugh or two. It consisted of a skin-tight, one-piece green latex bathing suit with a long, cotton-stuffed tail sewn to the back, a heavy rubber dragon head—including alligator-like snout and lots of foam rubber teeth—fitted tightly on top of her head, and green rubber sleeves with black claws at the ends strapped to her arms and legs. Cheap, hot and heavy. Desiree thought it made her look like Roseanne Barr being devoured by a plastic alligator, and she hated it.

Desiree had come to Mamasan's hoping to become one of the waitresses who lazily served bad food and

flirted with the customers while wearing topless ki-
monos, flaunting their proud breasts and seething
sexuality, laughing at the fawning men and raking in
the tips. But Howie McCracken, the half-owner and
full time manager of Mamasan's, had wiped a smear of
sticky whipped cream off his forehead—he was chas-
ing after a laughing waitress with a can of RediWhip
when Desiree walked in—and told her to try on the
ludicrous green costume. She was the only girl he had,
big enough to cart the damn thing around all night,
Howie said, grinning like the cat who just ate the ca-
nary. The truth, Desiree knew, was that she just didn't
measure up to the blonde-and-bosomy standard of
beauty Mamasan's set for its waitresses. She towered
over the rest of the waitresses, her hair was jet black,
her butt deserved its own zip code, and her breasts—
well, they were fine, she thought, but still white as
fish bellies, despite the recent afternoons she'd spent
sunbathing in her secret grotto. So she had meekly accepted the pro-offered stack of rubberized clothing,
peeled down to her underwear right there in Howie's
office, and wiggled into it. She had stopped halfway
through, slipped out of her bra and stood there smiling at Howie, hoping the sight of her unfettered
breasts might change his mind, but he had just smiled
back and gestured for her to finish dressing. She had;
to her chagrin, it fit perfectly.

So there she was: six-foot-one of big-butted geeky
girl, all wrapped up in a rubber lizard suit. She greeted
and seated customers from 6 till 2 five nights a week,
answered the phone, and rattled off the daily specials

the more comely waitresses could never seem to keep straight. As if anyone actually came to Mamasan's for the food.

At first she had studied each man coming in the door closely, watching for some recognition of her hidden sensual potential in each new pair of eyes. What she got instead was the same tired jokes about "draggin' her ass around" or "getting some tail." Eventually she stopped hoping and concentrated merely on getting through each degrading night. Desiree thought often about quitting, about spontaneously ripping off the absurd suit and stomping defiantly naked into the steamy Cedar Key night. But she needed the money, she had her days free, and the other girls were good about sharing their tips. Besides, where would she go? Back to school? Back to Daddy's bricks-and-ivy mansion in dreary dull Dayton? Not a chance. Desiree endured.

Days, she either kayaked the murky backwater bays of Cedar Key, looking for dolphins and sea turtles, or browsed through the funky little arts, antique and craft stores scattered along the central loop of the town. Downtown Cedar Key, if a place with less than a thousand permanent residents could really be said to have a downtown, was mostly one road that ran in a big circle around the small center harbor. The Loop ran from the bridge where C Street crossed the inlet, then east along the Gulf at Dock Street for about two city blocks, curved inland at A Street past what passed as a beach here on the mostly muddy Nature Coast, then ran back west along First Street, past the historic

Island Hotel, the L&M bar, the Cedar Inn breakfast emporium, and an incredible little grocery store that always had just what you were looking for, no matter how obscure, and then finally back to the bridge. The Loop. Everyone in Cedar Key walked that loop several times a day, whether tourists checking out the handmade art and fantastic seafood, or locals looking to gossip with and about other locals. Doing the Loop was a Cedar Key tradition. Besides, what else was there to do in Cedar Key?

For Desiree, a walk around the Loop ended as often as possible in the sweaty studio of Taylor Nichols. Tee Nichols, as he was widely known—and *everybody* knew Tee—was amazing. He was wiry as jute rope, his face framed by feathery, sun-whitened hair and a scruffy, sand-colored beard. His skin was the color of old honey, tough as the stringy bark on the southern red cedars the island was named for. Tee never wore shoes and seldom wore a shirt; some people said mosquitoes never bit Nichols as a matter of courtesy, as he was a distant relative to them, others said they just couldn't drive their needle noses through his leathery skin. Nichols was 50-something but didn't look it, and sure as hell didn't act it. He had a daughter just a few years older than Desiree—she had been an Olympic swimmer once, and set some sort of distance record for underwater swimming—but that didn't stop Tee from slipping a wiry paw onto Desiree's bottom when he'd had a few, or just when he had the chance. Nichols was father-confessor to half the people on the island, he was a painter, and at least one in every three of his sentences ended with a great, wide-open loving laugh. To Desiree, Nichols was the embodiment of the island spirit.

Tee was also her landlord. Desiree had been directed to him by a sympathetic clerk at Island Realty who had listened to Desiree describe her housing budget with an increasingly dismayed smile. She had followed the woman's directions with growing hopes, past the faded wood and worn paint of a dozen delightfully funky houses, only to find herself in front of a yard that looked like it could pass as a set from Gilligan's Island. She was only a few blocks away from C Street and one street back the ocean—right on the edge of the business district, actually—but the thirty or forty feet of yard in front of her looked practically primeval. Palm trees and red cedar, ferns and vines, a giant seagrape tree with its trunk twisted as red licorice, dagger-sharp saw palmettos reaching almost to her chin, bright blooming milkweed stalks and dangling purple bougainvillea flowers battling for space and sunshine with dust-gray Spanish moss and the fat green leaves of spindly live oaks. There were odd things hanging from the trees, with no pattern or apparent purpose whatsoever—a cow skull, adorned with fading dayglo paint. A bicycle wheel, four or five playing cards clothes-pinned to the spokes. Birdhouses, some brand new, some dilapidated as last year's campaign promise. Mardi Gras beads, strands of Christmas lights, a Chianti bottle suspended by thick fishing line. Three beer cans, strung together by their plastic holder, were hooked over the nose of a smiling four-foot-high wooden dolphin. A rope-and-plank swing hung expectantly from a limb of a red cedar too small to support any but the most slender swinger. A horseshoe crab big as Desiree's head clung to the side of a tall live oak, looking for all the world like it was climbing right on up to a nest in the treetops.

There was life here too. A mockingbird chittered angrily at her, and spread its wings in a feathery challenge before retreating into the jungle. Purple-and-white butterflies flitted among the flowers, bees buzzed in the bougainvillea. A grass green anole lizard darted out on a tree branch, bobbed its head up and down several times and skittered off again. A mosquito danced before her eyes, another announced its presence with a sharp nip at her bare calf. Something she hoped was a squirrel bounced off through the dead underbrush to her right, scrunching the fallen leaves as it went.

There was a house back there, so overgrown with moss and hanging plants it was hard to tell where wilderness ended and house began. A small house, wooden; Desiree guessed that it had once been painted white. A path of worn stones led through the underbrush to a screened-in porch, a porch that might have provided some protection from the swarming mosquitoes if its door weren't wide open. And sitting there in the doorway . . .

"Hey," he said. "Want a fig?"

"Um . . . excuse me?"

"A fig. Fresh picked, just this morning. Good and

juicy." The skinny gentleman sunning in the open doorway wore nothing but a pair of cut-off shorts and a leather necklace around his wiry neck. In one hand he held a longneck bottle of Budweiser, in the other, a garlic-shaped, light purple and definitely fresh fig.

"No, no thank you. I was looking for . . ." Desiree put down the hefty new suitcase she'd forgotten she was holding and dug in her pocket for the paper the realtor had given her. "For Taylor Nichols . . . ?"

"Found him. Want a beer?"

"A beer?"

"Fresh-picked, right out of the frigerator."

"It's ten in the morning."

"Yeah, 'bout that. Wanna beer?"

Desiree found herself smiling through her confusion. The part of her that had been raised on shopping malls and country club socials was appalled, but the part of her she really wanted to nurture, the part of her that would ignore the dangers and grab life by the horns, that part of her gave a happy little flutter. "Practice spontaneity," she told herself, repeating her new personal mantra. "Sure," she said. "What the heck." She picked up her suitcase and took a few bold steps forward on the stone pathway; suddenly, something small but lightning-fast darted across the path right before her. She gave a little squeak and took a step backward.

"Just a skink," Taylor Nichols said. "Good luck, a good sign. They won't hurt you, unless it's a brown skink, and that one wasn't, or unless you're a cat and you eat one. You ever seen a cat that's eaten a skink?"

"Um—no, I don't think so."

"Makes 'em crazy. Fucks with their nervous system, so they fall down a lot. Saw a cat once that had eaten a skink try to climb a tree. Ran right at it, full-speed, but when he got to the tree he forgot to jump. Rammed into it head first, knocked him right on his ass. Poor guy damn near died of embarrassment. You here about the apartment?"

"Yes."

"Thought so. Follow me. Here's your beer." Taylor handed her the beer he had been drinking and headed off down a branch of the stone path leading through the thick underbrush along the front of the house. Desiree quick-stepped after him, swatting at mosquitoes and watching the trail for skinks, suitcase in one hand and beer bottle in the other. Taylor disappeared around the corner of his house, and she scooted to catch up with him.

The side yard was much like the front; if anything, the undergrowth was even more dense. The nearest house was only thirty or forty feet away, but she could barely see it through a tangle of underbrush, live oak and dangling Spanish moss. Just to the right of Nichols' house stood a small building, little more than a large shed. Taylor was at the door of that shed, smiling back at her. She took a quick sip at her beer—practice spontaneity!—and trudged over to join him. The beer, she noticed, was warm.

"T'aint much, but it's home," Nichols said. He waved her inside the shed, flipping on an overhead light as he entered behind her. The apartment was a single room, maybe 25 foot square, hardwood floor; an aged wooden fan hung suspended from the low ceiling just above head height. A metal frame bed stood against one wall, a simple wooden table and two folding metal chairs against another. Across from the bed, looking out of place as a princess in a poor house, was a beautiful antique armoire, reddish cherry wood carved with intricate flowers and lively sea creatures. Most of one wall was a window, covered at the moment by a slat curtain. A hole had been cut in the wall above the table to allow the installation of a small window air-conditioning unit. Nichols went to the unit and turned the switch on and off several times, then gave it a good solid whack with the side of his hand. The AC coughed twice, like a tired automobile engine struggling for life, then clicked on and chugged into a happy rhythm.

"Okay then," Nichols said. "Can you pay five hundred a month?"

"Oh," Desiree said, crestfallen. "No, no I couldn't."

"How 'bout one hundred?"

"One hundred? Sure!"

"Two hundred?"

"Um—I don't know, really. I have to get a job, and—"

"Okay, two hundred a month when you can afford it and one hundred when you can't. I got a little refrigerator I'll put in here for you, and a hot plate. Bathroom is right around the corner here, but you'll have to shower with me."

"What?"

"Kidding. There's a shower out back too, open-air but fenced in. Don't let the tree frogs scare you. They like the water, and sometimes they'll join you in there, but they're harmless. Here's the key, I'll go get that fridge while you unpack." And he was gone.

Desiree stood for a moment in the middle of her new home, bemused but exhilarated. If her sorority sisters could see her now, or even Daddy! This was practically bohemian. "This was not proper," Daddy would say, "not the way you were raised to be. If your mother were here . . ."

Desiree scowled at the unbidden memory of her father's favorite litany, and couldn't quiet the sudden doubt it inspired. Suddenly she felt a little silly, and the room looked more grubby than quaint. A mosquito buzzed angrily at her ear, and she wondered if skinks liked showers too.

But no. Darn it all, this was her new life, this was what she had come looking for, and darned if she was going to let doubt drag her down. She dragged her suitcase across the room and heaved it up on the bed, which sagged alarmingly. Better unpack quick, she thought, before the silly thing collapses. But first, a bit more light in here.

Desiree stepped over to the wood-slat blind covering much of the northwest wall, on the side of the room opposite Nichol's house. She pulled gently with no results—stuck, apparently from disuse. She tugged, and then tugged harder still, until the curtain finally gave way. She pulled it all the way up, quickly, before glancing out the now-open window. But when she did . . .

Desiree gasped, and then clapped her hands together in delight. The window itself was dusty and streaked with clumped cobwebs—but outside! Right outside the window, outside *her* window, there was a beautiful natural grotto. A big old mulberry tree stood there, perhaps ten feet from the window. The tree was at least thirty feet tall, and half way up its twisted trunk exploded outward into a lush canopy of lime-green leaves as big as her head. The shadowy canopy had kept most of the wild underbrush that filled Nichols' yard from intruding here. Instead, there was a perfect circle of inviting green grass. Bright gold and purple butterflies flicked across the glade, darting from the violet wisteria on the right to a hedge of explosive white gardenias on the left. A single tall hibiscus flower stood at the very edge of the mulberry's shade, nodding it's red-framed yellow stem in the morning sun. And in the middle of it all, right beside the mulberry trunk, sat an ancient marble bench. One end of the bench swooped upwards, carved in the shape of a crashing wave, and a grinning stone dolphin danced at its edge. The white stone would be deliciously cool, Desiree knew instinctively, and she could picture herself lying there in the quiet glade of flowers, smooth marble against her back, pitcher of lemonade at her side. Book in one hand, some exotic fruit in the other. Figs, maybe. What a fantasy!

Desiree leaned her head against the dirty window and gave a little sigh of contentment. This would be her place, her refuge. At night she would dance and drink exotic drinks and command the attention of strangers, and in the mornings she would send her lovers home, no matter how much they begged to stay, and wash them away in the shower outside. And then she would come out here, toss her towel aside and lie naked and clean on the dolphin bench, alive and happy under her sheltering mulberry tree.

Desiree stood up straight again, not minding one bit the gleaming circle of sweat her forehead left on the dirty glass. She could hear Nichols dragging her refrigerator out the door of the main house, and she wondered what he would do if she accepted his offer of a shared shower. The old Desiree wouldn't even consider such a thing, of course—but the new one. . . .

Desiree smiled a secret little smile and took a big swallow from her half-empty beer bottle. It was warm and foamy and just a little bit flat, and without a doubt the best darn thing she had ever tasted.

The sound of drunken laughter brought Desiree back to the present. She shook the image of her wonderful cool glade out of her mind and blinked the smoky present of Mamasan's Chicks and Chinese back into focus. She poured a double handful of mints into the desktop bowl she was refilling, spilling only a very few, and then frowned at a sudden painful thought. What if it wasn't the suit? What if the two men in the corner were just laughing at her? She could hardly blame them if they were. She wasn't exactly graceful

at the best of times, and now that she was half blind—
Howie didn't want her wearing her glasses out front—
she kept running into things when she got busy.
So—a big blind babe in a lizard suit. Laughing? Heck,
they should be paying extra for the sideshow.

But that didn't make it right. She glanced over at
the two in the corner, still stealing glances at her and
guffawing into their hands, and felt her blood start to
boil. Darn this dragon suit, she thought, and darn
them too! Desiree wanted to be looked at, not
laughed at.

Chipmunk came out of the bar door at that moment, upturned sun-browned breasts and bare belly,
glistening with sweat. She was carrying a drink tray,
Desiree knew, that was destined for the two in the
corner. Without really thinking, Desiree lifted that
tray out of Chipmunk's grip and gently nudged her
back towards the kitchen. "Let me get this one," she
said. Chipmunk nodded gratefully and turned
around, digging into the change pocket sewn into the
topless kimono for a cigarette. Desiree squared her
shoulders, steeled her nerves, and headed off to con-
front the jokers.

"Good evening, gentlemen," she said when she
reached their table. "Having a good time?" The pair
stopped laughing when she approached them, but
they were still grinning like coots. The one sitting
against the wall, who had the remnants of a Singapore
Sling before him, said something to his buddy in a
quick sing-song voice. Now that she had a close-up
look at him, Desiree realized he wasn't Hispanic like

she'd thought, but rather some sort of Oriental. How embarrassing, she thought, to be serving pre-packed, re-heated chow mien to someone who actually knew how this cuisine was supposed to taste. She hoped he wasn't Chinese.

"My friend," said the man closer to Desiree, the one with a whiskey-and-water before him, "My friend is Chinese, visiting us at the university, and he wants you to know that he really likes your tattoo."

"Oh," Desiree said, "Well, please tell him I said thank you," her anger melting away. That made sense. The American, the whiskey and water, would be some sort of professor from the University of Florida, 90 minutes away up Route 24. And his companion, some sort of visiting scholar. Whiskey-and-water had decided to show Singapore Sling a bit of old rustic Florida, and they'd headed off through the backwoods and backroads to Cedar Key. Probably watched the sunset over grilled grouper at The Captain's Table, maybe knocked back a few drinks, and then what the heck, down to the titty bar for a nightcap. Or two.

As for their obnoxious laughter—well, it didn't matter. What mattered was that, in a roomful of bare-breasted, sun-bronzed backwoods beauties like Chipmunk and the rest, these two men had chosen to stare at *her*. Desiree felt herself melt in the warmth of their attention. She put the drink tray down, leaned in over the table, and pulled the corner of her bathing suit/costume down to give them a better view of her tattoo. She intentionally pulled it a bit farther than necessary, giving the guys a daring little flash of the top half of one nipple. "Would you like to hear what it means?"

"Oh, we know what it means," said Whiskey-and-water. "What my friend would like to know is, is hot sauce on your breast an American tradition?"

"Is—what?" The American was trying not to laugh; Singapore Sling was bouncing his head up and down and staring at her gleefully. Was this some sort of strange Far East pick-up line? Desiree couldn't decide if she should be flattered or insulted.

"With hot sauce," Whiskey-and-water said. "Your tattoo. That's what it says."

"No, no, it means, 'Stop staring at my boobs,'" Desiree insisted, but the joke she been anticipating so long seemed flat. Whiskey-and-water frowned and turned to his companion. The two exchanged a quick round of clicks and clacks while Desiree tried to fight off a sudden sick feeling in her stomach.

"It says, 'With hot sauce,'" Whiskey-and-water insisted. He was all business now, a drunk but determined professor lecturing to a particularly dense student. "In Mandarin, which is why I didn't recognize it, since my area is Cantonese. But my friend here noted it right away, found it really quite funny. With hot sauce. You see, the main staff of the character here—"

Desiree was no longer listening. She had dropped into a horrified trance, reliving each and every proud moment she had seen a man's eyes latched onto her golden dragon tattoo. Each time she'd practiced using her little pre-prepared line, every time she'd smiled to herself in smug self-assurance at her secret knowledge of its true meaning. Marching out of Pimlico Phil's with her head held high despite the throbbing pain in her freshly-pierced breast. Falling asleep at night with one hand resting on her inky badge of honor. Buying every low-cut shirt she could find, so she could proudly proclaim to the world that she was . . . that she was . . .

That she was with hot sauce.

The hot, smoky din of Mamasan's came rushing back to Desiree, along with a surge of humiliation that made her physically ill. She pushed herself away from the table, unsure if she was going to pass out or throw up. Instead, she rushed toward the door, ignoring the protests from the professor and his friend, ignoring the startled look on Chipmunk's face as she ran by. She smacked her knee hard on the temple dog by the door, ignored the pain and kept going. She slapped the glass door open and ran through, then came to an abrupt and painful halt, her tight bathing suit digging even tighter into her skin. She tried to take an uncomprehending step forward, felt the resistance at her rear end, and realized the door had closed on her costume tail. Caught, caught in Mamasan's at the worst moment of her life! Someone up the street laughed, laughed at her, and tears of frustration flooded Desiree's eyes.

She turned around, struggling not to sob. The tail was wedged tight in Mamasan's door, wedged at such an angle that she couldn't reach back to open the door without opening it right into her face. Desiree gave a desperate cry of anger and frustration, then grabbed the root of the tail hard with both hands and yanked. Once, twice—on the third yank, the tail suddenly slipped loose, and the off-balance Desiree tumbled hard to the asphalt surface of A Street. Pain ripped into one skinned knee, and she heard more laughter. She was on her hands and knees, hurt and humiliated, wishing with all her heart she would just up and die.

But then—a purpose. She could barely make out, through her confusion and tears, a literal light in the darkness. The shops along A Street had all long since closed for the night, but a dim light, candlelight, was flickering from one window. The window, Desiree knew immediately, of Pimlico Phil's Pinprick Palace.

A terrible strength flooded through Desiree's battered heart, and she clambered determinedly to her feet. The echo of laughter, the sting in her scraped knees, the hot tears cascading down her face, all receded into the distance, eclipsed by a burning, blazing anger. She straightened the rubber dragon's head atop her head and stepped back onto the sidewalk.

Desiree wasn't sure what she would do when she got to Phil's, but she knew it was going to be bad. Real bad. One way or another, she was going to spontaneously combust all over that wicked, wicked man.

Chapter Three

One thing Pimlico Phil's father never told him was, "Phil, don't never answer the door when the person knocking on it is a dragon. Not even if she's a well-built dragon with big tits and a pretty face, and not even if you're drunk." Not that Pop wasn't thinking of his son's future, or that he didn't care deeply what became of his favorite and only baby boy. It just never occurred to the elder Pimlico that such a situation would arise. Or maybe he just assumed that if it did, his level-headed boy would have the common sense not to open the door.

Papa Pimlico was wrong—the situation had indeed arisen. As Phil could plainly see—or at least partially see, drunk as he was and with the only light in his shop a genuine imitation antique seaman's lantern, casting peaceful shadows dancing around the dingy walls—there was in fact a dragon knocking rather insistently on his door. Pounding, in fact. Phil, who was celebrating his unfamiliar financial solvency with a solitary bottle of brandy and brandy-dipped beanie-weenies, couldn't think of a single reason why a dragon would be angry at him. The dragon at the door, he thought, might just be in urgent need of aid. Being the good-hearted person he was, Phil couldn't simply ignore such a cry for help, even if the, ah, person crying had green skin and long sharp nails. So, he opened the door—and regretted it right away. The dragon gave him a good hard shove in the chest and charged into the lantern-lit room, screaming at the confused and off-balance tattoo artist.

"Hot sauce! With hot sauce!" the dragon yelled in a very feminine and most un-dragon-like voice. "How could you!"

"Ah . . . um . . . do I know you?" Phil asked, though he already had a sinking feeling he did. The dragon, he could see now that she had stepped into the flickering light, was in fact a full-figured young woman in a dragon suit. A very cheap dragon suit. A very angry woman. The girl who looked like a lizard, Phil suspected, was in fact the dreaded chicken he had long feared coming home to roost.

"Do you know me? You've *destroyed* me! You humiliated me, you set me up, you—you *jerk!*" The dragon lady screamed again, took another step forward and swung at the air about two feet from Phil's head. *A drunk dragon*, Phil thought, *or a very nearsighted one.* Either way, he was very glad she had missed. That had been a pretty serious right hook, and Phil was in no shape for a fight.

Phil shook his head to clear the brandy-buzz and looked around for a weapon. He settled on the brandy bottle sitting on the nearby counter top, scooped it up and braced himself for the next on-slaught—but there was no swing forthcoming. His angry dragon had stopped her attack, and was instead wiping ineffectually at the tears rolling down her face with a not-very-absorbent green-scaly sleeve. Raising her arm like that pulled the bust of her costume aside just enough for Phil to see the all-too-familiar tattoo riding on her right breast. Phil's soft old heart, wounded by guilt and salted by the poor girl's tears, melted in his chest.

"Oh, you poor child," he said. "Don't cry, please. I'll make it all better, somehow, I promise. Here, dry your eyes." Phil transferred his half-filled juice glass to the hand he was using to hold the brandy bottle, pulled a faded handkerchief from a rear pocket with his other hand, and reached it out towards the dis-traught girl. The dragon girl looked at him gratefully and slowed her sobbing long enough to take it from him—almost. What she did instead was swing her gloved hand in the air about six inches above and a foot beyond Phil's pro-offered hankie, smacking his drinking hand and sending a nice dark shot of brandy splashing onto Phil's shirt. It looked like a gunshot wound, Phil thought abstractly, and right there over his heart. He and his odd visitor, each stupefied in his or her own way, shared a quiet moment staring at the slowly spreading spill before the dragon broke the silence.

"Oh, oh *darn* it all!" she said. "I am *so* sorry. I'm *such* a klutz, I'm sorry. Here, let me . . ." She reached out one green-sleeved arm to paw at Phil's brandy-splattered shirt. He could see she was moving very carefully this time, trying to compensate for her poor vision, trying to swab gently at the stain with her claw-tipped fingers. He watched in drunken fascination as the oddly attired and half-blind stranger reached for and missed his chest by a good six inches. No damage done—or at least, there would have been no damage done if not for the extra three inches of curved rubberized claws at the end of her she-monster sleeve. Those claws weren't very sharp, but they were fairly hard, and when they poked Phil's wrist, both he and the beast jumped. Not good. The rubber claws hooked around the neck of the brandy bottle in Phil's hand and ripped it out of his grasp. The mostly full bottle shattered at Phil's feet, sending glass shards and high priced liquor all over the floor of his shop.

"Well hell," Phil said, not because of the expense but because he suspected he was going to need another brandy, or two or three, if he ever got this walking disaster out of his shop. Said walking disaster, judging from the look of dismay on her face, was accustomed to making this sort of mess . . . and accustomed to feeling very bad about it.

"Oh God," she said. "Oh, I am *so* sorry. Here, let me . . ." She bent over at the waist, reaching for a large chunk of broken bottle. Unfortunately, she had failed to allow for the snarling headpiece resting on her own head, a stiff plastic-and-rubber headpiece that rammed Phil good and hard right in the gut. Phil "uffed" and staggered back a half step. "Young lady," he said, "Young lady, I am truly sorry about your tattoo, but really, are you *trying* to kill me?"

Phil regretted it the moment he said it. He had wronged this girl, and he needed to make that up to her somehow, and yet he'd just done exactly the wrong thing. The same sharp-eyed instinct that so often let him pinpoint what message a customer wanted to hear, and then wear on his or her flesh, gave Phil a bright and sudden insight into the miserable girl before him. The way she raised one hand to her face in dismay, the way she wrapped the other arm across her chest defensively, the waterworks streaming down her face . . . this girl didn't want to hurt anyone, not even someone who'd wronged her as badly as Phil had. She wanted nothing but to give compassion and get it in return. Yes, she was blind as a bat and a genuine menace to navigation, but so what? Her heart was good and kind and vulnerable and Phil in his selfish irritation had said exactly the worst thing he could say to her.

"Oh, no, listen, I'm sorry, I didn't mean that," Phil said. "Here, let's dry your eyes and get you something warm to wear." Phil stepped forward, meaning to put his arms around the girl in consolation, but he had not reckoned with the broken glass at his feet. He stepped on a nice sharp shard, let out an enthusiastic "Damn!" and danced backward, hopping on one foot. And the girl, of course, saw all this and let out another wail of her own.

"My God," she said, "I *am* killing you! I'm *so* sorry. I . . . I . . . Oh, darn!" The girl spun around, hands at her cheeks, meaning no doubt to run back out into the night and hide before she caused Phil any more harm.

Too late.

Phil saw it all coming in slow motion, like they say the world slows when you're heading into a car crash. The girl spun around, and her wire and rubber tail whipped up behind her and swept across the countertop to her right. Like a happy dumb Irish setter wagging his tail in a china shop, Phil thought, or one of those dinosaurs who was so big and so stupid it took five minutes for his head to realize what his tail was doing. The dragon tail swept across the counter as the girl turned, sending everything in its way crashing to the floor. A rack of temporary tattoos, a small stack of classical CDs, a bottle of colored ink and—tragically, terribly, predictably and inevitably as a train wreck—Phil's brightly blazing oil lamp.

Phil moved forward reflexively, trying to catch the falling lamp in midair. Not quick enough, and not smart either. The lamp floated gently downward, just past his outreaching fingertips, and he felt a distant stab as he trod on more glass. Phil saw it all in near freeze-frame—the lantern drifting downward, sheets of scattered paper floating by like flat lazy snowflakes, the green dragon's tail, its damage done, bouncing rubberishly on the hardwood floor . . . all very serene, almost peaceful . . .

Until the lantern hit the floor and the world exploded back into motion. The lamp shattered, splashing its oil reserve on top of the spilled brandy. The suddenly freed flame hit the combustible puddle at Phil's feet, and a lake of fire six feet around flashed into life. Phil was leaning over, reaching down in his misguided attempt to catch the lantern, and the sudden flame leapt right up at him and ignited the brandy on his shirt. Just like that, Phil and the floor were both on fire.

"Aiiiyyyyiiii!" Phil screamed, meaning every nonsyllable of it. He slapped frantically at the shirt front, scorching his fingers and serving only to fan the flames there. The shirt was too tight to pull over his head, and the buttons were blazing. Phil looked frantically around for something to smother the flames with. "The fire extinguisher!" he thought—but the fire extinguisher was on the wall beside the front door. Phil was towards the rear of the shop, cut off by broken glass and a rapidly spreading wall of fire. He had a vision of the fire spreading past him, leaping from one wall poster to another, igniting the stacks of newspapers and tattoo sample books carelessly stacked everywhere, until it hit the small workroom behind him and the bottles of alcohol and ink-mixing chemicals he kept stored there. His shop was doomed, Phil realized, and maybe himself as well, unless—

"There!" he shouted at the stunned dragon, who stood gaping at Phil over the flame. "On the wall, the fire extinguisher!" Phil couldn't tell if she'd gotten the message or not, and he couldn't spare any more time for her. The fire on his chest had mostly been just the alcohol burning off, but now the nylon itself was starting to burn—and it *hurt*. If he didn't get it off somehow, fast . . . Phil hooked his fat fingers under the hem of the shirt and jerked hard. Pain seared through his fingers. He coughed at the rising, chemical-smelling smoke, and jerked hard again. The scorched cloth parted suddenly; Phil ripped the shredded shirt off himself and threw it triumphantly aside. And looked up just in time to see a vision that was part Dante's *Inferno* and part Disney's *Fantasia*.

The flames engulfing his shop, now nearly tall as Phil and stretching from one side wall to the other, suddenly parted and a puff of wet white chemical cloud rolled toward Phil like a misty mushroom. And from behind it, green arms extended and fire extinguisher in hand, eyes clenched shut and mouth wide open, came the charging, screaming half-blind dragon. Phil had just enough time to open his own mouth, to scream "No!" before a layer of foamy chemical fire retardant splattered across his face and the dragon smacked into him.

Phil went down, hard, and lay dazed on the floor. From somewhere deep inside him an urgent voice told him to get up, to get out or die, but it was hard to concentrate on that voice with the bells pealing in his ears and the horrible chemical taste in his mouth. Perhaps, Phil thought dazedly, perhaps it would be easier to just stay right here.

That thought didn't last long. Something large and green swam into Phil's fuzzy field of vision, and insistent fingers grabbed his shoulders. "I'll save you!" an earnest voice said, and Phil felt himself hoisted off the floor. Then came a bony pressure in his stomach—a shoulder, Phil realized—and he was lifted off his feet. *Strong girl*, he thought hazily, and then, as his inverted vision focused on the upside view of the girl whose shoulder he was draped over, *Her tail's on fire*.

This was not a good thing, Phil knew, but the cotton-candy cloud that had descended over his thoughts made it difficult to determine exactly why. The girl under him took one staggering step and then another, and Phil watched dispassionately as the bottom-up view below him scrolled by. Hardwood floor reflecting the red flickers of the inferno behind them, smoke roiling all around like fog from a sailor's nightmare, that flaming dragon's tail rolling side to side with each step, dripping colorful globules of melted rubber as his mount moved along. The fire was moving slowly up the tail, well past the tip now, still a couple feet short of her backside and Phil's face, but progressing steadily. Along the center aisle of the shop they trudged, through the small workshop in the rear, through the cloth curtains that marked the small storeroom. *Oh good*, Phil thought, *The storeroom*. That was where the back door was. It was also where he kept his receipts and tax records, a few bottles of rubbing alcohol, inking chemicals, some odds and ends his landlords kept stored there, more oil for his lantern. Lots and lots of flammable things, Phil thought. Good thing there's no fire back here.

Except, of course, for the fire on the dragon's tail. That did it. Suddenly Phil was fully awake again, awake and yelling over the rushing whoosh of flames from the outer room. "Put me down before you kill us both!" he said, or at least tried to. With a shoulder in his gut and a mouthful of chemical retardant, what came out was more along the lines of "poofmekillsboof." But it was an emphatic "poofmakillsboof," and the girl got the message. She put him down.

Phil gave one quick tug on the rear doorknob— locked, of course—and began digging frantically through his pockets for the keys. The girl beside him started to whimper again, whether from fear or pain Phil didn't know or care. He found the key he was after, jammed it into the lock and twisted hard. The door clicked open and Phil stepped out into the alley behind his store, relishing the cool night air on his scorched skin. He spit chemicals and blood into the darkness, then turned to the girl standing in the doorway behind him, silhouetted by the flames inside the store. "Your tail is on fire," he said matter-of-factly.

The girl did the one thing Phil hadn't anticipated. Instead of leaping forward, or ripping the tail from her costume—she turned to look. That sent her flaming tail raking over most of the items in the storeroom. Blazing blobs of burning rubber glommed onto the newspapers, to the gallon jugs of mineral spirits, even to the half-gallon jug of lamp oil. How long, Phil wondered, till that oil explodes?

He decided not to wait. He grabbed the girl and jerked her out into the night, pushed her hard in one direction and sprinted off in the other. He'd gotten less than a half dozen steps when a fireball the size of a Volkswagen Beetle came roaring out of the open door. Phil covered his eyes against the sudden glare, and tripped as he staggered backwards.

"Ahhh," he thought as he fell. "That long."

Phil forced himself to roll over and sit up, wincing at the pain. He was on an old wooden boardwalk, maybe three feet wide, that ran along between the half dozen stores and warehouses on this side of A Street and the murky waters of the Gulf below him. Mostly store owners used the boardwalk to bring goods into and trash out of the back of their shops, though farther down Mamasan's Chinese had made a feeble attempt to broaden the boardwalk and set up outside dining. It hadn't worked; no one wanted to eat Chinese food amid the fishy vapors the Gulf Coast mudflats emitted at low tide, and now the topless waitresses used it for smoke breaks and moonlit trysts.

The tide was in at that moment, and the flames gouting from his shop lit up the night and reflected off the water below like liquid lightning. *Something's not right here*, Phil told himself. *Too much fire, too fast.* His papers, the brandy and some oil, sure, a couple gallons of mineral spirits, and maybe the wood of the place was even older and more rotted than it appeared. Still, he thought—and Phil had some experience in this area—that was a great deal of fire in a remarkably brief time.

Phil forced himself to his feet and wondered how long it would take the fire department to arrive.

Maybe they could still salvage something of his shop. His books and papers would all be gone, but maybe the cash register and some of his tools would still be intact if they got the fire out fast enough. There couldn't be anything else explosive in there; he'd only had a few bottles of mineral spirits and the single jug of oil. The fire seemed to already be subsiding a little bit; through the flames dancing out of his rear door he could catch glimpses of the dragon lady silhouetted against the open Gulf as she staggered down the boardwalk toward Mamasan's back door. Good Lord, was she injured? He hoped not; she seemed like a sweet kid, as raging lunatics go.

Phil took a hesitant step towards the flames and the madwoman—and then stopped. He was forgetting something, something important. He shook his head to clear the lingering cobwebs and started a mental inventory of the burning shop. The front room—sample books, display cases, posters: gone. Upstairs, his apartment: salvageable, he hoped; he didn't have many possessions but he would hate to lose his collection of classical CDs. Back downstairs, the bathroom: nothing important there. The small back room, with his tools and tattooing chair, check. The rear corridor, check. The storeroom—

"The storeroom," Phil whispered, and then he was shouting. "Run!" he screamed, as loud as he could. "Get away, run for your life!" The dragon lady turned and squinted in his direction; Phil waved his arm frantically before realizing she couldn't see him. "Get

away!" he screamed again. "It's going to explode!"
    And it did.

Pimlico Phil sat on the hood of his car, nursing a vending-machine diet soda and watching the distant firemen hose down the smoldering remains of his tattoo parlor. He was in a dark parking lot on 1st Street, close enough so he could follow the action on the far side of the Loop but far away enough that no one would notice him. He lifted his T-shirt and rolled the cool soda can across his singed chest. Not too bad, he hoped, but still, perhaps he should have it looked at.

    It had been maybe half an hour since the explosion in his shop ripped open the night sky and slammed the fleeing Phil facedown on the boardwalk. A mixed blessing, that. The explosion had ripped off the rear end of his shop and a big chunk of the boardwalk, but had also blown out the worst of the fire. It had awoken the entire slumbering town center, brought the late night revelers stumbling out of the bars to stare gape-mouthed at the sudden destruction on A Street. Phil himself had had a great view of the disaster; any closer, and he would have been blown right into the bay. As it was, it looked like his shop was totally destroyed, along with much of the warehouses on both sides and maybe even part of Mamasan's. A stretch of darkness 15 feet long had been smashed out of the boardwalk, like a missing tooth in a jack o' lantern's mouth.

    There was no sign of the girl in the dragon suit.

Phil sighed heavily and eased himself into the driver's seat of the Dart. He liked it here in Cedar Key, liked the salt-laden air and sunsets over the island, liked the saltwater taffy and the friendly people and the oh-so-somber pelicans perched on every empty post. He'd known it wouldn't last, because good things never do. But he would've liked to stay a little longer.

Phil cranked the Dart's balky engine into life and eased the car out of the parking lot without turning on his lights. He turned right on C Street, away from the fire and the curious people still trotting in that direction. Two blocks down and left on Third Street, then right onto State Road 24, heading east towards the mainland. Phil's shirt chaffed on his burned chest, but at least he had a shirt. It was part of the change of clothes he always kept in the trunk of the car, along with a half-pint of whiskey and an envelope holding a half-dozen 20-dollar bills. He already had a plan half formed in his mind—lie low for a bit, maybe head north and west, towards Mobile or New Orleans, eventually set up a new shop. Money would be no problem, not once all the paperwork was cleared. He allowed himself a half-smile at that thought, and raised the bottle in silent salute to his long departed father. Once again, Pop's good advice had served Phil well.

"Spot the trends before they get there," Pop always said. "Stay liquid."

Carry plenty of insurance.

Chapter Four

One of the McCracken brothers was happy, the other was miserable—nothing unusual about that. It was unusual, however, that the happy one was Stevie, and the miserable one was Howie. In the normal course of events, Howie McCracken was a genuinely jolly guy, unless, of course, brother Stevie was around. Unlike the affable Howie, Stevie seemed to travel through life with a scowl on his face and a dark cloud hovering unseen over his head. And Stevie McCracken was never more depressed or depressing than when faced with the prospect of losing money—something, Howie thought, that sure as hell seemed to be happening right now. But there they were, Howie kicking the ground in subdued dismay and Stevie trying not to grin, side by side on A Street, surveying the blackened ruins of Mamasan's Chicks and Chinese.

"Shit, Stevie, I just don't know what to say," Howie said when he couldn't stand the silence any more. "It was just a freak thing, some kinda crazy accident, that tattoo place catching fire and then spreading so fast like it did. The fire department, they got here as fast as they could, but you know . . ."

"Howard."

"Yeah, Stevie?"

"Don't call me Stevie."

"Oh, right, damn, sorry. Steven. Stephen, with a "p-h." I mean, just a fire, we'da been ok, we'da been fine. But that explosion! You know it knocked out four windows over to the Sea Breeze, just from the wind it put up?" Howie shook his head at the sheer magnitude of the thing. "What you think ol' Phil kept in there that would blow up like that? Chipmunk says maybe Phil was making bombs, like he was a terrorist or something, and blew himself up, but Sandy, she's got a cousin with the state law department who says maybe just air tanks, like scuba tanks, but Phil didn't dive, didn't even swim, so maybe he was storing gas or something back there, maybe like he was one of those survivite people and thought the end of the world is coming, or maybe—"

"Nitrous oxide."

"Um—nitrous oxide?"

"That's right."

"You mean, like the party drug? Like whippets?"

"I mean, like the big cylinders of nitrous oxide we get with our restaurant license, and use for baking pastries."

"At Mamasan's?"

"At Mamasan's."

"Stevie, Stephen, we don't make no pastries at Mamasan's. Hell, we don't make nothing at all you can't put in a microwave." Howie started to have a nice little chuckle at the Mamasan's cooking humor, but stopped when Stevie turned toward him and raised one knife-thin black eyebrow. Gotta watch that, Howie told himself. Damned if he could figure why, but Stevie was in a great mood—for Stevie—and Howie didn't want to ruin that. Howie had been dreading this moment all day, ever since he'd had to call Stevie out at his mansion up near Rosewood and tell him that the family restaurant Stevie had put in the care of his klutzy older brother had burned to the ground. Rosewood was only fifteen minutes away, but for some reason it had been nearly three hours before Stevie showed up. Three hours of Howie going through his story over and over, three hours of trying to figure how this godawful mess could be his fault. This time Howie was fairly sure he hadn't done anything wrong, and he was all ready to convince Stevie of that—and Stevie didn't even seem to care. Crazy as it was, Stevie seemed—happy.

Howie shook his head in confusion, then quick stepped after Stevie. His brother had his black leather notebook out and was scribbling in it again, walking up and down the burned remains of the East Dock landing. That whole pine plank and tar strip belonged to them, from the 35 yards of south-looking frontage next to the Sea Breeze Restaurant, around the corner of Dock and A streets, and north for 197.3 yards of Gulf frontage facing eastward, all the way to the thin bank of dirty brown sand that passed for Cedar Key's public beach. That was McCracken Strip—Mamasan's, the warehouse, Pimlico Phil's, the loading dock they used to unload the clams from the McCracken Brothers Seafood boats. A little of it they'd inherited from Mom, but most Stevie had connived and conned into their pockets over the last ten years. They'd paid a lot for it, in hard work and borrowed money, in lost friendships and hot sweat—and now it was gone. All, all gone—or a big chunk of it anyway.

So why was Stevie smiling?

"The exterior walls of the warehouse still seem pretty solid," Stevie said. Howie pounced on that, it was one of the few bits of good news he had ready to share.

"Oh yeah," he said. "Jeff Waters, he's bringing his crew out tomorrow to have a good look, but he did a walk through and said—"

"I want Tad Geery doing the construction."

"Tad Geery?" Howie frowned and studied his brother closely to see if he was joking. Fat chance of that; Stevie never joked. But Tad Geery? "But Stephen, Geery don't hardly work no more, not since he re-built the dock over to the Shipshape Motel and then the whole damn thing just fell into the ocean, and you know he drinks. Jeff Waters, he's the only—"

"Tad Geery," Stevie said in his end-of-discussion voice. Howie started to object, but then clamped his mouth shut and nodded glumly. Stevie must have noticed Howie was hurt, 'cause when he spoke again his voice was much softer.

"Howard," he said patiently. "We hold the mortgage on Geery Construction's warehouse and office, and he's got loans to us on half his equipment. He owes us more than he could ever re-pay."

"Oh, right," Howie said, mentally kicking himself and renewing his often-broken vow to pay more attention to the quarterly reports Stevie sent him. And then he brightened and looked at his brother in surprised approval. "So you're thinking we should give him the repair job? Get poor old Geery back on his feet? Stevie, that's awful damn nice of—"

Howie stopped in mid-sentenced, chilled by the unmistakable look of grave disappointment in Stevie's eyes. He'd screwed up again, somehow. He sucked his lower lip into his mouth and chewed on it for a minute, hard, looking down at his feet so he wouldn't have to face that withering look. Finally, Stephen sighed, and Howie dared to look up at him again.

"Howard," he said. "There won't be any repair job."

"No repair job?"

"No."

"But—what about Mamasan's? What about the warehouse?"

"Mamasan's is gone, and the warehouse is going. The Levy County building inspector is going to declare the whole block unsafe, and Tad Geery is going to bulldoze it down."

"Bulldoze it down? Mamasan's? But Stevie, you can't—" But Stevie had already turned away, was tapping on the side of the warehouse and taking more notes in his folder. Howie flapped his mouth open and closed a couple times, like a boated grouper sucking air. Mamasan's, gone? He loved that place! He was in charge there, his girls loved him—or at least acted like they did—and everybody did what he told them to. His girls! What would happen to his girls without Mamasan's? Sandy was supporting her kids, with her husband in the county lock-up for six months, and Chipmunk was seriously thinking about going to law school, and little Linda was saving up for that boob job she wanted so bad . . . how could he tell them?

There had to be some kind of mistake, Howie told himself. Maybe Stevie hadn't meant it, or more likely Howie had just misunderstood him, God knows that happens enough. That had to be it.

Howie snapped out of his stupor, convinced that he had just heard it all wrong. Stevie was down at the far end of the warehouse now, walking slow and still scribbling in that book. Howie took off after him, eager to get this all straight in his head. He caught up to his brother just as Stevie rounded the corner of the warehouse. Stevie was deep in thought, tapping his pen against one cheek, and Howie hesitantly reached out to tap him on one shoulder.

But then Howie heard something that froze him in mid-reach. Something absolutely eerie, something so wildly out of place—Howie couldn't have been more surprised if a manatee had swum up to the dock and ordered Mamasan's soup-of-the-day. It was a sound Howie hadn't heard in a lot of years and sure as hell never expected to hear again, and it left him frozen in his tracks in the midday sun, stunned, as his sour and dour bitter brother walked away—*whistling*.

Chapter Five

Florida State Parks Ranger Superintendent Jennifer Aly knelt over the blood-coated body of Bambi the beach deer and cried.

She cried not because she had known Bambi since she was a fawn, though she had, and not because the trail of gore through the roadside sand showed the doe had dragged herself crippled and in agony for nearly 20 yards before dying. Aly cried not because the fallen deer would never again gently nip snacks from the hands of charmed tourists and their squealing children, or because she would never again see Bambi delicately mincing along the sugary-soft sand near the Rye Key State Reserve swimming area. In fact, as much as Aly had loved the gangly whitetail doe, and as much as it broke her heart to see her lying unmoving among the sandspurs and fire ant hills, Jennifer Aly was not crying from sadness. She was crying tears of frustration and rage.

Frustration, because this should not have happened. Bambi had not been crossing the late-night drag strip that was the only road connecting Rye Key to Way Key and the town of Cedar Key. She had not been in a national forest where any lunatic with a six-pack and a hunting license could legally blast her soft flesh to bloody shreds. She was well within the grounds of Rye Key park, safe within the preserve that had been her home since she and two other emaciated young does had made the perilous swim across Number Four Channel from overpopulated Candy Island. One of the does had not completed that crossing, drowned or maybe been pulled under by an opportunistic shark; a second had died of exhaustion and exposure a few minutes after reaching Rye Key. But Bambi had survived, had struggled to her feet too weak to run from sympathetic picnickers offering the terrified deer chicken and cheese sandwiches and ice water from Styrofoam coolers. Bambi had learned to trust those people and the many others who came later, had learned to tolerate the cautious petting hands of children and expect the handfuls of grain tourists could buy from vending machines put near the park pavilion for just that reason. Bambi had learned to trust her human neighbors, and it had served her well. Until last night.

Jennifer wiped a hand across her sun-worn face and stood up, surveying the stretch of road before her. It was easy enough to see what had happened here. Bambi had been crossing the narrow road that ran from the park entrance to the main campground, making her way from her beachfront begging-ground back into the thick scrubland where she spent her nights. A car had come roaring around the curve where the road split toward the fishing pier, taken her by surprise. Bambi would have frozen instinctively, hoping the roaring predator speeding towards her would pass her by if she only stood still enough. It hadn't.

Aly looked back along the road and tried to imagine where Bambi had been standing when the car slammed into her. Jenny could see where she'd hit the ground, there, and plowed a trench through the roadside sand when she rolled over several times. She could see where the doe struggled to her feet and then staggered unsteadily a few steps toward the imagined safety of the scrub, leaving a trail of crimson and gore before collapsing, here, to die in the dark, in agony. The car had hit Bambi hard enough to split her abdomen like an overstuffed sausage. Judging from the off-kilter shape of her chest, it had also snapped several ribs. The driver had been hauling ass, and there were no skid marks along the tarmac-and-oyster-shell surface of the park's only street.

The speed limit on that road was 15 miles per hour.

Aly heard the distant rumble of the park's number two pick-up truck rounding the curve ahead. She stood, wiped the tears off her face with a khaki shirt-sleeve, and put her mirrored sunglasses on. By the time the truck lurched to a halt beside her, two wheels in the sand and two left carefully on the roadside, she was the stoic, stolid professional chief her two underlings were accustomed to seeing.

Rodney was the first one out of the truck. He jumped out of the passenger seat and took several quick steps toward Aly and the fallen deer. Jennifer could see the hope in his eyes fade as he got close enough to get a good look at Bambi's corpse.

"Ah shit," Rodney said. "Ah shit, Ms. Aly, I sure am sorry."

"Don't apologize to me," Aly said testily. "I'm not the one rotting by the roadside."

"Well yeah, but—well, yeah. I'm just sorry is all." Rodney bent down beside the crushed deer. He lifted her head and turned it gently to one side, making her look a little less twisted, and Jennifer was immediately sorry she'd snapped at him. He was a good kid, born and raised in Cedar Key, and she knew he genuinely cared for the deer, for the park, for this little chunk of wild Florida entrusted to their care. He wasn't just a local redneck who'd signed on for the summer because he was tired of digging clams in the sandy muck off Cedar Key. Rodney was basically a good kid, unlike—

"I got the shovel, like you said, Officer Aly," Caddy said. He shuffled to a stop a few feet from Jennifer, raised the shovel a bit and let its blade drop into the soft roadside sand with a half-hearted skish sound. He stared down at the sand rather than looking at Jenny when he spoke. "But I was just thinking. I know she was like a pet and all, but that's a lot of fresh venison, and—"

"No," Jennifer said, her voice flat as the Florida landscape.

"But it's not like it's gonna hurt any, and—"

"No," Jennifer said again. Caddy glared at her mirror-covered eyes and unwavering stance for a second, then looked back down at the ground and nodded.

"Where should we put her, Ms. Aly?" *Ms.* It always sounded odd when Rodney called her that, and she wondered where he'd picked it up. A college word, a politically correct phrase here in backwoods Florida where politics generally meant voting for the cousin you were least pissed at.

"Doesn't matter," she said. "Just take her back in the woods a bit, away from the road. Make it deep; the foxes will dig her up if they catch her scent."

"I will, Ms. Aly," Rodney said. It would be him doing the burying, no doubt, even though Caddy had brought two shovels. Jennifer knew Caddy would spend a lot more time bitching than digging, letting Rodney do the real work. Be a good chance for him to smoke the joint he no doubt had in his pocket. Come to think of it—"I'll take the truck back, leave you boys the air conditioning." She tossed the keys to her car to Rodney, though Caddy was a year or two older, had been with the park much longer, and by rights should be the one driving. She didn't give one good damn if Caddy sweated himself into a heat stroke, but she didn't want him trying to badger Rodney into making off with a haunch or two of fresh venison. No way he'd try that if it meant loading Bambi parts into Aly's own vehicle.

Jennifer allowed herself one more quick look at Bambi's body before pulling herself into the broiling interior of the Ford. She knew, in a way, who was responsible for it. Not a local. Not that everyone around here was above joy-riding through the state park, and God knows plenty of 'em knew how to get around the park's woefully inadequate front gate. But no local would have left a fresh deer to rot in the sun. Accident or intentional, wild animal or family pet, once a deer was dead it would be nothing more than a welcome change from their usual diet of mullet and shellfish.

And probably not a college kid either. It was Tuesday; the weekend invasion of University of Florida students looking for a little fun in the sun would have long before made the three-hour trek back to Gainesville. Besides, most of them drove sporty little cars with Japanese names that looked sharp but would have gotten bogged down in the off-road sand if they'd tried to Baja it around the park's fences.

Not locals, not students. It had to have been one of McCracken's men.

Jenny goosed the truck's engine to life and eased it back out onto the park road. It was a struggle not to slam the pedal down in frustration; just thinking of it made her that furious. The McCracken brothers had hired only a very few local people when they started to work on the brothers' seaside abomination in Cedar Key. Most of their crew were people who'd never been near Cedar Key before—lean, lazy men who worked slow, didn't worry too much about rules, and drank away their week's pay almost before they got it. Jenny could just imagine a few of those greasy mercenaries loading into a McCracken Brothers' truck, passing the whiskey around, and going for a joyride. Two miles down Bay Road to the preserve entrance, a quick veer around the gate, and they would have had the whole park to play in. Had they seen Bambi when they'd come roaring around the corner and caught her in their headlights? Were they so drunk they couldn't stop in time, or just so calloused that they didn't try?

Jennifer didn't know. It didn't really matter. What mattered is that the men in the truck were just the first of the invading army she'd hoped would never notice Cedar Key and her beloved park. The land-rapers had already decimated most of Florida's pristine sandy beaches; it was just a matter of time till they turned their greedy gaze on the quirky beauty of Levy County and the rest of the Nature Coast. South Florida and Tampa Bay had been destroyed and re-packaged for tourist consumption before Jennifer had been born, but she'd witnessed the rape of Panama City, of Key West and Destin and a dozen other no-longer-beautiful beach towns. Palm trees leveled for parking lots, sand dunes paved over for nightclubs and tacky gift stores, for T-shirt shops and hot dog stands for Ripley's Museums and amusement parks, until the natural beauty that had drawn people in the first place was nothing more than a doctored picture on a tourist brochure. It made Jennifer want to vomit.

Jenny Aly pulled the truck into its designated spot in front of the park's small ranger station and cut the engine. She let her head drop forward in despair on the steering wheel, ignoring the burn of hot plastic against her forehead. Poor Bambi hadn't been the first victim of the coming onslaught, God knew she wouldn't be the last. And there was absolutely noth-ing Jennifer could do about it.

Unless . . . Sitting as she was, head on the steering wheel, meant Jenny was looking straight down at the floor of the truck. There was a newspaper there, the weekly Cedar Key *Lantern*. Today's edition, no doubt brought in by Rodney and swept aside by Caddy. It took Jenny a moment to fully process the picture on the paper's front page, and not just because it was dark and grainy even by the Lighthouse's small-town standards. When she realized what it was, Jenny gave a little cry of delight and scooped up the paper. A fire on the dock at Cedar Key, three or four businesses destroyed including, thank God, that shitty little strip joint. Two people missing, lots of speculation about that. And something really odd, something about a monster from the sea . . .

State Park Ranger Superintendent Jennifer Aly leaned back in the front seat of her truck, drumming her fingers on the steering wheel, ignoring the blazing heat and the no-see-ums flitting in and out of the window. She was still sitting there when Caddy came driving her car in a half-hour later, covered with sand and sweat, a subdued Rodney sulking beside him and a nice quarter of venison wrapped in newspaper in the trunk.

Rodney put the car in park and checked himself again for telltale flecks of blood before daring to look over at the boss. He'd freaked when he'd seen her just sitting there in the parking lot, figured she must be on to him and was just waiting for him to pull in so she could fire his ass. But looking at her now, she didn't seem to be too upset.

In fact, she was smiling.

Chapter Six

Robin Chanterelles couldn't remember the last time she'd been so moved by the sight of a man crying. She couldn't, in fact, actually remember *any* time she'd been moved by the sight of a man crying, and she had seen more than her share. But here she was, standing in the middle of a small street in a seaside southern town, lump in her throat and long-suppressed maternal instincts screaming at her to *do* something, watching a painted man weep.

And she wasn't the only one. Pincushion wasn't exactly non-descript at the best of times, and right now he was hardly at his best. He was standing in the middle of A Street, wearing nothing but sandals, cut-off jeans and God knows how many gallons of tattooer's ink. Pincushion was over six feet tall and skinny as a stork. When he was smiling, which was most of the time, he radiated a kind of goofy infectious happiness, and his tattoos looked as perfectly natural as the Sunday funnies. But he wasn't smiling now. He wasn't sobbing, exactly, but tears were rolling unchecked down his cheeks, splashing on the multi-colored canvas of his chest. And he was slumping, somehow not just physically but spiritually. The tears of a clown, Robin thought. Or better, like that famous bronze sculpture of the defeated Indian warrior sitting on his weary horse. None of the tourists and Cedar Key locals who paused in their constant sidewalk circling to whisper and point at this gaudy gangly giant were laughing. This wasn't comedy, clearly, but tragedy.

Robin stepped up to Pincushion and gently put a hand on his arm. She had to reach up to do it; at five-foot-three, she normally looked Pincushion straight in the chin. He slowly turned his head and gazed down at her, hangdog eyes red and moist with tears.

"Yo, P," Robin said softly. "You okay?"

Pincushion nodded slowly and turned back to face the charred remnants of Pimlico Phil's Pinprick Palace. "It was a fucking shrine," he choked. "A fucking shrine."

It was a fucking tattoo parlor, Robin thought, and from what she'd heard so far, not particularly popular with the locals. Brought in the wrong sort of crowd, according to the lesbian owners of the clothing-and-coffee shop directly across A Street. Part of the "whoreification" of downtown Cedar Key, according to a bar owner who'd expressed sincere disappointment the fire had not also destroyed the Chinese restaurant two doors down.

But then there was Pincushion, who'd been excited as a child at Christmas, once he'd finally realized where they were going, about the idea of seeing the great Pimlico Phil. And there were other people grieving here—a fat-bellied biker with skulls tattooed on each fingertip sat on his Harley near the burned building with his head bowed; five minutes ago a pretty young redhead with florid Chinese symbols etched right below her tight little butt-cheeks had solemnly placed a bouquet of wildflowers where the parlor's door would have been. She'd been unable to answer Robin's questions, except to sob, "He was a prophet." A prophet in a tattoo parlor? *Bullshit*, Robin thought. People are so fucking gullible. But that, she grudgingly conceded, didn't make their pain any less real.

"A real tragedy, Cushion," Robin said. "But don't take it so hard. There are other parlors, other tattoo artists. . . ."

"You don't understand, man," Pincushion said. "They say he was a shaman, a seer, a great man. I had a special place on my heart for him."

"In your heart," Robin corrected absently.

"No, no, on my heart. See?" Pincushion pointed at his chest; sure enough, there among the prancing elves and slavering demon-dogs was a pale patch of untattooed flesh, about the size of a quarter. "I was going to get him to symbolize me right there. They say he could see right into your soul, and capture it in a single character for everybody to see. Now I'll never know who I really am!"

Okay, Robin thought, *compassion is fine, but enough is too much already*. Her bullshit meter had always been set on low, and she could only control her mouth for so long. She started to let loose on Pincushion, let him know what she thought of fools who place their faith in back-alley prophets. But at exactly that instant Pincushion squeezed her hand gratefully, then turned and walked toward the grieving biker. The biker stood, all jiggly belly and graying beard, and embraced Pincushion warmly. Strangers but comrades, sharing their pain. *Oh well*, Robin thought. She'd seen worse scams. And bullshit that brought people together was better than most bullshit. Like church, but less expensive. She shrugged her shoulders and bit her tongue.

To work, then. Max would love this new angle: Freaks weep after tattoo guru killed by mad monster. Pincushion, to his credit, had snapped a few shots of the girl with the flowers before descending into despair. Too bad he had all the cameras; a shot of him embracing the biker would be great theater. Serious violation of journalistic ethics for a photog to be personally involved in a shot, of course, but like Max always said, this ain't *The New York Times*.

True, and Robin Chanterelles knew she wasn't exactly Helen Thomas. But she had been a damn fine reporter once, and her instincts were still good enough to know when things didn't add up.

"And guess what, Robin ol' pal," Chanterelles mumbled under her breath. "Right here and now, things just don't quite add up." The tattoo parlor and the apartment above it were completely gone, burned beyond salvation by the time the Cedar Key Voluntary Fire Department had roared onto the scene. ("Voluntary, not volunteer," Robin reminded herself.

Nice bit of local color, that.) The warehouse next to the parlor was pretty much gutted too, but it had been empty. No one wanted to be next to that "horrible, horrible restaurant," according to the ladies at Loose Ladies Boutique and Coffee Shoppe. Said horrible restaurant, Mamasan's Chicks and Chinese, had lost part of an adjoining wall and suffered some smoke damage, but nothing serious. A Levy County inspector had told the St. Pete *Times* that the blaze undoubtedly started in Pimlico Phil's, and that there were some indications an accelerant had been present. He wasn't ruling arson—plenty of flammable chemicals on hand in a tattoo parlor, after all. Alcohol, some inks, lots of paper . . . still, he would be investigating further.

Fair enough, Robin thought. Maybe arson, maybe an insurance scam, maybe just an accident. Shit happens.

But why then had four different witnesses claimed that the sea monster was cursing Mamasan's Chinese, not the tattoo parlor, when it dove off the edge of the dock into the murky water below? Why were two people missing, but no bodies found? What was so special about this Pimlico Phil person? And why—

And why, Robin said to herself, *why am I worrying about all those facts? Not my job, not any more.* She had the meat of her story, had it before she'd set foot on the island. All she needed was another quote or two that she could manipulate into something juicy. Then back to the hotel to pound out a quick story, and send

it off to Max. With luck, she'd be finished in time for
whatever passed for happy hour around here. Or even
better, write the story now but hold off on filing for a
day or two. Drive Max crazy, run up a nice little expenses bill. Drinking on the company tab—the American way, right?

Before she could relax, though, Chanterelles
needed something sexy about the missing girl. Maybe
she'd had a premonition, or was phobic about lizards,
or just really crazy about seafood. Something like that
would make Max a happy boy even after she'd stuck
him for a couple days of hotel bills and gin and tonics.
Unfortunately, nobody here at the site seemed to
know much about the girl . . . to her home, then.
Sounded like it was only a short walk, and judging
from the smirks and knowing nods she'd gotten when
she mentioned his name, the girl's landlord was something of a local character anyway. Perfect.

Pincushion was deep in conversation with the
tattooed flower girl—mourning or making a move,
Robin couldn't tell—so she set off without interrupt-
ing him. It was mid-afternoon, and hot. She dug in her
purse for her sunglasses and slipped them on while
she walked.

Cedar Key, Robin thought, was actually a very
pretty little town. A little fancied up here along the
main drag, but that wasn't much more than a city
block long. On the way in, she and Pincushion had
passed over miles of mostly undisturbed saltwater
marsh, past quaint little hotels, wooden docks and old
clapboard buildings. Smiling sun-browned people

walked along and across the narrow streets without a whole lot of thought to traffic. There was a good feel to the place, a sort of sun-addled camaraderie everywhere. It reminded her of Destin 20 years ago, or Key West 25 years back, maybe St. George Island or a dozen other formerly pleasant beach towns before they'd gone the way of all Florida beachfronts. All of which meant, Robin knew, that Cedar Key was doomed.

Robin stopped to light a cigarette, remembering a chilling fact from her not-so-long-ago days as a straight reporter: Almost 1000 people moved to Florida every single day, and every damn one of them wanted to live on the coast. And of course, there was only a certain amount of coastline to go around. The law of supply and demand meant there was money to be made, truckloads of it, and plenty of people, more than willing to grab their share—environment and quality of life and sleepy quaint little towns be damned. Cedar Key had no real beach to speak of, just a stretch of dirty sand on a murky cove, but the developers would find a way around that. They always did.

Chanterelles had talked herself into a good cynical depression by the time she reached the western end of Dock Street; even the glum, fat brown pelican watching her from a piling by the D Street bridge couldn't get her to smile. Across the bridge and left on First, and there, just past the voluntary fire station, poking out of the comfortable tangle of weathered homes and folksy bed-and-breakfast spots, stood three, brand-spanking-new condominiums, way up on stilts to give their owner a view of the one-block-over Gulf. Just finished, apparently, "For Sale" signs in the front yard. They were pastel colored, lime green and peach pink and a sort of lemony yellow. They would have fit right in in Surfside, that godawful ready-made rich-folks-only Disneyfied abomination near Panama City. Here, among the rustic charm and backwater architecture of Cedar Key, they were appropriate as lipstick on a sand shark. Hideous. Robin flicked her cigarette butt disdainfully off a For Sale sign and fought the urge to break into her minibottle supply.

"Know just what you mean." Robin looked up, surprised to see a white-haired local on a rusty single-speed Schwinn coasting to a halt beside her. He gestured toward the pastel condos and grinned. "Never thought I'd see the day when they'd let coloreds move in. There goes the neighborhood."

Robin smiled despite herself and gave the cyclist a closer look. Not so old, really, the white hair and beard had fooled her. Mid-forties, maybe, or mid-fifties? Hard to tell; he had the agelessness that comes from a lifetime in the sun. Skinny, brown as a beachnut. He wore nothing but a pair of ragged cutoffs, though there was a T-shirt knotted around the bike's handlebar.

"I was just thinking," Robin said, "What a properly applied chainsaw would do to those support beams."

"Somebody tried that, while they were still under construction," the biker said. "Tried it three times, in fact, till they hired a night watchman. I hear you been looking for me."

"I have? Wait, are you, um, Tee Nichols? I was just trying to find your house."

"Just Tee, and you're on the right track. I got some sun tea brewing, why doncha come on over and we'll chat a bit." Tee grinned at Robin, then patted the handlebar of his bike. "Hop on."

"Um—thanks, but I'll walk," Robin said dubiously.

"Walk? All the way to my place? Come on, I do this all the time." Tee gave Robin an aw-shucks grin that must've melted many hearts harder than hers. "Trust me," he said, and for no reason whatsoever, Robin did.

"Okay," she said. "Just promise you'll be gentle." She slung her purse tightly over her shoulder, stepped up to Tee's bike, and after one false start managed to get herself up and balanced on the handlebar. She felt like an idiot—but an idiot who was having fun.

"Ready?" Tee said. "Brace yourself, here we go." He kicked off and pedaled the wobbly bike three or four good times. They coasted about twenty feet, catty-cornered across from the condos, and came to a stop in front of what Robin had thought was an overgrown empty lot. "Here we are," Tee said. "End of the line, everybody off."

Robin hopped down, trying her best not to smile. "My, that was exhilarating!" she said. "But I think I could have walked it."

"Yeah? What, you some kinda exercise freak?" Tee leaned the bike against a stunted, gnarled oak tree, then headed off down a narrow path through the underbrush. There was an old house back half-hidden behind the cabbage palms and Spanish moss, Robin realized. Warily, she followed.

Robin noted that Tee left his bike unlocked, in plain view of the street. Nobody was likely to steal something that battered, she thought, and if they did, well, big deal. But she was surprised to see Tee open his front door without using a key.

"You don't lock your door?" she said. Tee turned, halfway through the door, and looked at her like she'd just asked if frogs flew.

"If I lock the door, then how can people get in?" he said. "Watch out for the lizard—he likes little girl-toes, and he bites."

Robin looked where Tee had gestured. An ugly brown head the size of her thumb was peering out from between two coffee cans in a corner of the screened porch. A king skink, maybe the biggest she'd ever seen, and he did seem to be appraising her toes. She glared at it and stomped her foot menacingly; the skink didn't move. "Well, fuck you, buddy," she growled. The skink whipped its split tongue out—right at her, she thought—and Robin stepped quickly into the house.

Tee had already moved into the kitchen, leaving Robin alone in the main room. It took her a moment to adjust to the semi-darkness; the windows were open, but the light filtering in through the trees outside was dim and shadowy. Dust glittered like flecks of gold in a single beam of sunshine stabbing through one window. Robin blinked and swatted at a mosquito hovering before her eyes. The room, once she could make it out, was pretty much an extension of the wilderness and clutter outside. A bookcase took up most of one wall, overflowing with paperbacks, a few raggedy clothbound books and innumerable stacks of loose paper and faded magazines. A record player sat on the floor, speakers attached by two loops of worn wire, thirty or forty albums stacked beside it. A ragged armchair sat in one corner, reading lamp beside it, books and beer cars on the floor nearby. A faded gold couch was against the opposite wall, sagging so far down in the middle that it made Robin think of a swaybacked carnival pony she'd ridden as a child. Plants were everywhere, in coffee cans and fine handmade pottery, cactuses and ferns, flowers and creeping vines. Some were flourishing, others looked dried almost to death. Two coffee cans on the counter dividing main room from kitchen held nothing but dirt; Robin couldn't tell if the plants there were not yet sprouted or already long dead.

"Never got your name," Tee said from the kitchen. He was at the sink, pouring gasoline-colored liquid from a gallon jug into a jelly glass. That room was a kitcheny extension of the main room. Jars lined the cabinets, filled with dried fruits and pickled vegetables. One wall seemed devoted to nothing but bottles of vinegars and hot sauces. More plants. A card table groaned under the weight of more books and beer cans and the unwashed dishes of a long-finished meal. The walls were covered with pictures and posters of every shape and size, stuck there with yellowing tape

or plastic thumbtacks. Sky charts of unfamiliar con-
stellations, concert announcements, Buddhist tracts,
photographs of people and places all curling up from
the humidity. A naked Janis Joplin gazed somberly
out from a black and white poster, strands of beads
not quite covering her breasts, hands folded strategi-
cally over her bare abdomen. A single pickle floated
forlornly in a quart jar on the countertop; taped to the
jar was a handwritten note that said, "Please do not
feed the pickle."

"Chanterelles," Robin said. "Robin Chanterelles."

"Like the mushroom."

"Sorry?"

"Chanterelles mushroom. Bright yellow, sometimes black spots. Only grows in the sand. Honey?"

"No, thanks. Sweet and Low?"

Tee shook his head and gave Robin a wistful smile
that made her feel almost guilty. "Sorry," he said. "Try
some of this instead." He poked his upper body out
the wide-open unscreened kitchen window and
plucked something green and leafy from a window
box. Robin watched as he crumbled it into her glass;
when she raised the tea to her lips she smelled the
light vibrant scent of fresh mint.

"Delicious," she said, and meant it. Tee nodded
his acknowledgement and waved her toward the only
uncluttered seat at the table. He scooped a pile of
newspapers off a second chair, sat down, and looked at
Robin expectantly. Robin savored another sip of tea
before digging into her purse for pen and notepad.
She was, to her surprise, reluctant to shift into reporter

mode. It was relaxing here, almost peaceful. Despite the sweltering heat and the buzzing mosquitoes, she felt right at home. And that, she knew, was certain death for a reporter, especially for a hack reporter who specialized in bullshit and hatchet jobs. Gotta stay sharp, gotta stay distant. She remembered what Sam Puddler, her beloved once-upon-a-time news editor, had said her first day on the job: "Welcome to the *Apalachicola Sun*. Don't trust anyone, and kiss all your friends goodbye."

Shit, Sam, Chanterelles thought, *You may not speak to me anymore, but I still hear your voice. Damn you anyway.* She shook herself mentally. Might as well dive right in, blow this potential friendship out of the water before it gets started. She put down the mint-tanged tea and picked up her pen.

"Now then," she asked. "Why do you think a fire-breathing sea monster killed your tenant Desiree Dean?"

Tee didn't blink. "She's not dead," he said.

"I've talked to a half-dozen people who say she was in working at Mamasan's the night it burned down. The police list her as missing, and nobody's seen her since. Unless you have?"

"Nope. But she's not dead."

"You've talked to her, then?"

"Nope. No smoking in here, honey."

Robin grimaced and pushed the unlit Doral Light back into the pack. She hadn't even noticed she was preparing to light one. Old habits.

"Sorry. So, you know other people who've seen her?"

"Nope. You know, that's the quickest way to make a beautiful woman unattractive."

"Sorry?"

"Put a cigarette in her mouth. Makes you question her intelligence, ruins her breath. Kissing her is like licking an ashtray."

"I don't smoke that much. And I'm not beautiful."

"Yes you do, and yes you are. Desiree is the same way."

"You mean she smoked?"

"Smokes, and no, she doesn't. I mean she refuses to see how beautiful she is. Like you."

"I'm not—"

"You want to see a picture of her?"

"Yes, of course." Robin knew she'd been steered away from her questioning. An old trick, one she'd seen seasoned politicians try with much less grace than this aging beach bum. She decided to let him get away with it, because she did want to see Desiree's photo before Tee got too pissed off to show her. And she would piss him off, sooner or later. It was part of her job.

Tee stood up and started across the kitchen towards the refrigerator; Robin assumed one of the photos taped and magneted there was Desiree. Beat him to the punch, she thought, maybe intimidate him a little with my insight. She quickly scanned a half-dozen or so pictures taped to the rusty refrigerator before settling on one of a pretty young woman laughing at the cocker spaniel lapping her face. "That one," she said. "With the puppy."

"This one?" Tee pointed to a picture of a black-

and-white mutt on a dirty beach, yapping down at what looked like a crab hole.

"No, no the one beside it. With the cocker spaniel. That's Desiree, right?"

"Nope. That's my daughter." Tee opened the refrigerator and pulled out a strand of three Budweiser cans hanging together on a plastic ring. "Ready for dessert?"

"No thanks. Not while I'm working."

"Oh, right. I forgot. What paper did you say you were with again?"

Here we go, Robin thought. End of interview. "You've probably never heard of it. It's a weekly, published out of Orlando."

"You mean the *Weekly Alarm?*"

"Um—Yes."

"You're right, never heard of it. You want to see that picture of Desiree, you got to come this way." Tee walked off down the hallway past the refrigerator. Robin heard the soft cooosh of his beer can opening and jumped up to follow him.

There was a screen door at the end of the hallway and through it she could see some sort of garage-like outbuilding. She figured that's where Tee was heading, but at the last moment he turned left and opened a door into a room that must have been added on to the main house. Now what, she thought, would prompt this no-secrets-no-shame guy to actually keep a door closed? She braced herself for the worst, and followed him into the last thing she expected.

The room was at least as big as the kitchen, making

it the biggest room in the entire house, meticulously
organized, and blessedly cool. A small air conditioner
hummed quietly in one window, the only other window opened onto a beautiful little flower-filled courtyard. The walls were covered not with haphazard
odds and ends but rather more than a dozen paintings,
most in oil, others in acrylic or watercolors. Most were
Cedar Key scenes, the sort of subject matter you'd expect to find in any touristy gift shop, but something
about the tones, the shadings of light and fineness of
detail, made each painting seem ready to burst into
life. The craftsmanship itself was good—very good,
even—but there was something else, something
about the way each painting caught a story in the very
act of being told. A weathered fisherman checked his
empty net sadly, and the desperate worry so clear on
his face spoke of overdue bills and underfed children.
A sailboat leaned hard in the wind, crying out the joyous challenge of its unseen skipper. A child laughed at
some secret treasure he'd torn from the sand, and
Robin ached for the ability to laugh that freely again.
Soaring ospreys, a scarred old manatee, elderly lovers
embracing on a rickety dock—each one told a small
story, each one captured a lifetime. Robin realized she
was holding her breath. She forced herself to exhale
and tore her eyes from the paintings.

There were only three pieces of furniture in the
room. A three-legged easel holding a large canvas was
turned so Robin couldn't see, before it stood a worn
wooden bar stool. Beside them a simple wooden table
held paint and brushes, a paint-spattered rag, and—

"Fudge," Tee said. "Yum. Gotta have it. Want some?" He picked up a chipped blue plate on which rested a dozen or so fat chunks of gooey fudge, some brown, some white, several a soft yellow-green. "Try the key-lime fudge. Made right here in town, at a shop over on Dock Street. Best in the world."

"You're an artist," Robin said, trying to keep the awe out of her voice.

"Been accused of that, yeah, but mostly I just paint. The white chocolate is pretty good too. Had some peanut butter swirl earlier, but it all got ate. Sorry."

"Oh, no, that's fine, that's fine . . ." Robin moved slowly around the room, soaking in each painting before moving on to the next little masterpiece. This was not the way to maintain control of an interview, but she couldn't help herself. There were so many wonderful stories here, so many lives caught on canvas—the weary persistence of an oysterman harvesting his crop, a great blue heron standing patiently at the water's edge, a comical pelican gazing in solemn dignity right at the artist. She could sense Tee standing behind her, nibbling patiently on his fudge. "These are amazing," she said. "Beautiful, powerful—magnificent! Have you—I mean, I'm not an artist, or even a critic, but these are just amazing. Have you tried showing them, in a gallery, in a big city? These things could make you rich!"

"I *am* rich," Tee said. "Can't you tell?"

Robin turned and looked at Tee, wearing nothing but his ragged shorts and a lifetime's worth of sunburn. He was working away at what must have been a richly gooey chunk of fudge, mouth too full to speak, but he extended the plate toward her and raised his eyebrows in happy invitation. Robin laughed and stepped forward, reaching out to take a piece of the key lime fudge. Doing so brought her in view of the canvas on the easel, and she stopped in midreach.

"Desiree," she said. There was no doubt in her voice, and Tee didn't bother to answer. The painting spoke for itself.

The girl was standing in an outdoor shower, framed by the open wooden door. She was naked, full-figured but shapely, long midnight-black hair wet and slicked against her pale skin. She was leaning back toward the showerhead, soaking her in splashing water, so her bare abdomen leaned toward the viewer just a bit. One hand was over her pubic mound, but Robin couldn't tell if she were covering herself, or washing herself, or pleasing herself. Tee had apparently surprised her that way, her eyes barely open, lips parted just a touch. She was smiling ever so slightly in—embarrassment? Anticipation? Timid invitation? It didn't matter. Robin liked this woman right away. There was something delicate and important there, something fragile and familiar. . . .

"The Janis Joplin poster. She's got that same sort of hesitant sexuality."

"Yes," Tee said. "Like a scared, wild kitten that wants to be tamed. Or a tame, scared kitten that wants to be wild. That's Desiree."

"She *is* beautiful."

"Of course."

"She knew you were watching her shower?"

"Not that time. Later."

"So you spied on her?" Robin said it with no judgment in her voice, and when Tee answered he was not a bit defensive.

"Nah. She wanted to be seen."

Robin nodded and leaned in closer to the painting. Something small and green was clinging to the side of the shower just behind Desiree. Robin squinted, and then smiled.

"That's a tree frog."

"Yep. They love to hang out in that shower when the water's flowing."

Chanterelles grinned, thinking back to a weekend she'd spent camping at a state park near Panama City. The showers there had been inside, three or four in a big clean bathroom, but the tree frogs had gotten in nonetheless. They'd quietly creep up the shower wall while you showered, and for no reason she'd ever figured out, would suddenly let loose with a sharp amphibian bark and leap onto the bare back of the unsuspecting bather. Robin had set up her tent not far from the showers, and got a great kick out of listening to the steady chorus of screams from within.

"Now what," she mused, half to herself, "What is going to happen to that sweet smile when that frog leaps on her back?" Tee just shrugged and popped another piece of fudge in his mouth.

"Best fudge in the world," he said. "The guy who makes this, the fudge chef, he came to Cedar Key and spent like six months working on his recipes before he ever opened his shop. Went from one-hundred-sixty-pounds to two-thirty before he made a dime. Now people come from hundreds of miles for this stuff, and poor ol' Johnny Fudge can't have a bite."

"Tragic," Robin said. "Maybe I should try some, for poor ol' Johnny Fudge."

"It'd be the right thing to do," Tee said. He extended the plate toward Robin—it was down to a mere four pieces—and she had just picked one out when something slammed into the tin roof above them like a striking meteor. Robin jumped back into the wall and dropped to her knees, heart pounding like a trip hammer.

"What the fuck!" she shouted. Tee had jumped a touch at the explosion, but overall was being cool about it. He frowned and tromped out of the studio. Robin heard him open the side door and then yell out into the Cedar Key afternoon: "Chill out, Pris! I hardly know the girl, for God's sake!" He came back a moment later, shaking his head and holding something in one closed hand. He smiled reassuringly at Robin and helped her to her feet.

"Brace yourself," he said. "They usually come in sets of three."

"Three? Three whats?"

"Golf balls." Tee opened his hand to reveal a shiny new Titleist. Robin had her mouth half open to ask the obvious question when something hit the side of the house, not near as loud as the one on the roof but still loud enough to make her jump. "One more," Tee said. "Sorry."

"Tee, what the hell?"

"Priscilla. Ex-girlfriend. She moved into an apartment above that bookstore on the corner so she can keep an eye on me. When she sees I've got female company, she hits the roof with golf balls."

"Jesus H. Christ."

"Yep. Gets downright aggravating, sometimes. Hell of a thing to wake up to, golf balls slamming into that tin roof like the wrath of God after a long night of loving. Or not loving. I think sometimes she fires a shot or two just to keep me on my toes."

"From above the bookstore?"

"Yep."

"That bookstore is nearly two blocks away."

"Yep. She's got a big ol' rubber slingshot. Got a hell of an aim too. Get ready, we're 'bout due for the third shot." He was right, and Robin was ready, but she still jumped like a startled cat when the ball smacked into the roof. This time she heard it hit, bounced a couple times and then roll noisily down the slope of the tin roof.

Tee followed the sound of the rolling ball and nodded in satisfaction. "The good part of this is, every two–three weeks a fisherman friend of mine comes down and trades me fresh grouper for golf balls. Just too bad she switched to Titleist; Terry's more of a Maxfli man. So how you like the fudge?"

Robin followed Tee's eyes down to her right hand, feeling like an idiot. She'd had a piece of the key-lime in her hand when the first ball hit; in her fright she'd clenched her hand closed on it. Now she had soft green-yellow candy oozing out around her fingers like play-doh in a molding machine.

"Oops," Robin said. She smiled self-consciously and scooped a nice long smear of green fudge onto one finger. She looked around for some place to toss it; finding none, she shrugged and popped it into her mouth.

"Wow," she said after a moment. "Wow, that is good!"

"Toldja," Tee said. "Want a paper towel or something?"

"No, no, I got it. This is too good to waste." Robin scooped as much of the luscious green fudge off her fingers as she could, savoring every delicate citrus-flavored bite. Before she knew it she was licking her fingers clean, preening herself like a cat. She was going after one particularly sticky side of her thumb when she noticed Tee, framed between her splayed fingers and watching her studiously. Chanterelles fought off the urge to offer him a lick; instead, she slowly wiped her slick fingers on her slacks and slipped back into reporter mode.

"Mr. Nichols," she asked, "What do you think happened to Desiree Dean?"

Tee nodded thoughtfully, accepting without comment the sudden change in their interaction. He studied the ceiling a moment and pursed his lips before he answered.

"I believe," Tee said, "Pirates got her."

Chapter Seven

Desiree Dean awoke to pain and confusion.

The pain came first, pressing in on her even before she opened her eyes—a low burn/itch sensation from her upper chest, and a steady throb from her left knee. Distant pains, both of them, but undeniable. And uncomfortable.

Then came the confusion, beginning with the very basic, "Where the heck am I?" followed by the obvious "How did I get here?" and the not-so-expected "And who took my clothes off?" There was also the matter of the thick bandage strapped across her chest and the, now that she was thinking about it, not-so-distant pain in that same area. Plus, she had a headache. And she had to tinkle. Hungry too, and very, very thirsty.

"Just another happy Sunday morning," Desiree thought. Assuming it was still Sunday. It must be, because last night was Saturday, because she'd gone to work at Mamasan's, been working the door in that darned dragon suit, and—

Uh-oh.

Had charged into Pimlico Phil's with murder on her mind, and ended up in tears. Had set first Phil and then herself on fire. Fled Phil's in desperate search of help, pounded fruitlessly on the door of Mamasan's, and then there was bright light and sudden pain and . . . And then? She couldn't remember.

"Stay calm, Desiree," she whispered to herself. "Take stock, figure it out." Was she in a hospital? In jail? No—neither place, at least in her admittedly limited experience, would be constructed from weathered gray wood, neither would have bright sunlight leaking through holes in a tin ceiling, or windows covered over with thick burlap.

Dead and in Hell, then? It was certainly hot enough. But she didn't think Hell came with feather pillows and—yes!—water, in a quart orange juice bottle, resting invitingly on an overturned milk crate right beside her bed. There was fruit there too, several dates and a mango. But the water first. Desiree forced herself up on her elbows, wincing at the sharp pain from her chest and the discovery of numerous smaller aches from various corners of her body. The water was warm but delicious; she glugged half the bottle down before allowing her mind and her vision to turn to an examination of her injuries.

First, her chest. Desiree forced herself to sit up straight; the sheet clung to her sweaty torso for a moment before slipping down into her lap. Desiree took a sharp breath and fought against crying out. A handmade bandage the size of a handkerchief was taped expertly across the upper left side of her chest, covering most of her sternum and her left breast. She touched it gingerly and winced at the stab of pain. She tried to delicately lift the upper edge of the bandage to survey the damage underneath, and was partly relieved when the tightly taped bandage wouldn't allow her to do so.

Her knee, then. She grasped the edge of the sheet in the toes of her left foot and gingerly pulled it off her lower body. Naked all right, she noted, except for the strips of cloth wrapped tightly around her right leg from just below to just above the knee. The floral pattern on the strips matched both the bandage on her chest and the sheet she was sitting on. Very feminine, yellow flowers on a pale pink background. Not daisies, thank heaven. Slightly reassuring, too. The person who undressed her was a woman. Or at least had womanish tastes. Or maybe stole sheets from women. Kidnapped women, raped them, murdered them, and stole their sheets. Desiree swallowed hard and eased one hand between her thighs, hoping not to find the bruises she assumed would be there if she had been raped while unconscious.

"Ha! Nothing I like better than a girl who goes for her goodies first thing in the morning."

Desiree jerked her hand out of her crotch, grabbed for the sheet, spun around and winced in pain all at once. The door she hadn't noticed behind her—or rather, the thick burlap covering an opening in one wall—had been drawn back, and someone was standing there. She blinked and shaded her eyes against the bright sunlight flooding into the room, doing her best to cover herself with the sheet at the same time. There was a child at the door, or a teenaged girl perhaps—she couldn't really tell with the sun in her eyes. Small, at least, and female. Desiree felt a rush of relief, followed by a surge of embarrassment.

"Oh, no, I wasn't—"

"S'alright. I usually start the day that way myself. Get myself going before I get myself going. I like to roll over on my belly, put pressure on my hand in just the right place. You should try that."

"No, I—"

"Really, you should. I'll show you sometime." The girl stepped into the room, letting the burlap flop back into place behind her, and Desiree saw that she wasn't a child but a very short woman, 5'2" or 5'3" at the most. Slender, coppery-gold hair cut short around a sun-browned face, bright green eyes. She was wearing cut-off shorts, no shoes, and a garnet-and-gold Florida State University T-shirt. Early twenties, maybe, just a year or two older than Desiree herself.

The girl took several quick steps across the room and stuck her hand out toward Desiree.

"Hey," she said. "I'm Pambellina. Who the hell are you?"

"Pambellina?"

"No, I'm Pambellina. You'll have to be somebody else."

"I mean—"

"Kidding." Pambellina walked over to the bed, picked up the plate of fruit and plopped down on the milk carton. "Pambellina, actually, 'cause my real name is Pamela, but some people seem to think I'm a little small, so they started calling me Thumbellina, after the fairy tale. Then Pambellina, 'cause—well, because that's what people do with nicknames." She took an enthusiastic bite from the mango and looked at Desiree expectantly.

"I'm Desiree. Desiree Dean."

"Desiree Dean, the Dragon Queen?"

"Desiree the dummy," Desiree said glumly. And then, surprising herself, she blurted out, "I think I may have burned down Pimlico Phil's Pinprick Palace."

"Yeah, I heard about that. What'd you have against ol' fat Phil?"

"Nothing! I mean, lots, but I didn't mean to burn down his shop. It was an accident."

"Accelerants and explosives was an accident?"

"What and what?"

"Accelerants and explosives. Gasoline or maybe kerosene, the newspaper said, but they didn't know what kind of explosive. Of course, the paper also said you were dead, so whadda they know?"

"Dead? Me?"

"Yep. Well, missing and presumed dead. Just like ol' Phil."

"Phil's dead?"

"And presumed missing. Just like you."

"Oh no." I killed Phil, Desiree thought. I should

be really upset. I should be crying, or praying, or something. But I don't feel like crying, she realized with a pang of guilt, I don't feel like praying. I feel like—eating. "Could I have a bite of that mango?" she asked.

"Oh yeah. Help yourself, plenty more where that came from."

Pambellina ripped the mango slice roughly in half and handed one piece to Desiree. The two sat munching away in companionable silence for a bit. Finally, Desiree broke the quiet to address something that had been nibbling at a corner of her mind.

"You said I was in the newspaper?"

"Yep. Lots of 'em, I guess, but the one I read was the *Lantern*."

"But the *Lantern* only comes out once a week."

"Right."

"On Tuesday."

"Right."

"But it's Sunday."

"Wrong."

"Not Sunday?"

"Not close." Pambellina glanced over at Desiree and gave her a little half-smile. "It's Wednesday afternoon, girl. You been sleeping for three days."

"Three days!"

"Nights too, mostly. I got you up and made you pee a couple times, but I'm not sure you were ever really awake. You remember that?"

"Peeing? No, no I don't think so." Though in fact, Desiree did have a hazy memory of stumbling through sand, of strong arms supporting her while she squatted. There was something else there, too, a haze of gentle hands and soothing words, something painful and comforting at the same time . . .

"Too bad, you were kinda funny." Pambellina grinned and bit lustily into a plum-sized date the color of an early pumpkin. "Kept asking for paper; got all pissed off 'cause I didn't have any."

"How could I have slept for three days?" Desiree said, trying hard to keep the panic out of her voice. Had she been drugged after all?

"Doctor said that's not unusual for somebody who's got a concussion."

"A concussion? I had a concussion? How did I get a concussion?"

"Probably when you fell into my boat. That's how you hurt your knee too. The burn you got before you dropped in on me."

"Burn . . . ?" Desiree raised one hand tentatively to her bandaged breast. This time, Pambellina reacted to the fear in her voice.

"Hey, it's ok. Doc said it was mostly superficial burns, and you won't have much of a scar at all. He gave me some cream to put on there every night, too. Didn't have any bandages, though. Hope you don't mind the sheets."

"No, no, the sheets are just fine. Thank you." Desiree took a deep breath, forcing herself to calm down and stop imagining her breasts covered with blisters and horribly scarred. "Gosh, I have been so rude. I don't even know you, and you saved my life, you took me to a hospital and nursed me back to health, and I haven't even said thank you."

"Wadn't nothing. Besides, I feel a little responsible, seeing's how it was my boat you whacked yourself up on. But I didn't take you to a hospital."

"You didn't?"

"Nope."

"The doctor came here?"

"Sort of."

"He didn't come here?"

"He did come here. Sort of a doctor."

"'Sort of a doctor?'"

"He's a vet."

"A veterinarian!"

"Okay, a biologist. A marine biologist, mostly works on manatees and dolphins and such. But he's really good. I saw him one time, there was this bottlenose dolphin had a number 12 fishhook through his dorsal and about ten feet of heavy line, and Dr. Bill—"

"You let a veterinarian fondle my boobies and treat me for a concussion! I could've died!"

"Died from getting your boobs fondled?"

"No, I mean—"

"You couldn't have died, I told you, Bill's good. And he didn't fondle your boobs, he fixed 'em. Mostly, anyhow."

"Mostly?!"

"Well, yeah. I mean, he said you might have some discoloration there, where your tattoo was."

"Was?"

"Was. The burns kinda scrunched it up some. It's

still there, sort of, but mostly it's not. Hey, don't worry, once your skin heals up you can get the tattoo replaced. Or removed complete."

"Pimlico Phil gave me that tattoo," Desiree said, not bothering to disguise the anger in her voice. She blinked away the beginnings of a tear, and bit savagely into the mango. A bit of juice drooled down her chin; she tried to ignore it, feeling tough and mean, but after a moment her instincts won out and she delicately wiped it off with a fingertip.

"Okay," Desiree said after a minute. "Okay, then, I guess I'm not in a hospital."

"Not hardly."

"Or a police station."

"Ha!"

"Then where the heck am I?"

"You're in my home, of course. Welcome to the Tiltin' Hilton."

"Your home? You live here?" Desiree squinted hard. Her eyes had adjusted to the dim light a bit, and she could see better—but there just wasn't much to see. A chest over in one corner, with some candles and a stack of magazines on it. What looked like a broom handle had been jammed chest-high catty-cornered in one corner of the room, and a handful of clothes hung from it. A fishing rod stood in another corner, a plastic bucket beside it. The cot Desiree was on, the bedside crate . . . and that was pretty much it. No TV or telephone, no kitchen, and—groan!—no bathroom.

"Hey, I know it ain't' exactly the Ritz, but—"

"Oh no, no, I'm sorry, you have a lovely home. It's just that I'm, I guess I'm still a little confused. My head, you know."

"I know."

"So, um, your home. Where is it again?"

"On a island."

"An island. Cedar Key, you mean?"

"Nope."

"Atsinky Other Key?" Desiree said, knowing she was mangling the name of the little island directly south of Cedar Key.

"Atsena Otie," Pambellina corrected. "And no, not there either."

"Then Seahorse Key? Or one of the other little keys?"

"One of the others."

"Oh." Desiree nodded thoughtfully and nibbled the tip of a forefinger. Finally, she decided she couldn't wait for Pambellina to offer. "Um," she said hesitantly, "Um, you said there was a bathroom?"

"Sure. Right outside."

"Oh good, thank you." Desiree started to sit up, feeling more urgent with each passing second. The pain in her chest wasn't too bad, and she thought she could just hop on one leg if she needed to. But then—"Eek," she said.

"Eek?"

"My clothes?" Desiree pulled the sheet closer to her, blushing furiously. Silly, she thought, so anxious to show off her boobies at Mamasan's, but with Pambellina she felt—naked.

"Oh, right, your clothes. Burned, mostly, and we had to cut some of 'em off to get at your wounds. Lemme see what I got here." Pambellina stepped over to the makeshift closet and flipped through the clothes hanging there. "Hmmm, no way any of these are gonna fit you."

"I know. I'm so fat."

"What? No, I mean 'cause I'm so tiny. I buy most of my stuff in kids' departments, or get hand-me-downs from middle-school kids. Ah, maybe this'll do." She handed Desiree a faded orange Tampa Bay Buccaneers T-shirt with Warrick Dunn's name on the back. "It's way big for me, but sometimes I sleep in it when it's cold out."

Desiree nodded her thanks and reluctantly dropped the sheet. The shirt was a large, a little small for her. She squeezed into it slowly and carefully, wincing when the cloth pressed against her burned chest. Pambellina watched her impassively the entire time.

"Looks good," Pambellina said.

"Thanks. Um, panties?"

"Sorry. Maybe Dr. Bill will have some gym shorts or something we can borrow."

Desiree nodded, pulled the T-shirt down as far as it would go, and gingerly swung her legs over the side of the cot. Pambellina took one arm and helped her stand; Desiree had a dizzy flashback to that memory of someone holding her while she tinkled, and felt herself blush again.

"Okay," she said, testing her weight on her bad

knee. "Okay, I think I can walk all right. Wow, I really have to go."

"Well sure. I mean, three days."

"Yeah. Right outside, you said?"

"Uh huh. Follow me."

Desiree nodded and shuffled carefully along behind Pambellina. She stopped for a moment when they reached the door, leaning one hand on the wall and catching her breath. Then Pambellina pulled the burlap hanging aside, and Desiree stepped out into the blinding sunshine. She blinked for a moment, catching her breath and studying her surroundings.

"Well," she thought, "It's an island." An uninhabited island, as far as she could tell. With the Tiltin' Hilton behind her, Desiree was facing an intimidating, scraggly jungle of scrub pine, saw grass, ferns and palmetto bushes. There was a rough circle of bare sand maybe ten feet wide on each side of the shack. The ground sloped slowly down towards the left; there was a thick stand of mangrove there, but Desiree could smell salt water and hear waves on the far side of it. More jungle to her right, broken by a path through the tangled vines and brambles.

"Through there, to the oak tree with the split trunk and then to the right. You'll need these." Pambellina stepped around the side of the shack for a second; when she came back she handed Desiree a small shovel and—

"A bushel basket?"

"Uh huh." Pambellina smiled at Desiree for a moment, then frowned and took the tall, slender basket

back from her. "Like this," she said. Pambellina
flipped the basket over so the wide-open mouth was
facedown in the sand. The smaller bottom end had
been cut out; a thick layer of burlap padding was held
in place by a few strips of gray duct tape. "The
padding helps," Pambellina said, "But watch out for
splinters. And one more thing." She reached into her
back pocket, produced an old *Sporting News*, and
shrugged apologetically. "No paper," she said.

Desiree took the magazine, nodded and swallowed
hard.

Pambellina watched her odd new guest stagger hesitantly down the path towards the latrine and tried not
to laugh. *Poor kid's in pain*, she reminded herself. *And
so what if she actually says "eek"? Lotsa people say "eek."
Maybe where she comes from "eek" is a normal thing.*

The girl was walking kind of tiptoe through the
sand, trying to avoid sand spurs. Good strategy, but it
made the T-shirt rise up on her backside with each
step. Pambellina felt a little guilty about that; she
knew the gym shorts Doc Bill had left with her were
sitting comfortably in the bottom of her hope chest
right now. But it was such a nice backside, what
Madonna at the L&M would call a rump. Not a tight,
sexy, disco-queen ass, not a big ol' ride 'em cowboy
butt. A rump. Soft and rounded, Midwestern baby fat
curving out just enough on either side. And of course,
an angry red patch the size of the Pambellina's fist on
one cheek. Doc Bill had said it might scar there,

maybe big enough to show around the edge of a bikini bottom. Poor kid.

Pambellina started to call out to Desiree, to warn her to be careful when she eased herself down on the basket's edge. But no, she'd find that out soon enough. Let her alone, let her poop in peace. Give her a few minutes out there in the quiet wilderness to get herself together.

Pambellina would give her the rest of the bad news when she returned.

Chapter Eight

Pincushion was sitting at a wooden picnic bench beside a small coke and hot dog stand called Gulfside Cuisine when Robin found him again. He had a lime popsicle in one hand and the knee of a doe-eyed, mini-skirted, young brunette in the other; he was paying much more attention to the girl, even though the popsicle was dripping slick green juice over his fingers and down onto his camera bag. The girl was fairly wrapped up in Pincushion too, leaning in much closer than she really needed to study the inky alien invaders swooshing up Pincushion's left arm. The look she flashed when Robin plunked her notebook on the table and sat down across from Pincushion was not particularly friendly.

"Hey P," Robin said wearily. "Popsicle's melting."

"Hey Miss Robin," Pincushion switched the popsicle from his left hand to his right and began licking the sticky juice off his fingers, which meant the popsicle was now dripping right onto the sun-bronzed thigh of his companion. The girl hardly seemed to notice. In fact, Robin saw with a stirring of unhappy recognition in her gut, the girl was no longer paying attention to Pincushion at all. Her eyes were suddenly very wide, her pouty little lips had dropped in undisguised awe, and the look on her face had gone from wary to worship.

"Oh fuck," Robin thought.

"Robin Chanterelles!" the girl said, her voice hushed but rising, as if she had just begun a prayer. "Ohmigod I can't believe it's really you! I have been a fan of yours for just so long, I can't believe I'm really getting to meet you, I—oh, goodness, listen to me go on." The girl took a deep breath, composed herself, and with all the dignity she could muster extended one trembling hand across the table for Robin to shake. "Miss Chanterelles," she said, "It is an honor and a privilege to make your acquaintance."

Oh god, Robin thought. *Purple finger nail polish. With glitter.* But what she said, in her most well-behaved professional voice, was, "Well, thank you, thank you very much. It is always delightful to meet a fan."

"Delightful," the girl said, with an actual giggle. "God, she even talks like a famous writer! Oh, Pincushel, this is so exciting!"

"'Pincushel'?" Robin thought. She glanced at her photographer and raised one eyebrow slightly; Pincushion just grinned and licked more juice off his hand. "Yep, that's my partner, my colleague in crime, the famous Robin C," he said. "Robin, allow me to make you the introduction of The Chipmunk. The Chipmunk works at that fine eating establishment over there, the one with the missing wall. She is an entertainer."

"Pleased to meet you, Miss—The Chipmunk?"

"Oh, it's not *The* Chipmunk, it's just Chipmunk," Chipmunk said. "He just calls me The Chipmunk because . . . because . . ." Chipmunk half-turned and looked at Pincushion as if it had never before occurred to her to wonder why in fact Pincushion added the "the." She half-frowned, puckering up what even Robin had to admit were very nice lips. Then she suddenly brightened and turned back to Chanterelles. "My real name is Patricia, Patricia Pye," she said. "But Howie, he's my boss, he calls me Chipmunk 'cause he says I could crack walnuts in my cheeks." Chipmunk giggled again, and then, seeing that Robin was studying her face and hadn't gotten the reference, bounced to her feet, turned her back to Robin and hooked her girlish fingers under the hem of her skirt. "Not *those* cheeks," she said. "*These* cheeks. Wanna see?"

"Later, sweetpea, later," Pincushion said. Robin turned to him, grateful but surprised he had stopped The Chipmunk in mid-flash. Pincushion leaned conspiratorially across the table towards Robin, a suddenly excited, sticky-fingered little boy, and The Chipmunk dejectedly eased herself back onto the bench.

"Robin," Pincushion said earnestly, "The Chipmunk says they got pirates here!"

Robin nodded and reached into her shirt pocket for her cigarettes. "Yeah, I know. Gotta source who thinks that's who carried off the missing waitress."

"What?!" The Chipmunk exclaimed. "Red Luck has Desiree?"

"The ghost pirate kidnapped the she-dragon?" Pincushion chimed in. "Cool!"

"What? Red who? What ghost?" Robin glared from each of her companions to the other and back, debating if it was them or she who had been out in the sun too long. "I'm talking clam pirates. Claim jumpers. Apparently there's fishermen around here who are all pissed off because some fat cats have gotten a monopoly on the state-leased clam-breeding waters. So they come in late at night, these pirates, and scoop up clams when the legal owners aren't around, and then . . ." Robin let her voice trail off. Pincushion was looking right at her, shaking his head in disappointment, and Chipmunk seemed to have found something of great interest in the inlet behind her.

"Robin," Pincushion said gently. "Red Luck is the patron spirit of Cedar Key. He's a pirate, and a ghost. And he's *here.*"

"Right," Robin said. "Pirates. Ghosts. I gotta get me a Mountain Dew." She stood and started toward the hot dog stand—and suddenly someone grabbed her wrist.

"You shouldn't be laughing at Red Luck," The Chipmunk said ominously. "You don't want to do that."

The girl had a hell of a grip. She was still seated, so Robin had leverage on her, but she had the distinct impression she wouldn't be able to break free if she'd tried. And she wasn't going to try. There was something about the way The Chipmunk said those few words, not angry, but with a passion and intensity that caught Robin by surprise. And something else—the fire in the young girl's eyes made Robin wonder how much of Chipmunk's bimbo act was, well, an act. Robin eased slowly back to her seat.

"Tell me," she said.

Chipmunk nodded and leaned in over the table, all business now. "Well," she said. "Red Luck was a smuggler, and a pirate, back in the early 1800s— 1820,1830, something like that. He had a partner, a Frenchman who owned a bunch of land up on the Suwannee River. I guess you could say he was kind of Red Luck's fence. And the landowner, he had a daughter."

"Ah ha," Robin said. Chipmunk narrowed her eyelids in warning, and Robin shut up.

"The daughter, her name was Lura Lou, and she and Red Luck were in love. Her father found out, and he was really furious. He decided to kill Red Luck, and set up an ambush. But there were some fishermen from Cedar Key up there visiting, and they found out about it and told Red Luck. So Red Luck took Lura Lou aboard his ship and the two sailed off, and were never seen again. Alive, anyway. They sailed right into a hurricane, and the ship went down with all hands."

"But his ghost. . . ."

"Before he left, Red Luck swore he would pay back the fishermen for their help someday. And now, when Cedar Key fishermen are in trouble, the ghost of Red Luck shows up on his ghost ship, the *Lura Lou*, and saves them." Chipmunk sighed dreamily and leaned in to rest her head on her cradled elbows. "The *Lura Lou*. He named his boat after her. Isn't that romantic?"

"And you're saying he saved somebody recently?"

"What? Oh no." Chipmunk sat up again, and, eyes wide with excitement, reached across the picnic table to clutch Robin's forearm. "See, sometimes he shows up to warn people, like if there's a hurricane coming or something. And people are saying he was here four nights ago, when the dock blew up and poor Desiree got killed!"

"And Pimlico Phil," Pincushion added solemnly.

"Right, and Pimlico Phil."

"And these people who say this," Robin said, "Did they start saying Red Luck was around before the explosion, or after it?"

"Um—I don't know," Chipmunk said suspiciously. "What difference does that make?"

"No difference," Robin lied. "Just trying to establish a timeline. Got to have everything accurate for my story."

"Oh yeah," Chipmunk nodded sagely. "God, you are so, you know, *professional*." She frowned over Robin's shoulder and gave a hesitant wave. "Now what do you suppose they want?"

Robin turned to see what had diverted The Chipmunk. Across the street and down a bit, standing in front of the partly burned Mamasan's, were two women about Chipmunk's age, both buxom and beautiful, both scantily dressed. One was waving for Chipmunk to join them, the other seemed to be crying. Now what? Robin thought.

"That's Sandy and Linda, they work with me," Chipmunk said. "I better go see what's up. But I'll be right back, ok?" She popped up and jogged off down the street, her tiny heinie bouncing like a colt's tail. Pincushion, ever the professional, scooped up his camera and fired off a few shots of Chipmunk's retreating rear.

"So, whadda ya think?" he said over the rapid-fire click of his camera.

"I think she's lovely. I think she's smarter than she acts. I think she's a little too young to be working in a strip joint, and way too young for you to be fooling around with."

"Yeah," Pincushion agreed happily. "But what about her story? About the pirate?"

"Bullshit for the tourists," Robin said bitterly. "A local legend some P.R. genius made up a long time ago, and now even the locals buy into it. You notice nobody reporting seeing this ghost ship till after the disaster? Hysteria, or gossip anyway. Hell, maybe somebody even planted it. Who knows, who cares?"

Pincushion had finished off his roll of film and was busily loading another. He looked up from the open back of his camera, hurt-puppy disappointment etched on his face. "So you don't think it's a story?"

A story? Robin thought. *Jesus, this little town just had a big chunk blown out of the local economy, they got two peo-*

ple dead or at least missing, and I'm supposed to be writing about sea monsters and ghost ships? She opened her mouth to say something, bit back the anger she felt rising up, and then used her thumb and forefinger to rub her forehead against the headache she felt growing there. "Do I think it's a story?" she said. She put one hand on the side of her purse and felt the reassuring smoothness of the minibottles within. "Pincushion ol' pal—I think Max will love it."

Pincushion brightened and snapped his camera shut with a happy click. "Yeah, good ol' Max," he said. He popped off a few blank shots to advance the film, then suddenly raised the camera and aimed it at Robin. "Smile for the camera, Miss Famous Reporter Person!"

"Pincushion! No!" Robin recoiled, put one hand before her face and swung the other skyward. That hand was holding her purse; she swatted the end of Pincushion's long lens with it, knocking the camera off line. Robin wasn't sure if she'd meant to do that, or just gotten lucky. Either way, Pincushion got the message.

"Oh hey, jeez, sorry lady. Didn't know you were, like, so sensitive." He eyed the end of his lens appraisingly. "What, you think I'm gonna steal your soul or something like that?"

"Something like that," Robin said. "I didn't mean to hit your camera like that. Sorry."

"No biggie. I had much worse than that done to me. Once, when I was outside the Kennedy compound down at—hey, cool, a pelican! Smile for the camera, Mr. Famous Pelican Person!" Pincushion swung around to focus on the ponderous pelican coming to an unsteady landing on a dock piling a dozen feet out in the inlet. Robin watched him shoot for a minute, happily oblivious to her damnable temper, and then headed off to the hot dog booth. *Steal my soul*, she thought sourly. *What goddamn soul?*

Robin came back five minutes later, one finger stirring through the crushed ice in her paper cup, to find Pincushion consoling a teary-eyed Chipmunk. She sat down and wordlessly handed Pincushion a paper napkin; he accepted it with a glum nod and dabbed with surprising tenderness at Chipmunk's tears.

"They closed down the restaurant," Pincushion explained. "The Chipmunk's got no place to dance."

"I've got no *job!*" Chipmunk wailed. "And I really, *really* need the money. I've almost got enough for law school."

"For what?" Robin said.

"For because of the fire," Pincushion said.

"No, I mean, you're saving your money for—"

"Howie said that the fire did too much damage, and that they can't afford to fix it," Chipmunk said.

"No way," Robin said. "They gotta have bundles of insurance on a place like that. I mean, state law says—"

"It's not just the restaurant. Howie says the pier is all fucked up, and maybe the pilings too. He said they may have to re-do the whole thing, and that it could take months and months. And I've got my LSAT in three weeks!"

"That's not what the fire marshal said."

"The who?" Chipmunk snuffled. "Oh yeah, Howie said he came back and did it again, and that it's a lot worse than they thought."

"Looks fine to me," Robin said quietly.

"Well it's not. Nothing's fine, not anymore." Chipmunk honked loudly into the napkin and looked down at Pincushion's sheltering arm. "Oh look, Pincushel," she said plaintively, "I got tears on your dragon picture."

"Oh yeah, but that's ok," Pincushion said. "It's like he's crying, see? Hey look Robin, my dragon's crying. Idn't that cool?"

"Yeah, cool," Robin said, though she wasn't really listening. She took a deep draw from her drink, and then another, trying to drown out the insistent voice in the back of her head. The voice she had managed to keep fairly well sedated for quite a while now, the voice she had hoped she'd never have to listen to again.

The voice that was saying, *There's something wrong here.*

Chapter Nine

"Try these," Pambellina said. "I found 'em under some stuff in my trunk; I bet they'll fit." She handed a pair of gym shorts to the grateful Desiree, trying not to laugh. The poor kid was holding the bushel basket away from herself with two prissy fingers, like it was infectious or something, and already scratching at a bright pink mosquito bite on one hip. She was also blushing furiously. At running around with no shorts on? Because she'd had to go in the bushes? *Jesus God*, Pambellina thought, *hasn't this woman ever peed in the woods before?*

"Oh, thank you," Desiree said. "You've really been so kind . . ." She stood there uncertain for a moment, trying to balance basket in one hand and shorts and *Sporting News* in the other. Finally, Pambellina took the basket from her. She stepped around the corner of the Tiltin' Hilton to put the basket back in its storage spot; when she came back Desiree was sitting in the sand right before the front door, gym shorts about half-way up her sandy thighs.

"I fell," she said. "I guess my leg is weaker than I

thought, and when I put all my weight on it it sort of just slipped, and I fell." Desiree let out a sigh that sounded half-resigned and half barely contained despair. "I am such a klutz!"

"You're not a klutz," Pambellina said gently. "You're hurt. Here." She helped Desiree to her feet— awkward, since the girl insisted on pulling up her shorts as she stood. She would have tumbled backwards again if Pambellina hadn't had a good grip on her arm.

"There, see? I really am a klutz," Desiree said. "You know, they threw me out of ballet class when I was a kid because I kept kicking the other girls. And when Kathleen went riding when we were young, Daddy would never let me on the horses. He said I was too delicate, but it was really because he knew I'd just fall right off."

"Who's Kathleen?" *Horses*, Pambellina thought.

"My sister. She's a senior in college, majoring in business. And you know what happened the one night I got to fill in as a waitress at Mamasan's?"

"You spilled soup on a customer?"

"*Hot* soup. And I didn't just spill it on him, I *threw* it on him."

"Threw it on him."

"Un-huh. See, I had the soup bowl in my left hand, and a drink tray in my right, and I was taking them toward a table, just proud as could be, and then this guy said something crude to me about my . . . about my tattoo."

"Yeah. And?"

"So I turned towards him to say something back, and I plopped my left boobie right into the egg drop."

"Oh shit!" Pambellina barked out a little laugh, but cut it off short because Desiree was so seriously sad about it all.

"It was hot too, right out of the microwave, and it burned me, so without thinking I just jerked that bowl of soup away from myself."

"And right onto the jerk who'd said something nasty to you."

"No," Desiree said miserably. "I missed him by three or four feet. I poured it right down the back of a Baptist minister from South Carolina."

"Ha! Uh, I mean, huh, well, he probably deserved it. What the hell was a minister doing in a nudie joint anyway?"

"That's just what he said. Well, not the "hell" part, but he said it was his own fault, that he was being punished, and then he ran out the door without even paying." Desiree shook her head mournfully. "I had to pay his tab, and now Howie is never ever going to let me wait tables again."

Pambellina half opened her mouth, closed it again, and then held up one finger. "Wait," she said. "One minute." She swept aside the covering over her front door and stepped inside; a minute later she came back out carrying two folding chairs and a pack of Marlboro Reds. The chairs were those short-legged beach things that encourage the sitter to lean back and stretch her legs out in the sand, rusty but still functional. Pambellina opened them up and helped Desiree ease down into one before seating herself and lighting a cigarette. She offered one to Desiree, who politely declined.

"Okay," Pambellina said once they were both comfortable, "Okay, you gotta tell me what the hell you were doing working in a nasty place like Mamasan's in the first place."

"Oh it's not nasty, not really. I mean, sure, some of the customers are pretty sleazy, and the food . . ."— Desiree grinned mischievously; Pambellina got the impression she thought she was about to say something daring—"The food, well, it really *is* awful. But the other girls are nice, and Howie takes care of us." Desiree started to say more, then stopped and turned away, and Pambellina realized her serious disapproval must have been showing. She couldn't help it. Flashing tits to greasy old men and horny college boys, just to get a tip? She inhaled hard on her cigarette and bit her lip.

"And besides," Desiree added defensively, "I need the money."

"You need money? I thought . . . I mean, you said you had horses when you were a kid, and you and your sister are both in college. That takes a lot of money."

"Oh, sure. *Daddy's* money. Not my money."

"Oh, right. I get it," Pambellina said. Which was a lie. Her own dad was a distant memory, a smiling shadow who'd taken her fishing before the sea took him. And money? Money was something other people took away from you. Like the government, or a landlord. Or the fucking McCracken brothers. To have both a father and money, and walk away from them— that was just way beyond her. "So," she asked, "Does your dad know you're working in a tittie bar?"

"In a restaurant," Desiree corrected sternly. "No, of course not. He thinks I ran off to Hollywood to be an actress."

"To Hollywood? No shit?"

"No, really. See, I'm supposed to be in school, up in Ohio, but then I came to Florida on Spring Break, with my sorority, and I ran away down here, but first I mailed Daddy a letter saying I was running off to Hollywood. To be an actress."

"You ran away from college?" This was too fucking much. This girl, this child, had turned her back on things Pambellina could never even dream of having. College, for god's sake!

"Well, not college. Or not *just* college. I ran away from white picket fences and ivy columns."

"Your college had white picket fences?"

"No!" Desiree laughed and looked at Pambellina like she thought Pambellina was joking. "No," she continued after a moment. "But Daddy's house has ivy-covered columns. And the house he wants to put me in, the house he's been building for me all my life, that one's got a white picket fence. And a husband with a law degree, and two bright-faced children, and a Volvo station wagon in the garage, and bridge clubs on Tuesday and country clubs on the weekend. And club sandwiches, with toothpicks in the middle."

Desiree abruptly stopped talking, or maybe she just ran out of breath, and stared at Pambellina expectantly. Pambellina sucked on her Marlboro and exhaled thoughtfully. "You've got a garage?" she said.

"No! Not a real garage, not yet, and no kids and no Volvo. But they're out there, waiting for me, *stalking* me. Don't you get it? That's my destiny."

"Yeah, I get it. Doesn't sound so bad."

"Not bad? It's terrible!"

"Wait a minute, you're talking a nice car, and a house with screens in the windows, and clean sheets and regular dental care, and flush toilets and chocolate ice cream whenever you want it, and a garage, and you think that's terrible?"

"Yes! Well, no, not exactly all that, but . . ." Desiree frowned for a minute—pouty lips, Pambellina thought—and then started again. "Okay, what if I said that starting tomorrow you could never walk on the beach again?"

"I'd kick your ass."

"And you couldn't smoke cigarettes, and you had to wear shoes all the time, and dresses or at least nice slacks. And you couldn't say, 'ass.'"

"Fuck that noise."

"And you couldn't date anybody who wasn't in your own social class, and you couldn't go to a movie or a restaurant by yourself, and you couldn't go see Nsynch because they draw the wrong crowd."

"Insects?"

"Nsynch. And couldn't stay out late because people might get the wrong impression, and you had to join the bitchiest sorority on campus because they have the best connections, and you couldn't dye your hair or pierce your tongue or—" Desiree's hand fluttered toward the bandage over her upper chest, and Pambellina mentally finished the sentence. *Or get a tattoo.*

"Okay," she said. "So your dad's, what, some kind of religious fanatic or something?"

"No, not really. I mean, we go to church all the time, but that's mostly just to look good. He's just—oh, I don't know. He just has this idea of exactly how people are supposed to behave, and not behave, and people who act otherwise are just low-class. And no daughter of his is going to be low-class."

"What's your mom say about all this?"

"She's been gone a long time," Desiree said, and Pambellina wondered if "gone" meant "dead" or something else. "And it's not just Daddy. It was the teachers at Winslow Academy for Girls, and it's my minister, and it's my sorority sisters, and Kathleen, and my professors at college. Even my classmates, they all want me to be this little miss all American girl. And I hate it!"

"Fuck 'em. Do what you wanna do."

"I can't! Or I couldn't. I mean, I go to this small college, and everybody knows who I am and who Daddy is, and they know what sorority I'm in and who my sister is, she's the president of our sorority and the queen of campus, and they just expect me to act this certain way. And if I try to act any different they say I'm slumming, or that I'm a hypocrite, and then it all gets even worse. I went to a party once, and I drank two Grasshoppers and then threw up on the lawn. The next day, the very next day, the college counselor called me into her office and said she'd heard reports that I was bulimic and that she wanted to put me on Prozac. And the kids at the party all thought I'd narced on them, and the sorority gave me demerits, and Daddy said he was very, very disappointed in me and that if I acted that way I'd never find a decent man to marry."

"And live in a house with ivy-covered columns and a white picket fence."

"Yes!"

"So you ran away to Cedar Key."

"Yes."

"And got a tattoo."

"Yes. And I got a job, and I learned how to paddle a canoe and bait a hook, and I flirt with strangers and I don't go to church, and I take showers outside and sunbathe in the back yard, and sometimes I walk around with no shirt on."

"At the restaurant, or at home?"

"Both," Desiree said defiantly. And then, with just a hint of a smile, she added. "But you know, it's not really a restaurant. It's a tittie bar."

Pambellina smiled back at Desiree and nodded appreciatively. Not such a bad kid after all, she thought. Spoiled rotten and weird as hen's teeth, but she had some fire in her. Way down low and banked heavy, maybe, but it was there.

"So you see, that's why I have to get back to town

and try and make things right with Howie. Maybe if I promise to pay for the damage, and if I can straighten things up with the police, maybe I can get my job back."

"Ahh," Pambellina said. "Now there we've got a problem." Two problems, actually, she thought.

"A problem? A big problem?"

"Not a big problem, no. Kind of a middle-size problem, I guess, and a temporary one, but a problem. See," Pambellina inhaled on her cigarette and blew the smoke out through her nose. "See," she said, "We ain't got no boat."

"No boat?"

"No boat."

"But—we're on an island."

"Right."

"So how did we get out here if you don't have a boat?"

"Oh, I had a boat then. Still do, technically. But it's a boat with a big hole in the bottom."

"But—"

"You remember I told you how you fell off the dock there at Mamasan's, and dropped right into my boat, like you'd fell out of the sky?"

"Yes . . ."

"Well, you smacked down pretty hard, and my boat ain't nothing but a old wooden skiff. You knocked a nice little hole in the bottom, splintered a couple of the boards pretty good." Desiree reached for her bandaged knee, and Pambellina nodded. "Yep, that's where you hit. Dr. B says it was blind luck you didn't shatter your knee, or just break your fucking neck."

"But if I knocked a hole in the boat . . ."

"Not a hole, not really, that's kinda exaggerating. What you did was knock loose a couple of the boards in the bottom. I didn't even notice it at first, but on the way out here the water starting pouring in. So I really floored the motor, hoping to get home before we went down, and that pushed the boards apart even more. We were ankle deep in water by the time we hit my lagoon."

"But—well, why come back here in the first place? Why didn't you just take me to shore there in Cedar Key?"

"Hell, girl, all I knew was there were explosions and fire and you falling out of the sky like a angel in a dinosaur suit. Kinda freaked me out, ya know? I thought somebody was shooting at you, or maybe at me. And I knew the cops would be coming soon, and the McCrackens, and maybe some other people I can't afford to see right now. Once I saw you were still breathing, I just naturally lit out for home."

"And the boat?"

"I got it drug up on the shore and turned belly-up down by the lagoon. I can fix it, but I need some good cut wood, and some binding glue, and a bucket of lacquer. Dr. Bill is gonna bring all that the next time he swings by."

"And that would be?"

"Hard to say with Dr. B. He don't exactly keep to a tight schedule. Maybe any minute, maybe next week. But probably soon."

"Oh," Desiree said, and then again, "Oh." It didn't take a genius to read the concern on her face.

"Hey, relax already. You can stay right here, I got room. We'll have us some laughs, let things calm down a bit, and when you come waltzing back into town you'll be a celebrity. Like you came back from the dead or something."

"A celebrity?"

"Sure. Everybody will be so surprised to see you. You'll get in the paper again. It'll be fun."

"Well . . ." Desiree poked at the sand beside her, and when she looked up Pambellina could see a little sparkle in her eyes. "You're sure you don't mind?"

"No problem. I could use the company. You can tell me all about country clubs and sandwiches with toothpicks."

"Sure!" Desiree brightened, but quickly grew somber again. "I guess . . . I must look pretty silly to you, huh? I mean, running away to Cedar Key and all."

Damn straight, Pambellina thought, but what she said was, "Nah. Hell, half the people in Cedar Key are running away from something, and the other half were born here."

Desiree smiled at that. "And which half are you?" she asked.

"Me?" Pambellina frowned just a little. She dug a little trench in the sand, dropped her cigarette butt in it and covered it over before answering, patting the sand down like a Lilliputian's grave. "I'm a bit of both," she said. "Now come on. If we're gonna have any dinner tonight, we gotta go do some grocery shopping."

"Shopping?" Desiree asked, but Pambellina had already bounced up and disappeared once again into her house. She came back out a moment later, holding a fishing rod in one hand and a nylon cast net in the other.

"Grocery shopping," she said.

Chapter Ten

Howie McCracken sat in the middle of the Island Hotel's dining room, alone except for the six-foot stuffed manatee propped up on a piano bench facing the old Steinway, desperately wishing somebody would talk to him. He knew, of course, that the odds of that were pretty damn slim, even on a good day. And today had not been a good day.

It had been such a bad day, in fact, that not even the Neptune's Lounge bartender who occasionally passed through the lobby on her way to the ladies room or the front desk would look at him. Howie always tipped heavy, really heavy, and usually that got him fresh drinks and an occasional word. And sometimes, one of the guests in the hotel would join him, or even a local who was out of cash and knew Howie would stand him for a drink. If there were enough drinks, sometimes, they'd get to telling the old stories, and for a while manage to forget that Howie was the second-most hated man in Cedar Key. Sometimes. Not tonight.

Howie sighed and took a tiny nip at his almost-empty Jack and Coke. He could hear Madonna's horsy laugh echoing out of the hotel bar in the next room, and ached to go in there and tell the old girl to pour him another round. He wanted to rub Tom Willie's bald spot and ask him if he'd been hitting the headboards too hard, or have Chigger run through the history of the fish bones and turtle parts sewn into his fishing cap. Or maybe just sit there in that smoke-filled, cedar-paneled room, smile back at the gun-shot mural of Neptune and his naked mermaids over the bar, and drink in all the laughter and gossip like it was honeydew wine.

Howie toyed with the idea of driving to Stevie's spooky old Southern mansion near the cemetery on Rye Key to play with Sarah for a while, but he knew his little niece would have gone to bed hours ago, and besides Stevie didn't like Howie playing with his daughter when Howie had been drinking. Hell, Stevie wasn't all that crazy about Howie hanging out with Sarah when he was sober.

Howie breathed a bone-rattling sigh and clenched his heavy hand dangerously tight around the highball glass. All he really wanted was a little company, but he wanted it like a man six months at sea wants the sound of a woman's voice. Was that so damn much to ask, Howie told himself, just a little company? He knew that if he actually walked into the Neptune Lounge the laughter and talk would stop dead, and if he dared pull up a barstool people would get up and move away from him like he'd been skunk sprayed. Eventually they'd start wandering out, head down the street to the L&M or walk the three blocks to Frog's Landing, and no matter how much he tipped Madonna she'd never forgive him for running off a Saturday night crowd. Like she was ever gonna forgive him anyway.

"Shit, Howie," he said to the empty room. "You can clear out any bar in this damn town faster n' a fart in an elevator." He raised his glass high and let what was left of the blackjack drizzle down his throat. The stuffed manatee seemed to stare at him all blurry-eyed through the bottom of his glass, and when he'd sucked out all the whisky he could find he slammed the glass down and glared right back. "The fuck you looking at?" he said. He thought for a second about throwing the glass right at that big stuffed asshole, wiping that goofy grin right off its furry face, but the rage faded quick and it just didn't seem worth the trouble. So he just stared down into his empty glass and hoped the bartender would come out again soon.

Things hadn't been so bad when he was running Mamasan's. The girls there liked him, or at least acted like they did. Since he usually spent all night there and most days sleeping off the night before, he might go weeks at a time without really being reminded of what his long time neighbors thought of him. But Mamasan's was gone now, and all the pretty waitresses and shit-faced friendly customers with it. And Howie was, once again, all alone.

It hadn't started out to be a bad day. Started out pretty good in fact, a hot clear Cedar Key morning, sun shining and a little breeze blowing, and Stevie all happy and excited as a kid at Christmas. Well, maybe not that happy, Stevie never got that happy. But maybe like a little boy on, say, Presidents Day or Palm Sunday, or one of those other holidays you get off from school but don't really think much about. Happy like that.

Stevie had said the fine weather was a good sign, though Howie knew Stevie didn't believe in signs or omens or even luck, and Howie's own sense of trouble brewing had faded when he saw how nice things were set up outside of Mamasan's. There were balloons and colored banners, and folding tables loaded down with 25 boxes of pizza from the Dominos in Chiefland. There were ice-filled tubs of Coca-cola and 7-Up, and a tall wooden podium that Howie recognized as the hostess' stand from Mamasan's. There was a loud-speaker system, and a table the size of a plywood sheet right behind the podium, covered over with thick black cloth so nobody could see what was on it. There was a short row of chairs up there for dignitaries and special guests, and Stevie told Howie that's where he would be sitting. Stevie had gotten a special permit and roped off one side of A Street in front of Mamasan's so people would have a place to stand, and run ads in that week's *Lantern* and for three days running in the *Chiefland News*, inviting everybody out to celebrate a big new era in Cedar Key. And sure enough, everybody came.

Well, maybe not everybody, but sure as hell a lot of people. Stevie put Howie in one of the folding chairs alongside the podium, along with Willie Paul the mayor and Mr. Black, the quiet, stiff guy that Stevie said represented their silent partner. Howie didn't like that Mr. Black much and Willie Paul didn't speak to him at all, but still, he had a fine view of the crowd. There musta been two hundred people there, maybe more. Lots of them were tourists curious about all the hoo-ha, and plenty of kids and teenagers who were there for the free food. But there were lots of other people too, people Howie had known since he was a kid, and people who'd moved in and made a place for themselves over the last twenty years or so. Restaurant owners and shop clerks, charterboat captains, unemployed fishermen who didn't have nothing better to do and clammers who did. Howie saw preachers from three different churches, two of which was glaring hard at the Mamasan waitresses giving out pizza in their tiny shorts and tight shirts. Madonna from Neptune's was there, and Chigger, and most of the L&M gang. Fluffy was there, wearing the faded Garfield the cat T-shirt that earned him his nickname. Jennifer Aly from the state park, looking sweaty and out of place in her park ranger uniform. Tee Nichols, of course, standing with that reporter woman from Orlando and the skinny photographer with all the tattoos. Normally, you couldn't get a crowd that big in Cedar Key unless you were giving out free beer.

Howie got so wrapped up in studying the crowd, in fact, that he pretty much blanked out Reverend Ryan's prayer, and Willie Paul's welcome, and even most of Stevie's speech. He was making faces at a little boy in the crowd, trying to get the sleepy-eyed tyke to smile, when Stevie stopped talking and strode dramatically over to the covered table.

"And here it is," Stevie shouted. "Ladies and gentlemen, I give you—the Cedar Casino!" He whipped the coversheet off the table like a stripper flashing her wares, then stepped back and waved proudly at the uncovered model. And it was damn near pretty as a naked lady, Howie thought, in an architectural sort of way. The model showed A Street from the public beach past all of McCracken Row, right to where A Street veered west and became Dock Street. That whole strip, in Stevie's model, was one big complex including a parking garage, dockage space for boats, and the big central building that was the actual casino, all three stories of it. At the southern tip, where the plywood was painted blue to represent the Gulf, stood a mushroom shaped tower and observation deck that Stevie had promised would be the highest point in three counties. A blue and green flag hung from that tower. The colors, Stevie told Howie, stood for the blue of the sea and the green of the money their new casino would rake in. Stevie had got a little mad when Howie pointed out that the Gulf here was never really blue—it was too shallow and murky. Stevie said that Howie was missing the whole point, but Howie wasn't quite so sure.

The audience sure seemed to like the model though, at least at first. There was a big burst of applause when Stevie ripped the cover off, but it died fast. Howie saw clear that most of the applause was coming from the out-of-towners in the crowd, from the tourists and a handful of guys he knew were on the McCracken Brothers' payroll. The local people, if they reacted at all, sure as hell weren't clapping. They were glaring at Stevie, some of 'em nudging each other and talking low and mad. Stevie had already kinda turned his back on the crowd and was working his way along the VIP row, shaking hands and smiling, and for a moment Howie thought maybe they could just ignore their troubles away. And then that Jennifer Aly jumped on the stage, bold as brass, and walked up to the microphone.

"Mr. McCracken," the park ranger said in a voice that echoed like the word of God hisself, "You can't do that."

Stevie turned on the ranger slow, smile on his face but his eyebrows raised in that "oh really?" look that always gave Howie chills. He looked like a loving parent about to explain to a stubborn child why she couldn't have the keys to the car—but his eyes had gone killer-cold. Shark eyes, his workers called that look, and Howie figured they had that exactly right. Cold and empty and unblinking, moving in on you without no emotion until the teeth slammed closed and the blood spurted free. Stevie took a step toward Aly; she turned a little pale, Howie saw, but she didn't back off an inch.

"Of course I can, Miss Aly," Stevie said. He didn't have the mike and didn't seem to be talking loud, but Howie knew that snake-slick voice of his carried a lot farther than it had any right to. "As I said, we have most of the permits in hand, and Mayor Paul assures me that the rest are just a formality. We intend to start construction—"

"What about the charter? Doesn't the city charter say you can't do major construction without a referendum?" That was Cynie Sweet, one of the two women who ran the Loose Ladies Boutique and Coffee Shoppe. Howie frowned and shook his head at the interruption. Cynie and her girlfriend came down from Michigan ten, maybe twelve years ago, but they still had the manners of a damn Yankee.

"Now that's a good question, Miss Sweet," Stevie said, all southern gentleman and patient. "Mister Mayor, perhaps you could shed a little light on this issue for us." Stevie turned those cold eyes on Willie Paul, who slowly stood up and took the microphone. He stood there for a minute, frozen between smiling Stevie and the angry glare of Ranger Aly, until Stevie whispered something in his ear.

"Well then," Willie Paul said, "Well then, Cynie's right, she's right. The Cedar Key charter, as amended in 1987, requires that a public referendum be held before any major project can be constructed. Now there is some question as to whether the Cedar Casino actually qualifies as a major project . . ." Howie heard some quiet complaints from the crowd at that, and at least one muffled "bullshit!" The mayor seemed to lose his place there, like he was working from a speech and forgot his next line. He stood there working his lips like a beached mullet until Stevie gently nudged him aside.

"A referendum?" Stevie said. "We welcome a ref-

erendum. Why wouldn't we? Why would anyone op-
pose a project that will bring so many new jobs to our
town? And new jobs means more tax money, money
for our schools and streets. New jobs means a broader,
safer economy. New jobs means . . ."

"New jobs," Stevie said, and said and said and said.
Every time he said jobs he stared right into the eyes
of someone in the crowd, a different person every
time. Howie knew 'em all, and he could see that
magic word hit each one of them like a poisoned kiss.
Joe Kyller, who filled gallon jugs with fresh water at
the city park drinking fountain 'cause his busted-
down trailer didn't have plumbing. Jerry Folkman,
who'd been on welfare since he'd trimmed off three
fingers at the sawmill and couldn't hold a hammer no
more. Anne Jenkins, whose four kids went without
every month her asshole ex-husband didn't send the
child support. Even a lot of the old clammers, men
who had regular paychecks but hated working on
other men's leases—mostly Stevie and Howie's
leases. Stevie was talking to each and every one of
them, Howie thought. And one after one they'd turn
their eyes away, maybe wrestling their pride or counting their bills, and after a minute they'd slowly turn
back to Stevie.

Howie twisted his fingers together to keep himself
from counting on them, and did the math in his head.
Almost nine hundred people in Cedar Key. Toss out
the children, and the felons, and the people who
hated government or were just too ornery to vote, and
you had maybe five hundred eligible voters. That

means they needed two-hundred fifty, maybe three hundred votes to win. Howie thought of all the people already on the McCracken payroll, and all the favors and debts Stevie could call in, and the hungry eyes he'd just seen in the crowd, and then stared down at his knotted fingers. They had the votes, easy. Stevie wouldn't have started any of this if he didn't have the votes.

Jennifer Aly re-took the microphone then and said something about Florida's Growth Management Act. They had expected that; Mr. Black had gone through it all with Stevie and Howie the night before. Howie had had trouble listening then, and he was having trouble listening now. He was watching the crowd again. Most of them were sticking around, hoping maybe that the angry lady on the stage would take a swing at the man with the mike. And most of the newcomers to town were still listening too; Howie could almost see them trying to figure what a casino would do to the profit margins and the tax rates at their little shops and hotels.

And then Tee Nichols hopped up on the stage. He didn't take the microphone, but he didn't really need it. He just stood there for a minute, looking right at Stevie in that sleepy-cat way of his, and Jennifer Aly stopped talking, and there were a few "hushes" out in the crowd, and little by little the people stopped their shuffling and chatting until it seemed like the whole damn town was holding its breath waiting for what Tee Nichols had to say.

What he said was, "Cedar pencils." That's all.

That was enough.

Howie crunched the last chunk of ice from his empty glass and reluctantly rose from his chair. No booze, no waitress, nobody to talk to, no reason to hang around here. He thought again about going into Neptune's, but a surge of stubborn pride kept him from it. *The hell with 'em*, he thought, *hell with 'em all*. He'd just go down to the L&M. They wouldn't even let him in the door down there, 'cause they knew that some drunk or another would start a brawl with him the minute he stepped inside. That was fine with Howie; there were times when a good, bone-rattling fistfight was just what he needed. Needed it more than whiskey, needed it more than company, and some nights all he had to do was stand outside for a few minutes and somebody would come out to take him on.

Tonight, Howie figured, would be one of those nights.

Chapter Eleven

Desiree whipped the supple fiberglass rod through the air over her head, feeling delightfully self-sufficient. She popped her restraining index finger off the line at precisely the right moment, and hook, weight and bait went whizzing out over the gentle swells of Pambellina's lagoon. The rig came down with a satisfying *sploosh* a good twenty yards out.

"Not bad," Desiree told herself. "Not bad at all." She looked around to see if Pambellina had seen that particular cast, but her host was still out of sight around the nearby bend in the shoreline. Desiree turned her attention back out towards her line, determined to reel something in this time. So far, she'd lost her bait three times and managed only to catch one slimy sailcat. Pambellina had had to get that off the hook for her; its mouth was leathery gray skin that seemed impossible to pry off a barb. Desiree had learned the hard way, while fishing off the Cedar Key public pier, that the tall dorsal spine and the bony fins on each side of a sailcat were razor sharp and dangerous. The coating of slime on the cat not only kept it warm, but was also a mild poison that would quickly infect any untreated wound opened by those sharp fins. "Mother Nature's biological warfare," Pambellina had said. "Birds and other fish learn not to mess with sailcats pretty quick."

Pambellina herself had already raked in nearly a dozen fat Gulf shrimp, plus a pair of pan-sized whiting. She was amazing. She'd wade out until she was about thigh-deep, then stand still as stork, eyes scanning the water, cast net coiled and ready. When she saw something, or just when her instincts told her it was time, she'd swivel her hips back, coiling like a spring, and then snap forward, arms outcast, and send the net flying through the air. That net was taller than Pambellina was, and weighted down on the edges by six-ounce lead shots, but still she tossed it a good fifteen feet on every cast. The net would open in midflight like an airborne jellyfish, forming a perfect knotted-nylon circle some eight feet around. When it hit the water the weights would pull the net down over anything underneath it, and Pambellina would reel it in by the rope she kept looped around one wrist.

Opening the net was like getting a mystery package on Christmas morning. There would be seaweed, sure, and sticks and loose turtle grass, but also crabs and minnows, sometimes, shrimp and any nature of fish. Once a foot-long eel had squiggled through the net just as they dragged it up on the shore. Pambellina had coaxed her into holding a soft-ball-sized cannonball jellyfish—slimy but harmless, just as Pambellina said—and had gently pushed aside the rust-colored leaves of a clump of seaweed to show Desiree the colony of tiny crabs and quarter-inch shrimp residing within. Each netfull had a surprise or two in it, and Pambellina seemed to enjoy revealing them to Desiree as much as Desiree enjoyed seeing them.

Pambellina had also shown her how to dig thumb-sized sand fleas out of the sand just at the waterline. They were bullet-shaped little creatures with lots of legs and a hard white carapace. "Some people call 'em sand crabs, but Doctor B says they're more arachnid than crab," Pambellina said. "All I know is, redfish love 'em."

Redfish. That was Desiree's target. She'd seen a few pulled in at the pier, and Heaven knows there were enough pictures of grinning tourists holding big redfish on the walls of darn near every bar and restaurant in town. Beautiful fish, long and slender, silver in the sun, with a blood-red spot the size of a quarter right back near the rear fins. And tasty, too. Desiree had eaten plenty of them. She'd just never caught one.

Desiree squinted into the late afternoon sun and carefully checked the tension on her line. A slow, steady pull, she'd quickly learned, was only the tide tugging at her rig. A series of little pull-and-releases meant that crabs had found her bait, and she needed to move it or lose it. And when a redfish hit—well, Pambellina insisted she'd know when a redfish hit.

Desiree ran an exploratory thumb over the bridge of her nose—already a little tender, despite the Beelzebubba's Bait and Guitars Shop baseball cap Pambellina had loaned her. It didn't matter—Desiree was having the time of her life. Cool, salt water gently lapped against her knees, and soft, warm sand scrunched playfully through her toes with every step. The only sound was the quit sploush of waves on the shore behind her and the occasional complaining cries of seagulls overhead. There was a slight breeze blowing, just enough to keep her cool, and when the sun got too much, Desiree simply knelt down in the water. It was all so peaceful! Part of Desiree knew that she had problems to deal with, that she really needed to get back to town and find out how bad the accident had been, find out if Pimlico Phil was really dead. But for the moment—well, for the moment, the whole world felt just right.

Desiree cast a quick glance back towards the shore, looking for her wild new friend. Not only had Pambellina saved her life, but she was smart, and funny, and helpful. So what if she cursed like a sailor? No, not a sailor, Desiree corrected herself. A pirate! A true outlaw, an honest-to-gosh pirate. She could hardly believe it when Pambellina had told her that, when they first got to the beach.

"A clam pirate," Pambellina had said. "I paddle over to the acres that are leased to the big owners for aquaculture, late at night when nobody's around, and I scoop up clams. That's what I was doing out in my skiff so late at night when you dropped in."

"But—I thought clams just, you know, grew wild, like oysters?"

"They do, some. But if you go for wild clams, you have to spend all your time hunting for them. With aquaculture, you just plant baby clams in your leased acres, inside these special bags. Then you just let 'em grow, scoop up the bags, and plant some more. Just like growing corn or something. Much easier than going for wild clams, much more productive. Lots more money."

"So why don't you have your own clam farm?"

"I did, once." Pambellina scowled and jerked harder than necessary at the knot in the net she was untangling. "Okay, it used to be people around here made most of their money on fish—mullet, mackerel, that sort of thing. Clams were just a sideline they'd go after when the season was right or the mullet weren't running. But in 1995, Florida passed this goddamn law, banning nets."

"Nets?" Desiree said. "You mean like this one?"

"No, no, the big nets, the ones the commercial fishermen used. They said we were overfishing, destroying the fish stock and ruining it for everyone."

"Was that true?"

"No! Or only partly, anyway. There were a few really big companies who really were doing damage. They'd go out in huge fleets, with spotter planes to track the fish, and then they'd surround a whole school and just wipe it out. Wouldn't leave hardly any left to breed, and they killed a lot of other things they caught in those huge nets by accident—turtles, crabs, sharks, that kind of thing. Usually they killed more than they caught."

"God, that's terrible!"

"Yeah. But like I said, that was only a few really big operations. Most commercial fishermen, like the people around here, they had one or two boats, and one or two big nets. They'd catch lots of fish, sure, but they also left a lot out there to keep breeding. That's the way families have done it here, and in places like Apalachicola and Pensacola Bay and Tarpon Springs and Panama City, and on and on, for whole generations.

"And then they passed that fucking net ban, and suddenly all those people were out of work." Pambellina had stopped working then, and just stood there staring down at her cast net. Desiree could practically feel the anger boiling off of her, and could see defeat and despair in the slump of her shoulders. She looked away, then dropped to her knees to dig for more sand fleas. After a minute, she heard Pambellina snort playfully and looked up at her.

"Damn, girl," she said. "Even squatting down you practically reach my waist. You're a great big thing, you know that?"

"Yes," Desiree said defensively. "And you're a little bitty thing. So what?"

"So nothing. I'm only saying." Desiree could hear the smile in Pambellina's voice. She grinned back, looking up at Pambellina and admired how her coppery hair stood out so sharp against the bright blue sky behind her. Pambellina looked right back at her. Desiree could see laughter in her eyes, and something else too that she wasn't quite ready to think about.

"So," Desiree said, "So how did all that lead to your clam farm?"

"Oh, right," Pambellina said. She scratched her nose for a second, then eased herself down onto the sand beside Desiree. "Well, after the government saw all these people were gonna be out of work, and that they were gonna have to foot the bill for welfare and food stamps and all, they came up with this idea of aquaculture. They sent people down here to teach us how, and then they gave out leases to everybody who had a seafood harvesting license."

"A what?"

"Something you gotta have to commercial fish in Florida. Like a hunting license, or a restaurant license."

"Oh."

"And they gave out these leases depending on how many boats you had, and how much fish you'd caught the year before, that kind of thing. My dad had busted up his leg really bad the year before so he hadn't caught as much as usual, so his lease wasn't all that big."

"Well that's not fair."

"Damn straight. Still, I gotta admit the state was pretty generous about it. We each got our own little acreage to grow clams on, good places where the water flow and temperature are right, and we set in to planting. Next thing you know, Cedar Key is one of the biggest clam-producing regions in the whole damn country."

"Great!"

"Yeah, at first. But then the people with the big leases, people like your buddy Howie McCracken and his asshole brother, they started buying up leases from other people. Waving big chunks of money around, more than these dumb-shit mullet men had ever seen before. They'd sell their leases, buy a new boat and go on a six-month drinking binge. Next thing you know, they're outta money, the boat's repossessed, and they're working for the McCrackens, harvesting somebody else's clams on the leases they used to own."

"Well that stinks. But it's also pretty—" Desiree stopped herself in mid-sentence and glanced sideways at Pambellina.

"Pretty stupid? Yeah, it was, but you gotta understand most people around here had never seen real money before. They never thought they'd have a chance to get some, and didn't know what to do with it when they did."

"Is that what happened to your lease?"

"Hell no, Pop was smarter than that. He musta run Steve McCracken off three or four times when he came around with his smooth talk and big checks," Pambellina said proudly. "Even though his leg never really got right after he broke it and he had a hell of a time working that lease. But he held onto it as long as he could."

"So what happened?"

"Economics."

"Economics?"

"Yep. Clams brought fresh money into Cedar Key, a lot of it. People opened new shops and restaurants, and that brought more tourists, and that brought more money. Some of the tourists bought summer houses here, or investment homes. Property values went up. Rent went up. Taxes went up. Next thing you know, people who'd lived here their whole lives couldn't afford to stay in their own homes. Lotsa folks moved out of town, up to Sumner or Rosewood, or to trailer parks out along the forest roads. Now they have to drive miles and miles to work and their kids take buses to school."

"And your dad?"

"My dad held on as long as he could. He loved it here and he knew how much I love it, and he promised me we wouldn't leave. I didn't know it then, but he was borrowing money just to get through. Lots of money. And one day a note came due that he just couldn't pay. And that same day, Steve McCracken came back."

"Oh no."

"Yeah. Pop sold out, but he refused to work for those bastards. He paid off his bills, put what he had left in a trust fund for me. Then he left me with my aunt and went off to Alabama to find work on the fishing boats outta Mobile Bay. He was gonna send for me when he got settled, but then . . ." Pambellina stopped talking and dug in the sand blindly for a moment. Desiree was about to give her a hug when Pambellina started up her story again.

"I got letters for a while, lots of them at first. And then they just stopped coming. I think he musta fell into the sea—that happens, sometimes. And I went up there once, and there wasn't anybody who could remember him leaving. So I think that's what musta happened."

Desiree blinked back tears and stared down at the sand, trying to swallow around the lump in her throat. What a sad story! And what an idiot Pambellina must think she was, moaning about Daddy's money and country club dinners and her pathetic little life. She was trying to figure some way to apologize for it all when Pambellina slapped her playfully on the back.

"Why so glum, chum?" Pambellina said. "It's all good. I got me a good life now, damn good. I don't owe nobody nothing, got a house of my own and a boat that floats, most times. Got plenty of friends and a little money in the bank, and every time I make a midnight raid on McCracken leases, I'm getting me a little revenge. Life is good, girl! You oughta grab yourself some."

"God, Pambellina," Desiree said. "You are just . . . you are just amazing."

"Damn straight," Pambellina said. She bounced to her feet, swiped the sand off her butt and extended a hand to Desiree. "Now get up off your ass and get to work, girl. Them fish ain't gonna catch themselves."

Them fish, Desiree thought. She'd settle for just one fish now, even if it were just another bony little whiting. Just something, anything, to contribute to dinner. She'd done nothing but sponge off Pambellina since she'd gotten here. Food, a place to sleep, the clothes she was wearing—God, for a while she hadn't even been able to pee without Pambellina's help! Pambellina was wonderful, hadn't complained or criticized one little bit, but still. It was starting to feel like being back home, like all those years of being so dependent on Daddy for, well, for everything. No way she was going to let that start up again.

Desiree crinkled her nose and checked the tension on her line. If she couldn't provide any food, she'd just have to work for her keep—maybe she could clean up Pambellina's house, or do some sewing or something. And tomorrow, Dr. Bill would come and they'd fix up Pambellina's boat. Maybe she could even get a ride back to Cedar Key with Dr. Bill. And then—

And then the fishing rod in Desiree's hands jerked so violently that she almost fell over face-first into the water. Desiree let out a little grunt and locked both hands hard on the rod handle. The line was suddenly tight as a kite string in a summer storm, cutting a tiny wake in the water as it ran diagonally away from her. The line went slack for just a moment as the fish turned towards her, then tightened like a bowstring when it turned to run again. Desiree could feel the power of the fish right into her shoulders, and sensed the line stretching to its limits. "Too tight!" she thought. "It'll break the line!" She slipped her left hand down to the drag wheel at the rear of the reel, trying to remember Pambellina's instructions. "Righty tighty," she'd said, "And lefty loosy." Desiree gave the wheel a tentative nudge to the left, and then a full turn. The loosened line whipped off the open face of the reel, and the tension in the rod eased.

The fish turned again and headed straight out to sea. Ten, fifteen, twenty yards of 12-pound-test spun off the open-face reel, and Desiree wondered how much line she had to give. *Do something!* she told herself. She tried to picture the people she'd seen fishing off the pier, and suddenly remembered one afternoon watching from her kayak as an elderly man in big baggy waders patiently worked a fish to the shore. He'd been using a fly rod, and she didn't think it had been a redfish, but still . . .

Desiree eased one hand to the butt of the reel and twisted the drag a half turn back to the right. Then, both hands firmly on the handle again, she slowly swung the rod to the side and down, down till it almost touched the water beside her. *Turn him sideways,* she thought. *Make him stop running.* For a minute the fish kept driving forward and Desiree feared again that he'd break the line. But the hook in his mouth was pulling him sideways now, like a horse trying to run straight while the bit in his mouth and the reins in the hands of his rider forced his head to the side. Finally, the fish gave in. He turned slowly to the right, and the tension on the line eased a bit. He was still running hard, but he was running parallel to the beach now, tiring himself out but not stripping any more line.

Desiree set her feet deep in the sand and let herself draw a deep breath. The fish ran parallel to the shore before her; when he reached the limit of the line he even cut back towards land just a little, and Desiree cranked the reel several times to keep the line taunt. When the fish suddenly turned out toward deep water again, she repeated the whole operation, let him run just a bit and then brought the rod around and to her left. Again, the fish turned with her, and this time she reeled in a good five feet of line.

The battle went on like that until Desiree lost all track of time. Her world shrank down to only what was immediate and important—the tension of the rod, the rippling arrow of fishing line knifing through the gray-green water, each tiny change in the strength and direction of her unseen opponent. Desiree's arms ached and her eyes burned from sweat dripping off her forehead, and still they fought on. Until finally, finally!—she saw a flash of silver under the water ten feet in front of her. The fish was almost in.

Without really knowing why, Desiree began backing up towards the beach behind her, using her legs and not the line to bring the fish closer to land. She could sense his exhaustion. His tugs against the line were half-hearted, his runs toward open water seldom and much shorter. Back and back she went, reeling in line when she could, but mostly using her legs to haul the fish landward. The water was barely above her ankles now, and then her toes—until finally she was completely on dry land. The fish was a long streak of silver in the water just a few feet out. Just a few more feet from the frying pan and Desiree's first catch.

And then Desiree backed into a solid chunk of driftwood embedded in the sand and fell on her ass.

Desiree tumbled over backwards, crying out in surprise and frustration as she went. She held on tight to the fishing rod, jerking it backwards as she fell. That meant she couldn't put out her arms to soften her landing; she hit the sand with a solid whap! that knocked the rod from her hands, the breath from her lungs and the hope from her heart. "Oh no," she thought. "Oh stinking no!"

Desiree lay where she had fallen for a moment, eyes closed, gathering her breath and her composure. When she opened her eyes she found herself looking right up at the inverted face of Pambellina, smiling down at her.

"Oh Pambellina!" Desiree cried. "There was this fish, this great big beautiful fish, and I—"

"And you got him," Pambellina said. "See?" She swung her left arm into Desiree's field of vision; suspended from her hand by a foot of nylon line, gasping in the bright Florida sunshine, was the most beautiful redfish Desiree had even seen.

Desiree let out a little gasp, then rolled over and bounced up to her knees, ignoring the pain from her injured knee, to kneel right before Pambellina and her prize. It was a fully mature redfish, easily two feet long, red-tinted silver glistening in the sun. The scarlet spot at its tail winked at Desiree like a ruby. And it was hers!

"Ohmigosh," Desiree said. "It's magnificent!"

"'bout four and a half pounds of magnificent, I'd say. You did good, girl. We're eating good tonight!"

Desiree raised one hand to her mouth and reached the other out hesitantly toward the fish, as if she feared it would suddenly vanish. "I did it," she said tentatively.

Pambellina frowned down at Desiree and tilted her head slightly. "Of course you did it," she said. "You're a fucking star."

Desiree glanced at Pambellina, then back at her beautiful redfish. A delighted smile slowly spread across her sun-reddened face.

"I did it," she said again. "I'm a *star*."

First, they released the two whiting Pambellina had caught and kept alive in a white plastic bucket. The redfish would be more than enough, she explained, and the whiting would be there to catch some other day. Then Pambellina put Desiree to work gathering firewood while she gutted and cleaned the redfish.

They made a nice little fire in a stone pit behind the Tiltin' Hilton, away from the beach. Once the flames died a bit, Pambellina used one half of a metal U.S. Army mess kit to boil the shrimp. "Hors d'oeuvres," she said with a smile. She produced four tepid Budweisers she kept tied to a rope and cooling in the surf; the girls sipped on those and munched boiled shrimp until the fire had burned itself down to a nice bed of hot coals. Then Pambellina showed Desiree how to wrap fillets of the redfish in tin foil and bury them in the coals. When they pulled the packets out a half-hour later, the fish inside was grilled to delicious white flakes that they scooped out and ate with their bare fingers, with mangos on the side. It was without a doubt, Desiree thought, the most satisfying meal she had ever had.

After dinner they built the fire back up and sat around trading stories till their tongues got tired. Desiree learned about growing up by the sea, about hot days working the fishing nets and cool afternoons swimming with manatees. She tried again to explain how stifling money could be, about mannered luncheons and formalized conversations, about how she'd always tried to be the good girl Daddy wanted and ended up with no idea of who she wanted to be. When the no-see-ums drove them inside the house, Pambellina lit candles and tossed a blanket on the sandy floor so they could stretch out and keep talking.

Desiree had no idea what time it was when she slipped outside to, as Pambellina put it, water the lawn. When she came back in she stretched out flat on her back, and immediately regretted it. Even by the dim candlelight, Pambellina saw her wince.

"Your wounds hurting you?" Pambellina asked.

"No—well, maybe a little. By my back burns! I thought that T-shirt would protect me, but. . . ."

"Nothing'll protect you from the Cedar Key sun for long, especially not a pale-face white thing like you. But don't worry, I got the cure for what ails you." Pambellina popped to her feet and walked toward the door, stopping to pull a diver's knife from its case hung by a nail in one wall. "There's a big ol' aloe plant just a little up the pee path. You take your shirt off, and I'll be right back." And she was gone.

Desiree sat up and stared at the softly swaying blanket-door where Pambellina had just exited. "Take your shirt off," she thought. "Just like that." Well, why not? Pambellina was her friend, there was nobody else around for miles—and her back really did hurt. Some aloe lotion might just feel great.

Desiree carefully pulled the T-shirt over her head, wincing when it scraped along her tender skin. Then she spun around and lay down quickly, on her belly, feeling self-conscious even though the room was empty. She put the T-shirt under her breasts, arranging it carefully to cover as much skin as possible. Then she folded her arms on the soft sand, rested her head, and tried to loosen up.

Loosen up. *Loose women.* The phrase popped into her mind, unbidden and unwanted. Daddy's words; in fact, Desiree didn't think she'd ever heard anyone else use that phrase, at least not seriously. Even the Loose Ladies Gallery back in Cedar Key was a playful name, a pride and defiant comment on the owners' lifestyle. But when Daddy said it . . .

"Those loose women . . ." he'd say, shaking his head sadly. Or, "No, you can't watch MTV, it shows nothing but profanity and loose women." Once, even, "I worry about your sister being away at that college, Desiree. I fear she may be in danger of becoming a loose woman." Desiree smiled at that one. "Daddy," she thought, "You have no idea." Desiree loved Kathleen dearly, and looked up to her, but everyone at the entire college knew that Kathy Dean loved boys. Especially athletes. "It's those muscles," Kathy would say, all dreamy-eyed. "They just make me all weak in the knees. If I ever find a real man with money and muscles and a mind, lord, I would never let him go. Half a mind, even."

"Well," Desiree thought, "At least Kathy goes after what she wants. Me, I'm not even sure I know what I want." She tried to picture the few guys she'd gotten physical with, all groping fingers and gooey tongues, but what came to mind instead was an image of Pambellina stretched out and smiling on the beach. Desiree was still pondering that image when Pambellina come in through the door behind her.

Pambellina knelt beside Desiree and began sawing at the thick green aloe stem she'd brought with her, chatting in that soft Cracker accent Desiree had already learned to trust. "Okay," she said. "Okay, this will be a little cold at first, but it'll cool off that burn right away. You'll see." Desiree felt a kiss of something cool and wet on her shoulders, and then Pambellina's soft hands spreading the aloe around. It did feel good. Felt great, in fact. Desiree felt herself relax just a little.

Loose women, she thought again. She remembered the one and only time Daddy had used that phrase to describe Desiree's mother. She must've been four or five at the time, Kathy about eight, so Desiree was old enough to begin asking why they didn't have a mother like the other children. Daddy had tried to tell her his old vague story, that Mommy had to go away and could never come back, but Desiree had kept pushing for more details. Finally Daddy exploded. "You will never ask me about that *loose woman* again!" he shouted. He'd scared Desiree badly, and seeing Kathy crying had scared her even more. Desiree never asked again.

The delicious cooling sensation along her spine brought Desiree from her troubling memories back into the much-more-interesting present. Pambellina had finished massaging her shoulders and moved down to the center of her back, down to the hollow just above her beltline. She wasn't burned much there, and Pambellina seemed to have run out of aloe, but so what? It still felt good. Desiree arched her back and smiled a secret smile. She was still smiling when Pambellina slipped her hand under the elastic band of Desiree's borrowed gym shorts and started rubbing places that were not at all sunburned. That smile changed only a little when Pambellina's clever fingers journeyed on down to places where the sun never, ever shone. When Pambellina pulled back and sat up to pull her own shirt off, Desiree surprised herself— practice spontaneity!—by rolling over on her back, leaving that protective T-shirt right where it lay.

If only, Desiree thought as the smiling Pambellina slipped into her arms, *If only Daddy could see me now.*

Chapter Twelve

Robin Chanterelles was back at the picnic table beside the Dock Street hot dog stand, hoping the afternoon sun would burn off some of her hangover, when Pincushion sauntered up. He had one hand nestled companionably in a rear pocket of the very tight shorts of The Chipmunk, who in turn was nestled companionably in the crook of Pincushion's tattoo-covered arm. In his free hand, Pincushion held several sheets of shiny paper, which he dropped unceremoniously on the table in front of Robin.

"Mail's in," Pincushion said. "And Max called. He wants to know when we're gonna quit running up his expense account and get our asses home."

Robin acknowledged all that with a nod and picked up the top sheet of the fax; Pincushion and Chipmunk somehow slipped onto the bench opposite her without ever removing hand from rump or shoulder from side.

"Pincushel says that's some really important investigative reporter documents that you had to send all the way to Tallahassee for, Miss Chanterelles," Chipmunk said. "I just think that's so cool."

"Not so important, and not so cool," Robin said absently. "And call me Robin."

"Really? Robin? Oh, wow!" Robin flinched inwardly at the admiration in Chipmunk's voice, but didn't look up from the articles of corporate organization in front of her. It was pretty much what she'd suspected—the absolute minimum amount of information required by Florida's public disclosure laws. Cedar Casino, Inc. listed Stephen McCracken as president; vice-president was a vaguely familiar name with a New York City address. Treasurer was Noel Black of the Miami law firm Black, Black, and Blecker; Robin wondered absently if he had been the stiff suit on the stage yesterday afternoon. The fourth name, the secretary, was unknown to her, but his name was also on the second form, the certification of minority ownership.

"Damn," Robin said. "They got an Indian."

"A what?" Chipmunk said. She was watching Robin intently, of course, while Pincushion set to work building a tiny log cabin from Robin's discarded cigarette butts. There were a lot of those butts there, Robin realized. She'd been sitting here thinking longer than she'd thought.

"An Indian," she said. "A Native American, specifically, a Seminole. Or at least a one-quarter Seminole, that's all the law requires."

Chipmunk said, "Ahh," and nodded her head as if that explained everything; Robin tried not to smile and pressed on. "Florida's state constitution prohibits gambling, unless it's licensed by the state and approved by the public, like the lottery. But there's a loophole—Seminole and Micossukee Indians have the right to establish gambling halls on their reservations. That's how they got those money-mills disguised as bingo parlors out in the 'glades near Miami."

"But the Cedar Casino isn't on a reservation. It's right here," Chipmunk objected.

"Right," Robin said, noting how Chipmunk had jumped right to the heart of the issue. "But there's loopholes there too. One of them allows a county commission to designate a certain property as an extension of a reservation, and thus exempt from a lot of state regulations."

"And the McCrackens own the county commission, or at least most of it. That's how they got approval for Mamasan's," Chipmunk said. She leaned in over the table to study the documents before Robin; Robin registered something that was part envy and part sympathy when Chipmunk had to carefully maneuver her cantaloupe breasts to avoid slapping them on the table's edge. "So what about this growth manglement thingie that park ranger was talking about yesterday?"

"Management. The Florida Growth Management Act of 1985." Pincushion looked up at that; he knew Robin had spent much of the prior afternoon in the Cedar Key library reviewing that law, and much of the evening trying to wash away her findings with gin tonics. "Back in the early eighties," Robin said, "people finally realized that the tremendous influx of immigrants moving to Florida was going to overwhelm the infrastructure and the environment. There was one famous study that said the equivalent of the entire state of Georgia would be moving to Florida by the end of the decade."

"What?" Pincushion said. "You mean they'd just leave Atlanta?"

Chipmunk glanced at Pincushion, confused; Robin ignored him and pushed on. "So, the legislature spent like three years putting together this huge bill, the Growth Management Act, that set all sorts of regulations on who could build where, what kind of construction would be allowed, what kind of permits they'd need and what sort of infrastructure improvements they'd have to make, all that sort of thing. A lot of it was aimed at protecting desirable but vulnerable areas, especially the coast. It even sets limits on how close to the water you can do construction."

"What's an infrastruction?" Pincushion asked.

Robin opened her mouth to answer that, but Chipmunk beat her to it. "Infrastructure," she said, "roads and sewers, schools, wastewater facilities, that kind of thing. That sounds like a really good idea."

"It was a good idea, a great idea, and it's done a hell of a lot to protect the environment," Robin said. "But the developers and private property nuts fought it tooth and nail, and they managed to slip in a lot of loopholes of their own. One of them says you can build beyond the coastal protection line, build closer to the water than the law normally allows, if you're actually rebuilding an existing property."

"So somebody could rebuild their beachhouse if it got zapped by, like, a hurricane or something."

"Exactly, as long as the original foundation is still there. The idea was to avoid taking away the rights of people who'd lived on the beach for years, while still prohibiting new construction right on the beaches. That's why if you go places like Pensacola or Destin you'll see old houses right near the water and new hotels and condos fifty yards farther back."

Chipmunk frowned and absently shook off the lean-to of cigarette butts Pincushion had begun building against her forearm. "So the McCrackens—"

"So the McCrackens, even though they obviously have one hell of a loophole lawyer, could never have built a brand new casino on the coastline. None of the boat rides for the gamblers' kids and seaside bars for the adults they were touting yesterday, no swimming with dolphins or fishing from the waterside bar between poker games."

"No *new* construction," Chipmunk said pointedly.

Robin nodded. "But since the fire, they now have existing but bare infrastructure—the pilings and the concrete overhang—and they have the right to build any damn thing they want on it."

"Including a casino."

"Including a casino."

"Well, those bastards," Chipmunk said. "Those nasty bastards."

Robin shrugged her agreement and reached for

another cigarette. Pincushion had extricated his hand from The Chipmunk's pocket and was preparing to launch a butt field-goal kicker style towards the inlet behind Robin; she reached across the table and swatted his hand like she'd caught him trying to steal cookies. "Not in the water, P," she said. "Fish think they're bread and swallow them, and it fucks up their insides."

"Oh," Pincushion said. His face darkened for a moment, then he brightened and turned to Chipmunk. "But that'll work out all right for you, right Pumpkin Butt? Casinos need dancers, and hostesses and cigarette girls and all like that. You'll get your job back!"

Chipmunk turned to Pincushion, mouth half open, and Robin thought she was going to let him have it for the Pumpkin Butt crack. Instead, she just sort of crumpled into the surprised Pincushion's arms, looking like she might just cry. "Pincushel," she wailed, "Cedar Key is my *home*."

"Yeah," Pincushion said hesitantly. He wrapped his arms tight around the unhappy girl and looked pleadingly at Robin. "Yeah, and so. . . ."

"And so," Robin took up, "So imagine what D Street is going to look like when you've got tourists' cars backed up all the way to Chiefland. Imagine what the city park will be like with a thousand bratty kids and two hundred barking dogs dumped on it every day. Imagine what walking the Loop will be like when there's hundreds of pissed-off losers stumbling along it every night. Think what's gonna happen to all the great little shops when property value along Dock

Street suddenly triples or quadruples, and their taxes go through the roof. Think what happens to the fishing, and to the clamming, and to the manatees and the pelicans when construction goes way up and the water quality goes way down."

Robin wanted to go on, to let her growing anger take her through the all-too-familiar litany of environmental disasters and paradise lost a casino would mean, but she could see the lights going on in Pincushion's eyes.

"No more quiet little town," he said. "No more pelicans eating outta children's hands. No more hot dog stand by the road. No more key lime fudge!"

"No more Cedar Key," The Chipmunk whimpered.

"No more Cedar Key," Robin agreed. She picked angrily at a loose splinter along the table's edge. "But look, Chipmunk, what about the referendum? Your own charter says—"

"The McCrackens own a whole lot of people in this town," Chipmunk snuffled. "Own the mortgage on their property, own the notes on their boats. And they got a lot more on their payrolls, a whole lot more. And there's other people here who want development, not many, but some. When you add 'em all up . . ." Chipmunk let the sentence go unfinished and dug further down into Pincushion's arms.

"Okay then," Robin said. "Okay then, so maybe that won't help either." She tugged at the edge of the table a bit more, chewing on her lower lip, until she remembered something that had bothered her all day.

"Chipmunk, what was that that Tee Nichols said about pencils?"

"What?" Chipmunk asked sadly. She peeked up out of Pincushion's arms; he produced a fire-hydrant-red handkerchief and gently pressed it into her hand.

"At the end of the unveiling ceremony yesterday. Tee said something about pencils, and suddenly a lot of people who were watching Stevie McCracken pretty close just turned around and walked off."

"Cedar pencils," Chipmunk answered. "That's what he said."

"Cedar pencils?"

"Yeah." Chipmunk honked into the handkerchief with a rumble like a sore-throated Canada goose, and then handed it back to Pincushion. "It's like a historical reference, back to, to ummm. . . ." Chipmunk stumbled a little, and Robin feared she would start bawling again. But Pincushion took her hand and whispered something in her ear. The girl nodded bravely, squeezed Pincushion's hand, and forced herself to sit up straight.

"See," she said, "back in the 1870s, 1880s or so, a couple big pencil companies discovered our red cedar. That's what gives Cedar Key its name, you know." Robin nodded; she'd seen several of the twisted, stringy-barked reddish evergreens with electric green needles and baby blue berries around town. "Turns out red cedar was great for pencils. The best pencil wood in the world, in fact.

"So next thing you know, there's something like fifteen or twenty sawmills in the cedar keys, most of 'em chopping up red cedar for companies like Eagle and Faber-Castell. Cedar Key was already a big seaport 'cause it had one end of the only cross-Florida railroad, and now they had all that wood to ship out. It was a boomtown for a couple decades there, mostly 'cause of pencils. And everybody thought things were set forever, 'cause the pencil companies said the supply of red cedar was inexhaustible."

"Inexhaustible," Robin said. Different place, same story, she thought.

"Yeah. So, after about twenty years, the red cedar was all gone, or damn near. The pencil companies pulled out, the mills closed down. Ships started going to Tampa instead of Cedar Key. The railroad got old and fell apart, and nobody saw much reason to fix it. Something like twenty-five hundred people lost their jobs in a few months. Twenty-five hundred! That's like three times as many people who even live here now. Times got real bad for a whole lot of people real fast."

"I can imagine."

"And most people around here know that story. Lots of 'em had it handed down to them by grandparents or great grandparents who lived through it. So when Tee said that yesterday, everybody who really knows Cedar Key knew just what he was talking about."

"Exploitation," Pincushion said, and Robin was surprised to see him nodding his head mournfully.

"Economic colonization," Chipmunk added gloomily.

"Globalization," Robin said. The colorful couple across from her nodded their heads in quiet confirmation for a moment. Then a tiny frown slowly wrinkled Chipmunk's brow. She looked at Pincushion, who coughed once, then again, and finally shrugged his shoulders and turned back to Robin.

"Um, you know, Robin dear Robin, that globalization stuff, that's a word you hear a lot nowadays, and as a full-fledged member of the working press I know what it's all about, of course, but The Chipmunk here . . ."

"Globalization," Robin said, "is pretty much what you just described. A big company comes into a small place and uses its money or muscle to take advantage of whatever that place has—natural resources or cheap labor, usually. Everybody's happy for awhile, till the trees or the oil or the ivory is all gone, or till the company finds someplace where they can get their blue jeans or their athletic shoes made cheaper, and they pack up and go."

"And the place they left behind . . ."

"The place they left behind suddenly has no jobs, no local economy, and no natural resources left to build from. They're dependent on outside resources they can no longer afford," Robin said. "They're screwed, just like Cedar Key was when the pencil-people left. The only difference now is the companies are corporations, and they've got trade agreements and international regulations to make it easier than ever to pull it off."

"Well shit," Pincushion said. "That ain't right."

"Welcome to the real world, P," Robin said.

"And what Cedar Key has now," Chipmunk said thoughtfully, "Is location—the Gulf."

"And a local government too small and poor to stand up to big money. And people who are hungry enough for jobs to ignore the long-term costs," Robin said. "And a beautiful environment for the kids and wives to enjoy while the dads gamble their life savings away."

"And the wives and kids are gonna want things to do while daddy gambles," Chipmunk said. "Arcades. Amusement parks."

"Golf courses," Pincushion chimed in. "Jet skis. Plane rides."

"Shopping centers," Chipmunk wailed. "A Wal-Mart!"

"And somewhere down the line," Robin said, feeling the familiar anger and helpless frustration in her stomach like a living thing. "When people get tired of gambling, or someone builds a casino closer to home, and all the jobs go away again but the environment has been tackified into a smaller version of Panama City Beach, what will you have left?"

"Nothing," Chipmunk whispered. "Not even our souls."

"Your souls are part of the deal," Robin said. She lit up a fresh cigarette and breathed in hard, letting the hot smoke punish her lungs. "It's all part of the deal."

Pincushion reached into his pocket for his big red hankie; instead of handing it to Chipmunk he gave it a prodigious honk of his own. A seagull passing overhead screeched back like she was answering a mating call, and the three sat listening to the mournful echoes. It was The Chipmunk who broke the brief silence.

"But this is a little different, right?" she said. "Because it's local people who are doing it, and maybe we can talk them out of it? It's not like some humongous multinational is behind all this. It's just, you know, Stevie and Howie."

"Is it?" Robin said quietly. She ran one forefinger down the articles of incorporation spread before her, letting it linger on that tantalizingly familiar name with the New York address. She just couldn't place it, not exactly, but something about that name made her stomach muscles tighten.

Robin was still glaring at that name and searching her memory when one of Chipmunk's companions from Mamasan's came pounding down the street and staggered up to their table. She was covered with sweat and completely out of breath, Robin realized, and there was some sort of growing commotion down Dock Street in the direction she'd come from.

"God, Sandy, what's wrong?" Chipmunk asked. "You look like you've seen a ghost!"

Sandy nodded her head, and then shook it. She reached across the table to take the cup of Mountain Dew Robin offered her, knocked half of it back, apparently without noticing the layer of gin, and then turned her excited gaze to Pincushion.

"You gotta come quick," Sandy said. "And bring your camera. Some old couple just got attacked by the sea monster!"

Chapter Thirteen

Not that morning, or the next, but the third morning after her first night in the arms of Pambellina, Desiree woke to find a strange and hairy man staring down at her.

"Good morning," he said. "Show me your tits."

Desiree was too surprised to speak. Not so Pambellina, who let out a joyous war-whoop, tossed aside her blanket and bounced up and into the arms of the grinning intruder. Since Desiree had been more or less covered by that same blanket, Pam's abrupt action left her suddenly much more exposed than she had ever before been in the presence of a strange and hairy man. She grabbed the blanket and tried to wrap herself in it while Pambellina assaulted their unexpected guest with hugs and kisses.

"Careful, little Elf, you'll make me spill!" the man laughed. He was holding a silvery cylinder in one hand that Desiree recognized as a martini mixer. Pambellina saw the mixer and groaned, then took a playful swipe at it. The stranger growled in a sleepy bear-like way and raised his arm up over his head; he was not a tall man, but that still put the mixer out of the reach of the diminutive Pambellina. She jumped for it ineffectively a couple times, looking all the world like a clumsy kitten swatting at a string, before collapsing happily against the bare belly and breast of the stranger.

"Desiree," Pambellina said, "Allow me to introduce Dr. William Beelzebubba, PhD."

"Doc B to my friends," Beelzebubba said. "Or just B, if you're pretty and naked." He leaned over Pambellina's shoulder and flopped one shaggy paw on her stomach, then spider-walked his hand downward. Pamela giggled and stopped his hand before—but only *just* before—it reached the northernmost border of her Bermuda Triangle.

Desiree sat up and extended one hand tentatively towards the stranger, trying hard to maintain both her dignity and her hold on the blanket. "Dr. B," she said, "Pleased to make your acquaintance."

"And I yours, my dear," Dr. B said, taking her hand gently. Desiree couldn't help but smile at the contrast between B's formal words and his wild-man appearance. He had a bristly black beard covering his face from ear to ear, and kinky black hair that would have reached his shoulders if it hadn't sprouted up and out rather than down. He was a stout little guy, probably three or four inches shorter than Desiree's six-foot-one, with a barrel chest and a rounded beer belly. A great thatch of dark hair spread across his chest, narrowed into a Mohawk streak and plunged down his belly into his ragged cutoffs. His legs were just as hairy and, yes, more than a little bow-legged.

"You look quite a bit improved from the last time I saw you," Dr. B said. "How's the leg?"

"Better. It still hurts sometimes, like if I walk a lot or turn suddenly."

"Uh-huh." Dr. B knelt in the sand beside Desiree, slid the blanket aside and poked gently at the palm-sized bruise surrounding her knee. "It's a miracle you didn't just shatter your knee all to shit, falling in the Elf's boat like that."

"Or just dropped right in the water and drowned," Desiree said. "Though I guess maybe the shock of hitting the water would have woken me up."

"It wouldn't have, not the way you were concussed. Speaking of which—little Elf, open those curtains for us, would you?" Pambellina pulled aside the gunnysack draperies and sunlight stabbed into the room. B took Desiree's chin gently in one hand and turned her head from side to side, staring intently into each eye. "Any headaches? Lightheadedness? No? Good, good. All right, now the chest."

Desiree hesitated, hearing the echoes of a lifetime of warnings from her preachers and teachers, her parents and sorority sisters. But there was nothing salacious about Dr. B; despite his appearance and their un-office-like surroundings, he seemed to be as professional and concerned as any physician she'd ever seen. Desiree glanced at Pambellina, whose trust and faith in Dr. B was obvious. She slipped one corner of the blanket aside to show the final mark of her misadventure, and then abruptly, brazenly, dropped the entire blanket into her lap.

"Ahhh," Dr. B said thoughtfully. He turned Desiree to one side so the sunlight shone full on her chest. An egg-shaped patch the size of a baseball spread across the top and inner side of her left breast, glaring angrily red against the cloud-white background. B ran one forefinger around the edge of the burn, apologizing each time he saw Desiree flinch.

"Not bad, Desiree, not bad at all. Still tender, I see, but for the most part it seems to be healing nicely. I've got some ointment for you down in my boat that'll help a bit." Then he frowned and leaned in so close that Desiree felt the bristles of his beard tickle the side of her right breast. "I'm a little concerned about this slight discoloration here. . . ."

Dr. B rocked back on his ankles, crossed his arms and pursed his lips in thought. Desiree felt a little icicle of fear dart through her, and raised one hand protectively towards the offending red splotch. Silence hung like tropical humidity in the air. Then B gave a decisive nod. "Only one thing to do," he said, reaching reached past Desiree to grab the chipped coffee mug off Pambellina's bedside table. Suddenly the martini mixer was in his other hand and his eyes were twinkling above a wicked grin, like silvery minnows in sunlit water.

"You'll have to drink this," he said.

"Bubba! No!" Pambellina shouted. She dropped to the sand beside Dr. B, laughing, and tried to swat the mixer from his hand; he held her off effortlessly with one extended arm. "Doctor's orders!" he shouted. "Doctor's orders!"

Desiree watched the two of them, envying their comfortable playfulness, then leaned in and sniffed suspiciously as B poured a cupful of thick, greenish liquid from the mixer into the mug. "What is it?" she asked dubiously.

"Mother's milk," Dr. B said.

"Pirate's poison. Shark shit," Pambellina added. "Eel squeezings. Don't touch it!"

B shot Pamela a dramatically evil glare; she rocked back on her heels, mumbled something about it being Des' funeral, and then pantomimed running a zipper across her lips. Dr. B turned back to Desiree and handed her the mug.

"It's a margarita," he said. "You like margaritas, don't you?"

Desiree nodded. She did like margaritas, and daiquiris and pina coladas, and just about every other frozen fruity drink she'd ever tried. This wasn't frozen, of course, though she could see little ice cubes bobbing around in the pea-green mixture. But it didn't look like any margarita she'd ever seen, frozen or otherwise. She sniffed at the mug suspiciously, catching a heady mix of herbs and seawater.

"Don't sniff—swallow!" Dr. B ordered—and Desiree did. She shoved aside all the distracting reservations swelling up in her brain, raised the mug to her lips and drained it all in one big long slurp. She turned the mug over and smacked it face-down into the sand, shot-glass style, and grinned proudly at B and Pambellina. Not so bad, she thought. Salty, mostly, with the warm undertone of something that might have been tequila, plus something vaguely celery-like, something slippery and oysterish, and—and then it hit her.

"Oh my God," Desiree squeaked. Her eyes suddenly flooded with tears, her stomach flipped like a frog in a frying pan, and the air seemed to vanish from her lungs. She gasped for breath, flapped one hand frantically in front of her open mouth and tried not to retch. Pambellina slapped the orange juice jug of water into Desiree's hand, the lid already removed, and Des' raised it over her head and sucked at it desperately, pounding on the sand beside her all the while.

"Damn," Dr. B said mournfully. "Still too much sea slug."

"Sea slug?!" Desiree demanded, once she'd regained enough equilibrium to do so. *"Sea slug!?"*

"Sure," Dr. B said. "Dry 'em out, chop 'em up, toss 'em in the blender. Helps balance out the bitterness from the urchins, but sometimes people react to them funny, if they're not used to it."

"Used to it?" Desiree said weakly. She accepted a handful of dried figs from Pambellina and gratefully popped them into her mouth. "My gosh, who would drink enough of that nasty stuff to ever get used to it?" She saw the hurt in B's eyes too late to take it back.

"Three years," he said, sadly. "Three years of research and experimentation, of scorching days and long nights searching for the perfect marine margarita, and still they scoff. I tell you, Elf, sometimes I fear I'll never find the right formula."

"Aw, now, B," Pambellina said gently. She put one arm over Beelzebubba's shoulder and slipped her delicate hand over his gnarled knuckles. "You'll find it, someday. You just have to remember that most people aren't as, um, accustomed to these flavorings as you are."

"Sure, that's right," Desiree chimed in. "It wasn't that bad, really. It was, um, it was . . . ah, what was it, anyway?"

"Sea cucumber, mostly," B said. "Distilled sea grapes. Pureed oyster, for body and vitamins. Extract of turtle grass for color. A little ground urchin, some sea slug, a dozen other secret spices. Mangos, when they're in season. And . . . figs?"

"Figs?" Pambellina said.

"Figs!" Dr. B shouted. He grabbed Desiree's hand, staring at the partially eaten fig sitting there as if it were a gold nugget. "Of course, figs, for tartness! Perfect, perfect, why didn't I think of it before! Not strictly aquatic of course, but close enough for government work. Elf, where did you pick those—"

"Down the piss path, right at the scrub pine that looks like an old woman's hands. Can't miss it."

Dr B nodded enthusiastically, jumped to his feet and bolted to the door. "Figs!" he said gleefully. He rushed out, but almost immediately pushed the curtain aside and poked his head back in. "Desiree, you go cleanse your palate," he said. "When I get back, we'll try again. Figs!" And then, before Desiree could do more than open her mouth to protest, he was gone.

"And that," Pambellina said, "Is why they call him Beelzebubba."

Desiree balanced carefully on the bow of Dr. B's boat, amazed at the chaos before her. The word "ship-shape" came to mind, and she immediately drew a mental circle-and-slash around it. The *Sailcat's Revenge* was many things, but orderly was not one of them.

The boat was a sturdy old Chriscraft, aluminum hulled, with a battered Evinrude motor clinging to the stern like a weathered barnacle. Desiree guessed she was sixteen or seventeen feet long—no bigger, really, than the sleek and polished crafts she had watched Kathy ski behind back in Ohio. But the resemblance ended there. The hull of the *Sailcat's Revenge* was a silvery landscape of dents and dings. Streaks and spots of various colored paint spoke of numerous collisions with—what, other boats? Docks? Whatever. A chrome railing stretching around two-thirds of the bow ended abruptly in a knot of heavy duct tape, a spotlight mounted beside the captain's seat was held in place by a spider's web of knotted bungee cords. A small electric trolling motor clung to the bow beside the Evinrude; the wires leading from it were more electricians' tape than original wiring. The name itself, *Sailcat's Revenge*, was painted proudly in purple reflective paint on the bow, but a circular rip that looked suspiciously like a bullet hole had taken

out most of the "v" and part of the second "e." Desiree decided not to think about how that had come
about.

The interior was no better. The third of the boat
aft of the console looked like it had once been a comfortable place to sit—but no more. The horseshoe-
shaped strip of foam-filled seating was covered with
an array of tools and trash, torn in numerous places
and streaked with grease. A pair of swim fins sat on
one side of the seat, though no mask or snorkel were
in sight. A chicken-wire crab trap was wedged between one edge of the seat and the lip of the railing; a
cinder-block anchor with a yellow ski-rope knotted
through it took up much of the narrow front deck. A
long aluminum pole with a crook at the end, the sort
the lifeguards at Daddy's country club might use to
haul a struggling swimmer out of the pool, was roped
to the starboard railing.

The captain's and passenger's seats aft of the console were a little better, but not much. Two battered
boxes hung beneath the console in front of the
captain's chair—a radio and depth finder, Desiree
guessed, though she would hate to rely on either one
of them in time of trouble. A fat snub-nosed flare gun
hung in a wire cage beneath the boat's speed stick.
Two short, stout wooden poles with single shot-gun
shells mounted on the end were wedged between
the seat and the boat's side—bang sticks, Desiree
thought, for fending off an attacking shark.

The passenger's seat was occupied by a mid-size
cooler, strapped in place by two frayed bungee cords.

In front of the seat, where a passenger's legs would go, was a rolled-up sleeping bag and a plastic box packed tight with what looked like spare towels and a change of clothes. The deck behind the seats was a mélange of more mess: three brightly painted gallon, milk-jug marker buoys, each tied to a red brick by more ski rope. Two plastic bags bulging with trash; one with aluminum cans, the other an assortment of plastic and paper. A heavy tackle box leaned against one gunwale, though there was no fishing pole in sight. The storage rack running along each gunwale was packed with items nautical and nonsensical: two quarts of motor oil, a squirrels' nest knot of heavy line, a water-stained copy of Rachel Carson's *Silent Spring*, a row of Busch beer cans, pliers, heavy wire cutters, three bottles of water, a bag of pretzel rods and half a dozen little cans of Vienna sausages.

The only island of order in this ocean of mess was a rectangular metal box bolted to the floor behind the captain's chair. It was probably three feet tall, two feet wide and a foot deep—a mechanic's tool chest, the kind you'd expect to find in an auto repair shop. The cabinet's door was secured by a length of heavy chain, and locked tight with a sturdy Yale lock, just like Beelzebubba had said. Desiree took a deep breath and, watching where she put each foot, carefully wound her way from the bow back to the chest. The key Dr. B had given her slipped easily into the Yale; after just a moment's pressure the heavy lock popped open. Desiree pulled the chain aside, opened the cabinet's double doors, and caught her breath. The rest of the *Sailcat's Revenge* looked like it had been through a typhoon, but this cabinet had all the sterile precision of an hospital operating room.

Desiree reached for the first drawer hesitantly, curious but reluctant to disturb anything. The cabinet was filled, mostly, with medical supplies—boxes of sterile bandages, syringes and packets of large-bore hypodermic needles. Rows of little medicine bottles, some pills but most injectable fluids—Desiree recognized a few as antibiotics, but most of the names were unfamiliar. Sewing needles, the sewing-up-wounds kind, and boxes of thick suture cord. She saw a tube of antibiotic cream and reflexively raised one hand to her burned breast.

The second drawer was mostly tools. Desiree was surprised at first to find a pistol there; then she saw the package of heavy sedatives beside it and realized the gun was designed to fire darts. A worn leather case the size of a hardback novel rested beside the pistol— surgical tools, Desiree guessed. The drawer also held three hard-worn books, one on marine biology, a second a physician's desk reference to drugs. The third book was actually a journal; Desiree shuddered when she saw "Margarita Research" handwritten in felt-tip along the book's spine.

The third drawer, the one Desiree was supposed to have gone for right away, was divided into twenty or so individual compartments, each containing its own little bottle or tube. Desiree counted three over and one row down, just as Dr. B had instructed, and picked up the finger-sized tube of ointment he had said would be there. Burn cream, to speed healing and minimize scarring. Scarring—Pambellina had told Desiree over and over that she had beautiful breasts, and that no blemish or burn could change that, but still the idea of going through life with a disfigured bosom chilled Desiree to the bone. She imagined customers at Mamasan's turning away in disgust, and gripped B's magic cream a little tighter.

Desiree closed the cabinet doors, pulled the chain back in place and locked it up tight. She looped the key through the waist of her pocketless gym shorts—the key ring also held the boat key and a half-size Swiss army knife—grateful that the chain was knotted to a fat red-and-white fisherman's bobber, to keep the keys afloat should they fall overboard. How great would that be, she thought, if B trusted her with his keys and she let them sink to bottom of the sea!

Desiree squeezed a dollop of the burn cream on one forefinger and pulled up the bottom of her T-shirt, trying to expose her injury but not flash the whole world. Then she realized what she was doing, shook her head and smiled. There was nobody around to flash, for gosh sakes! The *Sailcat's Revenge* was resting peacefully in a quiet little cove a good hundred yards from the beach where Pambellina and Dr. B were working on Pam's boat, tied to one of the mangrove trees lining the banks all around her. It was open to the Gulf, of course, but the mangroves blocked all but a straight-on view, and she would hear any boat approaching long before it came into sight. Even so, Desiree allowed herself one more look around before peeling the shirt over her head and off.

That made it much easier to apply the salve—and there was a delicious sense of naughtiness to it, too. Desiree smiled and wondered if she would ever stop feeling that little rush of pure animal pleasure that came with being naked outside. She remembered her first outdoor shower back at Tee's place, the exhilarating, forbidden touch of fresh air on naked skin. The shower had a door to it, of course, weathered cedar that covered her from mid-calf to upper shoulders. But the wood had expanded over time and it was darned hard to keep that door shut. Usually, you had to keep one hand on the door to keep it from creaking open, which was a real nuisance when you were trying to shampoo. Tee had promised he would fix it the moment it started bothering him—and of course, it never did. He would just stand there naked to all the world, soap in one hand and beer can in the other, singing one of his dirty sailor songs. Nobody was there to look, he said, and so what if there were? Desiree thought about that, accepted that no one could see into the shower unless they were stationed right in Tee's studio, and eventually she stopped worrying about the darn door.

And when she'd realized that Tee was watching her, that he was actually painting her! The flush that memory brought to Desiree's cheeks was part embarrassment and part pride.

She had finished her ministrations and was trying to screw the cap back on the tube with her ointment-slippery fingers when Desiree was startled by an abrupt, loud cough. Desiree's eyes popped open wide, and she grabbed for her T-shirt. She spun around to study the shoreline, expecting to see someone staring back at her—a hairy pirate holding his sword aloft, perhaps, or an emaciated castaway lurking furtively among the tightly packed mangrove bushes. What she saw instead was—nothing.

"Dr. B, is that you?" Desiree said, trying to keep her voice steady. "Pambellina?" No answer, and no movement she could see. She put the ointment down on the seat beneath her and reached blindly for the paddle tucked between the seat and the gunwales, watching the shore and trying to keep the shirt over her chest all the while. Probably nothing, she told herself, probably just the wind. And then she heard the cough again, louder, closer and from behind her. There was someone in the water!

Desiree jumped up, dropped the shirt and raised the paddle high in both hands, ready to smash it down on top of whomever was sneaking up behind her. The splintered paddle held heroically overhead, expression on her face frightened but resolute, bare and ointment-anointed breasts glistening in the sun, Desiree stood tall and strong, like a Gulf Coast Amazon.

And stood there. And stood there, and stood there. And then, feeling more and more foolish, she slowly lowered the paddle, inched her way over to the railing, and peeped over the side of the boat.

Nothing. The greenish-brown water of the cove was undisturbed except for the gentle swells rolling in from the Gulf. A soft breeze teased a strand of hair over Desiree's face, off in the distance a gull cried out its strident complaint. Just another peaceful day on Pambellina's island.

"Idiot," Desiree said to herself. She lowered herself onto the boat seat and tucked the paddle back into its niche, feeling sheepish, relieved that Pambellina and Dr. B hadn't been around to see her freak out. Still, she could have sworn she heard something . . .

Desiree hesitantly looked back over the side of the boat and noticed, about ten feet out, a stream of fat white bubbles come bobbing up to the surface. Bubbles, she thought, now what would cause bubbles in a cove like this? Did the ocean have swamp gas? Did fish have gas? She cupped one hand above her eyes, trying to cut down the glare from the sun, and gasped. Her bubbles had all but stopped, but a large black shadow was appearing in the water right where they had been.

"A scuba diver!" Desiree said. There was a scuba diver in her cove, turned now and coming right at her. She put one hand on the paddle and the other on her shirt, not sure if she should be modest or macho. She decided on modest and turned to grab the shirt. When she turned back, the shadow was even closer—and bigger. Much bigger. In fact, she realized with a giddy little rush in her stomach, she was either looking at the world's fattest scuba diver, or—

The shadow broke the surface at the end nearest Desiree and the *Sailcat's Revenge*. A walrus-like head the size of a basketball rose a few inches out of the water, elephantine gray skin, long bristly whiskers on a nose broad as a bread loaf, big brown eyes soft as a golden retriever's, set over a mouth trailing vibrant green strands of turtle grass. The beast turned towards Desiree, regarded her dispassionately for a moment, let out a heavy "huff" sound through the nostrils atop its nose, and then slowly slipped back below the waves.

"A manatee!" Desiree said, with all the delight of a child on Christmas. "A real life wild manatee, right here in Pambellina's cove!"

Desiree scrambled up to kneel on the boat seat, leaning over the side so she could get a better look. The manatee was maybe five feet away now, turned parallel to the boat and moving slowly towards the shore. Desiree could see her outline clearly—at least eight feet long, she guessed, maybe ten. Its body too was vaguely walrus-like, but with a big flat ping-pong-paddle-shaped tail. Fat stubby flippers that looked too small for its body protruded from each side. Grazing on the turtle grass on the cove bottom, Desiree realized, and didn't give a hoot one way or another about the girl in the boat right beside it. Wonderful!

Desiree watched fascinated as the manatee worked its way slowly across the cove. She tried to remember what little she knew about the creatures— they were marine mammals, she knew, like dolphins and seals. Vegetarians, obviously, and absolutely harmless. They were supposed to be curious about people, friendly even. In fact . . . Desiree smiled a secret smile, then stood and scanned the mangrove shoreline for any sign of Pambellina or Dr. B. Seeing no one, she slipped off her gym shorts—they were all she had to wear, after all—and eased herself over the side of the *Catfish* and into the cool blue water.

This was one horsie ride, Desiree decided, that she was *not* going to miss.

Chapter Fourteen

The crowd, when Robin, Pincushion, Sandy and The Chipmunk arrived, was pretty equally divided between people gathered around an older couple, sitting in one of the big, porch-style swings at the Faraway Inn, and a second group on the low-tide sandbar near Goose Cove. A few of those on the sand were pulling a big fiber-glass canoe up out of the tide's reach, while the rest pointed at various spots out on the Gulf and jabbered excitedly among themselves. Robin decided to talk to the victims first; that would give those on the bar time to talk themselves into even more outlandish versions of what really happened before she got to them. Pincushion, who knew that photos of old people talking don't sell papers, went off with the girls in tow to get some shots of the beach and canoe.

The couple on the deck were not really that old— mid-fifties, maybe, but out of shape and puffy-fat from too many hours in front of too many TVs. They both wore gym suits way too heavy for the Cedar Key weather, his powder blue, hers a pale pink. The dozen or so people gathered around them had provided glasses of water and a place to sit, and were mostly mumbling among themselves about how horrible it all was, despite the woman-in-pink's attempts to keep the focus on herself with a mild case of hysterics. She was talking to a thirty-ish black man kneeling beside her; from the look on his face Robin guessed he was a doctor or some such who had long since ascertained the woman wasn't injured, and was looking for some way to extricate himself from her grasp. Her husband—and clearly the man in powder blue had been married to her for a long time—patted her absently on one thick thigh, staring out to sea and drinking dispassionately from his cup. Water, Robin guessed, was probably not what he wanted to be drinking at that particular time.

She slipped through the row of onlookers to stand beside him, pulled the little silver flask from her purse and offered it in the man's direction. His eyes lit up, he shot a quick glance toward his wife and then turned to one side so Robin could drizzle a nice shot into his cup without too much fuss.

"Hell of a day," Robin said. The man nodded, took a slug from his freshend drink, and then nodded again.

"Hell of a day," he agreed.

"Want to tell me what happened?" Robin produced her slender reporter's notebook and flipped it open with a dramatic flair. That was a trick she'd developed in her first few months with the *Alarm;* subjects would realize they were talking to a reporter without ever really knowing whom that reporter worked for. When you worked for a notorious rag like the *Alarm*, it was best if you could delay that information as long as possible.

"Damndest thing," the man said. "Damndest thing. Me and Joycie were out in the canoe, just paddling around, looking for dolphins and such, you know? And suddenly, this big green thing came out of the water and attacked us!"

"Attacked you? How? Did it bite?"

"No, no biting. But it grabbed the canoe and shook it, really hard, trying to turn us over. I figure it was going to really tear into us once we were in the water."

"Uh-huh," Robin nodded. "You say it grabbed the canoe—with what? Tentacles? Claws?"

The man took another nip at his gin-and-water, shaking his head. "Hands. It had hands just like a person, except they were dark green, like a frog's. And claws at the end, long white things with blood on the ends."

"Did you see its face? Its head?"

"Only a little, what with the boat shaking and Joycie screaming and all. But it had that same green rubbery skin all over, and a row of black spikes running down its back."

"And horns!" asserted Joycie, who had noticed the reporter with her husband and quickly abandoned the recalcitrant doctor for bigger game. "Don't forget the horns, Arthur."

"Horns?" Robin asked.

"I don't think it had horns, Joycie. I didn't see any horns," said Arthur.

"Of course it did! Big long ones, on either side of its head, pointed like an antelope, or a bull. And those eyes! Lord Jesus help me, I just know I'll never forget those horrible eyes."

"I didn't see any eyes, Joycie."

"Eyes like red coals, big as tea cups they were, and staring right at me. I thought I was a dead woman for certain!"

"My, my," Robin commiserated. "And why aren't you?"

"Why . . . excuse me?"

"Why aren't you? Dead, I mean. After all, attacked by a ravenous sea monster far from shore, just the two of you all alone in that little boat. How did you manage to get away?"

"Well," Joycie said slowly, as if this part of the story hadn't really occurred to her before now. "Well, because Arthur hit it."

"You hit the sea monster?"

"Well—yes," Arthur said. "I had the paddle in my hand, you see, and that thing was coming up out of the water towards my Joycie, and when she screamed, I just sort of hit it."

"With the paddle?"

"Yes."

"And it went away?"

"Yes. It let go of the boat and dropped back into the water."

"But it screamed first!" Joycie interjected. "A horrible inhuman cry of pain and anger. Or hunger, maybe."

"An inhuman scream, huh?" Robin said, writing all the while.

"Not so much a scream," Arthur said, "As it was a complaint. It was more of a loud 'ouch,' I think."

"But an inhuman 'ouch,' I'll bet."

"Oh yes, very inhuman. As inhuman as anything I've ever heard."

"I see, I see. Well, Mister. . . ."

"Willingham. Arthur and Joyce Willingham, from Karaoke Falls, Nebraska, just south of Lincoln. I'm in siding."

"Well, Mr. Willingham," Robin said, snapping her notebook shut, "You must be a very brave man."

"What?" Arthur said. Joyce started to say something, but stopped when she saw Robin's notebook was closed. She turned from Robin to her husband with an odd new light in her eyes.

"Sure, very brave," Robin said. "Fighting off a vicious sea monster like that with your bare hands." She shook her head appreciatively. "You must really love your wife, Mr. Willingham. Really love her a lot."

"Well of course I do," Arthur said. "I've always loved my Joycie." He puffed his chest up a little and wrapped one arm protectively around Joyce, who was gazing at him with something approaching admiration. She gently pulled Arthur closer to her and was whispering something in his ear when Robin walked away.

Next stop, Robin thought, was the growing knot of

people gathered on the sand bar thirty or forty yards away. They had worked themselves into quite a lather, and seemed to be divided into two camps, arguing over whether the beast had actually been breathing fire or simply dripping blood from its horrendous mouth. Robin braced herself, thinking longingly of the gin she'd given Mr. Willingham, and was heading toward the knot of knot-heads when she noticed two men standing near the grounded canoe. One of them, a local judging from his fish-blood stained overalls and T-shirt, had turned away from the boat and was gazing thoughtfully out to sea. The other was Tee Nichols.

Tee was kneeling beside the canoe when Robin reached him. He was holding one of the paddles, studying the flat broad working end of it.

"Hey Tee," Robin said. "Find something?"

Tee looked up at her and smiled. He stood and slipped the paddle back in the canoe, but not before Robin noticed the chips of green paint on its blade.

"Hey, Miss Mushroom. How you doing?" Tee stepped forward and wrapped Robin in a friendly embrace before she could react; one hand was on her back and moving steadily down toward her butt when Robin put both hands on Tee's chest and pushed him firmly away.

"I'm doing fine, Mr. Nichols," she said. "You see the monster?"

"Not me, Miss C. I just got here. But I bet those people up there can tell you about it," Tee said, pointing out the group of people on the bar with a jut of his bristly chin. "Seems every damn one of them saw the whole thing."

"I'm sure," Robin said. "Listen, I—"

"I know you."

Robin stopped in mid-sentence and turned to the man who'd interrupted her, the one who'd been studying the Gulf when she approached. He was tall and thin, almost gaunt, salt-and-pepper hair and a curly ZZ Top beard that reached the top of his worn and torn T-shirt. He had the tanned-leather skin of someone who'd spent his days on the water, and the thick calloused hands that came from working hard every day. His eyes were sky blue, still as swamp water, and very very sad.

"Terry Turtle," Tee said, "This is Robin Chanterelles. Robin, Turtle."

"I know you," Turtle said again, his voice deadpan and still as a sand dollar. Robin knew she had never seen the man before, and groaned inwardly when he produced a thin brown wallet from the inner recesses of his coveralls, looked through it for a moment and then pulled out a single square of paper. What, had Chipmunk Pumpkinbutt been talking about her all over the island?

"Look, Mr. Turtle, I'm flattered and all, but really, you need to understand that I'm just a lousy writer for a lousy tabloid. My autograph isn't worth a damn thing, I promise you."

Turtle didn't say anything, he just unfolded his scrap of paper and handed it to Robin. It was a newspaper clipping, she realized, and when she saw what it was she felt like she'd been kicked in the stomach.

"You helped us then," Turtle said. "Help us now."

"Oh my God," Robin said. "You don't . . . I didn't help then, I didn't help anybody, and now . . ." She looked wildly from Turtle to Tee and back again. She thrust the clipping at Turtle, spun around and half-ran away, nearly bowling over the approaching Pincushion as she did so. Behind her, the newspaper clipping fluttered softly to the sand.

"Well, shit. Shit fire and pee blood, Mr. Tee," Pincushion said. "What'd you say to the Ice Queen? Never seen her so freaked out before."

"Not me," Tee said. "Him." He waved a thumb at Turtle, who had recovered the clipping and was carefully smoothing it out. "I believe Terry Turtle here just slapped her in the face with a bit of her own past."

"Her past? No shit, I didn't know Robin the C had a past. She sure never talks about it." He swung his camera to his face and popped off a quick shot of Turtle, who gazed back at him expressionless as a sleepy hound dog. "She keeps to herself, you know, quiet like, doesn't ever come out to the bars or lunch or nothing with the gang. She came from some little paper in North Florida, and Mr. Maxmillian Pyre says she's hot stuff, you know, but that's about all I know. You know?"

"The *Apalachicola Sun*," Turtle said. Tee looked at him and nodded, then gently took the clipping from his hands and passed it to Pincushion.

"You know about the net ban, Pincushion? Passed into law back in 1994?"

"Sure, yeah, Chipmunk was telling me all about it just yesterday. Really fucked up a lot of people around here, she said."

"Fucked 'em up bad," Tee agreed. "Put a lot of people outta work. Lotta proud people suddenly taking welfare checks and selling their granddaddies' boats before clam farming came along to get things going again. But most voters never thought about any of that. All they saw was the stories about how people like Turtle were wiping out all the fish."

"Lies," Turtle said.

"Yeah, mostly, though there were some people . . ." Tee threw a quick glance at Turtle, and stopped whatever he was about to say. "Anyway, the rich sport fishermen, the guys who spend twenty thousand on a boat and ten thousand more on gear and guides and fish-finders, they hired these big-shot lobbyists to work the state officials, and to talk to all the newspapers and TV stations. And that's all that most people saw, these hired guns getting quoted about saving the fish. That's all the reporters ever reported."

"Not her," Turtle said.

"Yeah, not her. Robin was one of the only reporters out there who ever went after the other side of the story. She talked to real people, to fishermen and their families, wrote about how thousands of people were gonna be out of work if it passed. She went to all the hearings, all over the state. She wrote columns about it, and just generally raised hell."

"Robin? Far fucking out," Pincushion said. "You knew that all along?"

"Sure," Tee said. "Didn't you?"

"Ummmm, don't think so. Not sure, though. I don't always know what I know, ya know?" Pincushion unfolded the clipping Tee had given him and studied it closely. He recognized the setting—the big conference room at the Capitol where the governor and other big wigs held their press briefings. The picture had been taken from the side of the room, so it showed both the audience and the podium at the front. Most of the audience were reporters; Pincushion could tell that by all the cameras and by the way they held their notepads. They were all sitting down, except for one he recognized as Robin, despite her much-longer hair and how she was all dressed up. She was holding a little tape recorder, thrusting it toward the guy at the podium like an accusing finger. The guy at the podium, some stuffed shirt who looked like he'd been born wearing a three-piece suit, was glaring at Robin. And she was glaring right back.

"She fought for us," Turtle said.

"She thought we were worth fighting for," Tee agreed. "She fought for us, and she always said that we had a chance."

"But this net law thingy—"

"It passed, by a three-to-one margin," Tee said. "A landslide."

"Whoa shit," Pincushion said. "So that's why Robin . . . well, you know, that's why Robin."

"You gotta figure," Tee said.

"Man oh man oh man oh. I gotta go talk to her, gotta see if I can help. I'm kinda like her best friend, ya know."

"Right," Tee said.

"Right. Here's your picture, dude. See ya." Pincushion turned and had taken maybe one step when a set of strong bony fingers descended on his shoulder and stopped him in his tracks. He turned to find himself looking right into the quiet brown eyes of Terry Turtle.

"One thing, Mister Photographer," Turtle said. "You be good to my sister." And he turned and walked away.

Pincushion stood with his mouth open for a moment, watching as Turtle trudged slowly off across the sand. "Holy shitski," he said at last. "He's The Chipmunk's brother?"

"Sure is, and if I were you, Mister P, I'd do like he said." Tee gazed after the departing Turtle and shook his head in wonder. "I've known that man all his life, and I swear, I have never seen him that all-fired worked up before."

Chapter Fifteen

"Well, hell," Pambellina said. "If I'd known that's all it took to get your drawers off, I'da taken you looking for manatees long ago."

Desiree swept the wet black hair off her face, her eyes shinning with wild joy. Pambellina and Dr. B were on the thin spit of sand by the path through the mangroves; they'd shown up while she was under water stroking her new friend. Desiree raised one hand and waved enthusiastically, keeping the other hand resting on the submerged back of the manatee.

"Oh gosh, Pam, Dr. B, look!" she cried. "It's a manatee!"

"Aw, ain't nothing but a fat old sea cow," Pambellina said, but she was grinning. She stripped her Tampa Buy Bucs jersey over her head and tossed it on the sand before wading out to join Des.

"He's not a cow, he's a manatee!" Desiree protested. "And he's beautiful!"

"He's not a he either," Dr. B said. "That there is a she cow. A she sea cow." He waded over to the rope holding the *Sailcat's Revenge* and reeled the boat in,

then braced both hands on the bow and hoisted himself up and in. "Let's see now," he said, studying the
barely submerged manatee from his higher vantage
point. "Let's see, that's Molly. Desiree Dragon, meet
Molly the manatee."

"Molly," Desiree breathed, enchanted. "A beautiful name for a beautiful girl." Molly chose that moment to lift her head just a bit out of the water, letting
out another "chuff" of exhaled air. She hadn't had to
come up yet, Desiree knew, she'd already timed
Molly's average dive at about five minutes. But the
manatee was curious, Desiree could see that in the
way she turned her head to gaze at the newly arrived
Pambellina. Des ran her hand along Molly's back,
scratching firmly, and she could swear she saw grati-
tude in the manatee's eyes before Molly slipped back
under water.

Pambellina swam up to Desiree and gave her a
quick kiss, then tried to stand up and gave a gurgling
little yelp. Desiree laughed; standing on her tiptoes
kept her head just above water, but poor little Elf was
out of her depth. Desiree took Pamela's elbow and
steadied her, enjoying the soft warmth that came
when Pambellina slipped one arm around Desiree's
waist.

"Hey wait a minute," Desiree said, loud enough
for Dr. B to hear above his rummaging around in the
Sailcat. "How can you tell?"

"That she's a female? Look under her flukes.
Those long fatty bulbs are manatee mammaries."

"No, I mean how can you tell that it's Molly?"

"Ah," B said. He stood up, holding a wood-handled scrub brush. "When Molly comes up again, check out her right shoulder, just before her fluke."

Desiree didn't have to wait, she knew immediately what B was referring to. There was a long white scar etched along the manatee's back, nearly a foot long, the raised tissue forming a rough speed bump on Molly's otherwise smooth skin. The scar didn't seem to bother Molly, but Desiree ached in sympathy every time her hand touched it.

"Prop scars," Desiree said quietly.

"There's another on her left fluke, and a nice little chunk missing from her tail," Dr B said. "Not too bad, actually, for a manatee who's been in these waters as long as Molly has."

"Not too bad?" Desiree said sadly. She'd noticed the chunk missing from Molly's tail, but not the scar on her fluke. "I thought maybe the, uh, the wound on her tail was maybe a shark bite."

"Sharks don't hurt manatees," Pambellina said. "Neither do barracudas, or anything else in the water. Only people."

"And that's why we really shouldn't be loving her so," B said. "People are ok, but you don't want manatees associating boats with kindness, or food, or anything else good. You want them to stay the hell away from boats."

"And they usually do—or at least they try to," Pambellina added. "But then some asshole comes roaring through a manatee area in his speedboat, not paying a damn bit of attention, and smacks the poor manatee right in the back before it can get out of the way. Cuts 'em all to hell, then drives off and leaves the manatee to suffer and bleed."

"But there's laws about that, right?" Desiree protested. "I've seen the "slow down for manatees" signs . . ."

"Right, there's a law, and there's lots of signs," Pambellina said. "But there's also lots of assholes."

"That's why every damn year seventy or eighty manatees get killed by boats, and God knows how many are crippled or cut, and there's only something like three thousand of them left in the wild." B shook his head sadly. "And now we've got the damned jet skiers to worry about too."

"Yeah, though not as many of 'em as we had a couple months ago," Pambellina said, grinning at Dr. B. "Seems somebody's been monkey-wrenching them pretty good."

"Yeah," B said, grinning back, "Amazing what just a single cup of sugar in the gas tank will do to a Sea-Do. But I can't do that much longer; I can't get within a hundred yards of McKenna's rentals without him going for his shotgun."

"You . . . destroy people's jet skis?" Desiree asked, aghast. She didn't know how much, exactly, but she knew personal watercraft were expensive. An image of Daddy lecturing about the importance of expensive items came unbidden to Desiree's mind, and she couldn't keep the shock out of her voice. Dr. B heard it, and when he answered he had a coldness in his eyes Desiree had never expected to see there.

"You think that's wrong?" he said. "When Molly comes up again, you take a good look at that fluke. She could hardly swim for weeks, and if I hadn't been around to bring her fresh food . . ."

Desiree stared back at Dr. B, confused, stung by his anger. She glanced over at Pambellina, who crinkled her nose and shrugged. And then, because she didn't know what else to do, Desiree inhaled a lungful of air and dove under the water.

She swam straight for Molly, keeping her eyes open despite the salt-water sting. Molly was perpendicular to the shore, still grazing on the turtle grass; Desiree slipped right under the manatee's big round abdomen and up on her far side. She reached out and took Molly's long flat fluke in one hand, pulling it close to her face to study it. There was another scar there, a big white blotch Des could see clearly even in the not-so-clear water of the cove. Desiree could also feel the residual hand bones in Molly's fluke, almost human-like, left over from the days when the manatees waded ashore like hippos. One of those bones felt odd, twisted under her probing fingers, and Desiree realized with a surge of horror that the foremost joints had been crushed and pushed far out of place. Molly turned her eyes toward Desiree, eyes sad and trusting as a basset hound's, and for the very first time, pushed herself away from Desiree. When Desiree surfaced a moment later, the tears in her eyes were not there solely because of the salt water.

"Dr. B," she said. "I'm so sorry. I didn't mean—"

"Ain't no big thing," Beelzebubba said, cutting her

off. "Here, when Molly comes back up, you give her this, and she'll love ya for life." He tossed the plastic water bottle he was holding out toward Desiree; it splashed down a few feet away and she tiptoed her way over to get it.

"Water?"

"Sure," B said. "Remember, she's a mammal, just like us. She needs water, lots of it, and she can't drink seawater. She gets all her water from the vegetation she eats, and that takes a long time and a lot of plants. To a manatee, straight fresh water is manna from heaven."

Molly surfaced just then, and Desiree waved the water bottle before her face, then twisted the cap off and poured a little on the manatee's head. Molly turned toward Desiree, moving with surprising grace for something shaped like an aquatic zeppelin. She opened her wide mouth beseechingly, and Desiree carefully poured a little water in. To her surprise, Molly wrapped her horse-like soft lips around the bottle's neck and began sucking the water in like a nursing child.

"Ha!" Pambellina laughed. "Knock it back, Molly! Look at that mermaid go!"

"Molly the mermaid," Desiree said. "I like it!"

"Well, that's what they used to think manatees were, ya know. Mermaids."

"They did?" Desiree said dubiously. "Mermaids?"

"Damn straight," Pambellina said. She had paddled a few feet closer to shore, where she could stand on her own. "Sailors way out at sea looked over the side of their ships and saw these long shapes moving gracefully through the water, big flat tail and those flippers on each side, and they didn't see sea cows. They saw mermaids."

"Wow," Desiree said. She looked at the bald head and bewhiskered face of the manatee suckling beside her and grinned. "Well, they say beauty is in the eye of the beholder."

"That's what they say," Dr. B chimed in. "They're wrong."

"They are?"

"Yep. Or at least, only partially right." Beelzebubba was still in the boat, but he'd swung his legs over the side so he could sit on the gunwale and splash his feet in the water. "That eye of the beholder stuff is only true of mothers of ugly children and horny drunks at last call. Truth is, beauty is in the mind of the beholden."

"The beholden? Is that a word?"

"Take Miss Molly, for instance. She's big and broad, slow as a sloth, got moss on her back and whiskers like an ancient mariner. Look at her that way, a piece at a time, and it adds up to one ugly critter."

"Molly is not ugly!"

"Of course not," B said. "And do you know why?" Desiree glared at him, then turned to study Molly for a moment. She turned back to B without saying a word. "Because," B continued, "She's beautiful within herself. She doesn't know you're not supposed to be fat and hairy, all she knows is she was born for the water and that sea grass tastes fine. All she's got within her is a peaceful, gentle soul—and that's what shines through."

"Well sure," Pambellina said. "But she's a wild animal. All animals are beautiful."

"Oh, I dunno," B said. "I think opossums know they're ugly. But you're right, it's different with people, 'cause we've got all kinds of crap in our heads telling us how we should look."

"Like a Barbie doll, but with better hair," Desiree said.

"Like Melissa Etheridge," Pambellina said. She crossed her hands over her heart and rolled her head back dramatically; Desiree splashed her in mock jealousy, but B was not to be deterred.

"Take Elf, for instance," he said.

"Hey!"

"Pambellina is beautiful," Desiree sighed.

"Pambellina," Dr. B said, "Is a runt. She's a magical little runt, which is why I call her Elf, but she's still a runt. She's got a butt like a board and enough freckles to spot a leopard. "But," he said forcefully, cutting off the protests from the two women, "But she's got a wild, happy soul, and she likes herself, and she doesn't much care what other people think. So, she is beautiful."

"Well that's what I said!"

"But Desiree, on the other hand," Dr. B continued, lecturing to himself now as much as his audience, "Desiree has luxurious black hair, thick pouty lips, tits to die for and a voluptuous Rubenesque figure. But instead of rejoicing in what she is, she worries about what she should be, and so. . . ."

"B . . ." Pambellina warned.

"And so what?" Desiree said. "Go on."

"And so she walks around slumped over, with her shoulders tucked in and her eyes on the ground, trying to hide her beauty instead of celebrating it. And to a certain degree, she succeeds."

"B, you asshole," Pambellina growled.

"Is that what I do?" Desiree said. "Well, if I do it's only because I'm not pretty, because I'm . . ." She noticed the I-told-you-so grin on Dr B's face and stopped herself.

"Okay, smart-ass," Pambellina said. "What about you, you hairy little dwarf?"

"Me?" B said in mock surprise. "I am an Adonis!" He turned to one side, clenched his biceps in the classic he-man pose, and made a great show of sucking in his beer belly. Pambellina raked her arm through the water, trying to splash him, and even Desiree managed a little smile.

And Molly farted. She was underwater again, having finished off the water bottle and returned to her grazing, but even so her emission produced an audible little thump. A cascade of not-so-little bubbles rose to the surface and popped, bringing with them a tang of fresh-turned earth and week-old trash.

"Why Miss Molly!" Pambellina chided. "That was not lady-like!"

Desiree laughed, waving one hand in the air before her nose. "My gosh," she said. "Why does she do that?"

"Because she can," B laughed. "Because she has to. You can't eat all that grass and not work up a little gas, you know."

"I wouldn't know," Desiree said. "But whoosh, what a stinker! It smells like . . . well, you know."

"I do know," B said. "It smells like methane. And that's what it is, pure methane gas. She's a ruminant, just like cows and goats, and when she processes all that vegetable matter, the methane is an inevitable by-product." He sighed heavily, gazing thoughtfully at Molly's undersea shadow. "I just wish I could figure out some way to bottle it."

"Bottle it? You want to bottle manatee poots?"

"Not poots. Methane. It's a combustible gas, like propane. If I could figure some way to capture it, to bottle it and put it on the market . . ."

"Mermaid Methane, made from pure manatee farts," Pambellina said. "I can see it now, on your grocer's shelf right beside the baked beans and prune juice."

"Don't laugh, little Elf. It's not practical, I know, but there really is commercial potential there."

"B, you really are something else. First marine margaritas, and now this." Desiree shook her head in amusement. "What would you do with all that money anyway?"

"Money?" B said, confused. He looked at Pambellina for assistance.

"B doesn't want to make any money, Des," Pambellina said. "He wants to save the world."

"With manatee poots?"

"With a sustainable local economy, based on non-consumptive use of naturally occurring resources," B said, somewhat huffily. This time it was Desiree who turned to Pambellina for a translation.

"If he can come up with a decent margarita made from nothing but local, natural crops, it would create jobs without hurting anything. People wouldn't have to leave to get work, and we wouldn't have to let in bullshit businesses like Mamasan's and McDonald's."

"And not just here," B added. "Any time you can create an industry that works with the environment without destroying it, you've got a commercial motivation for conservation. Like eco-tourism in Central America, or medicinal plants from the Amazon. Sometimes the only way you can stop greedy people from doing damage is to find a way to give them what they want—money—in a way that doesn't do harm."

"Like margaritas and manatee gas."

"Like margaritas and manatee gas."

Desiree wiped a little saltwater off her brow and turned her head slightly, looking at Dr. B in a whole different way. "And you wouldn't keep any of that money for yourself?"

"Not a bit," B said, and then, with a slight grin, "Well, maybe enough to open my bait-and-guitar shop. But that's all!"

"Yeah, he's a regular saint, our Dr. B," Pambellina said. She swam over to the *Sailcat's Revenge* with a few easy strokes and raised one hand for B to grab. "Now gimmie a hand getting in that boat, Saint Beelze-bubba. I wanna dry off."

Desiree saw it coming long before B did, or maybe he saw it too and fell for it anyway. At any rate, B leaned over and took Pambellina's hand, she quickly latched on to his arm with both hands and swung her legs up to brace them against the side of the boat. "Now who you callin' a runt, Runt?" she shouted. Pam pushed hard with her feet and pulled down with her arms, and Dr. B tumbled head-first into the water.

He came up sputtering and cussing. Pambellina took off for the shore, laughing, but B caught her in the shallows. He scooped her up, all pretend anger, and tossed her effortlessly back out into deeper water.

"I am the king of the beach!" Dr. B cried. "No one can topple me from my sandy throne!"

"Oh no?" Desiree said. She ducked low in the water and started in B's direction, keeping her eyes just above the water like a stalking alligator. *I just need to be careful about my hurt leg,* she thought. *And remember to keep my shoulders back, and my head held high.*

Five minutes later she'd forgotten all that, wrapped up in an energetically playful battle for the beach with B and Pambellina. Laughing and shout-ing, they dunked and splashed one another, stirring up the sand and generally raising hell. From the far side of the cove, Molly the manatee raised her great gray head out of the water to see what all the ruckus was about, and gave an exasperated huff. Just people at play, moving fast and making a mess of everything. As usual.

Molly gave one leisurely swoop of her powerful tail and eased off through the murky water, leaving a trail of silvery gaseous bubbles as she went.

Chapter Sixteen

Robin sat at the darkest table in the darkest corner of Frog's Landing, sipping her frozen drink and staring out at the dark and foggy Gulf. Despite her best efforts to appear unapproachable, she had already had to deal with three different guys hitting on her, one of whom just couldn't believe she was serious until she threatened him with a dinner fork. She was nearing the bottom of her third frogarita, much to the surprise of the dozen or so other customers in the bar, but she did not feel particularly intoxicated. She also did not feel one iota less guilty than she had all damn day, which of course was the whole point of being there.

Well, half the point. The other half was to avoid Pincushion, who had been yipping at her heels like a lap dog ever since her encounter with Terry Turtle two days earlier. Pincushion really truly wanted to help her, and Robin really truly did not want to be helped. Or comforted, or pitied, or analyzed, or listened to. She wanted only to be left alone with her liquor, which had provided all the damn solace she needed for many years now, thank you very much. Still, she also didn't want to punch any holes in Pincushion's gentle heart, even though he was driving her nuts. So rather than screaming at him, she hid.

Pincushion would know she was in a bar, of course, but he also knew that Frog's Landing was her least favorite place in Cedar Key, despite its magnificent second-story view of the Gulf. Frogs had only been around twenty years or so—an infant, by Cedar Key bar standards—and it was designed to draw in the tourists. Cutesy posters on the walls, clever names for drinks and sandwiches, kare-fucking-okie twice a week and second-rate Jimmy Buffet imitations on weekends. She much preferred the laid-back funkiness of the historic old lounge at the Island Hotel, or the down-home grittiness of the L&M Bar. After all, she was feeling pretty damn gritty at the moment herself.

Robin hadn't left the Beachfront hotel that day till early afternoon, hoping that sleeping in and a long soak in the pool might ease her memory-inspired and gin-birthed hangover from the night before. Even so, the half-mile hike to Dock Street and the center of town had been painful—and it got worse along the way.

She ran across the first roadside vender when she was still about two blocks from the Loop. He was working from a battered step-van parked beside the road, thanking an elderly couple in Hawaiian shirts for their business when Robin walked up. Towards the Loop on past him she could see a steady stream of out-of-towners walking briskly towards Dock Street. Her mental, early warning system, dazed as it was, started to jingle.

"T-shirt, lady?" the vendor said in an accent that had nothing of the slightly country, slightly southern tones of Cedar Key. "Just twenty bucks, cheaper than anything you'll find downtown."

"T-shirt?" Robin said. "Downtown?"

"Got 'em in three sizes and four colors. You'd look really hot in the pink." The vendor pulled down one of the bubble-gum colored shirts hanging from the side of the van, flipped it around and held it up against Robin's chest. It took her a minute to read it that way, upside as it was, but she didn't really need the words to understand what it meant. The shirt sported the ironed-on likeness of a greenish, be-clawed, bug-eyed figure vaguely reminiscent of the old "Creature from the Black Lagoon" movies. It reached threateningly outward, dripping what she supposed was blood from its impossibly toothsome mouth. The legend underneath it read, "I Survived the Cedar Key Sea Monster."

"Ohmigod," Robin said.

"Yeah, scary, ain't it?" the vendor said. "I got others too. I got "I got sea-monstered at Cedar Key," and I got, "My Boyfriend Saw the Cedar Key Beast and All I Got Was This Lousy—" "Hey, wait!" But Robin was already gone, loping toward the Loop as fast as her hammering head would allow.

Things were even worse than she had feared. Cars were parked bumper to bumper along D Street coming into town; most had Florida tags but there were plenty from Alabama and Georgia, a few from Ohio, New York and points north. She spotted copies of *The Alarm* on the seats of three different cars before she stopped looking.

The bridge over the marina inlet was so tightly packed with people that the line of cars waiting to get across was at a standstill. Over the bridge there were more vendors, and more people, and still more vendors. The fishing pier was packed with people taking pictures of people, while displaced pelicans and seagulls looked on in avian disapproval from perches on nearby pylons. From the front door of the Captain's Table, on down Dock Street past the Red Luck Cafe and Island Fudge, past Annie's Other Place and the Sawgrass Gallery, past Frog's Landing on down to the curve at A Street where Mamasan's and her neighboring buildings were already buckling under the assault of crayon-yellow bulldozers. Dock Street was packed with more people and pandemonium than Robin would have imagined possible. Vendors loudly hawked monster T-shirts and bumper stickers, plastic monster action figures and aerosol cans labeled "Monster Repellent." A whining six-year old sat on the life-size plaster dolphin in front of the Sawgrass Gallery, picking her nose and holding a shiny mylar balloon in the shape of a grinning monster head. Her father stood beside her, sipping a murky green liquid from an elongated plastic bottle shaped somewhat like an alligator, while bemused locals looked down on it all from the windows and balconies of their restaurants and stores. Two of the charcoal-and-chalk portrait artists seen at every two-bit fair and festival had set up shop and were cranking out scenes of children riding beast-back, or fisherman fathers standing proudly beside monsters strung upside down from marlin hooks. Some of the monster reproductions were fanciful and comical, some seemed to be honest attempts at sea creature re-construction, a few looked like hastily re-worked versions of the University of Florida's alligator mascot. Way too many of them, Robin saw, were modeled after the artist's conception of the Cedar Key Creature on page one of the new issue of the *Weekly Alarm*. The picture drawn to accompany her story.

Robin Chanterelles had looked upon the fruit of her works and felt her world spin. She pushed through the crowd to the D Street bridge, braced her hands on the hot concrete railing, and puked heavily into the salty water below.

Robin scowled and took another nip of her margarita (and it was a *margarita*, god damn it, no matter what the chowderhead behind the bar insisted on calling it). Pincushion had found her there at the railing, she remembered, drooling vomit and barely able to stand. He'd half-carried her back to the hotel, tried to make her eat something, and fled the room when she started throwing ash trays and Gideon Bibles at him. Once alone, she'd called up *The Alarm's* website on her laptop and discovered to her dismay that Pyre had actually done very little editing of her story. He'd added an end-of-the-world headline and the cartoonish artist conception, but mostly, it was Robin's own words staring back at her. Her own accurate representation of the few facts at hand, her quotes from the Willinghams and the sandbar yahoos, her recapitulation of Desiree's disappearance and the resultant monster reports. All of it a completely accurate representation of the facts, and all of it a total distortion of the truth.

Now it seemed like every lame-brain, thrill seeker out there who ever bought a grocery checkout-line scandal sheet, every conspiracy nut and flying saucer chaser in the country, every lonely loser looking for a sign that things were going to change real soon had latched on to the *Alarm*'s report and come a'lookin' for the Cedar Key Sea Beast, followed closely by those who fed on and profited from mass hysteria. It was Nessie and Big Foot and the Easter Bunny all rolled into one, located a convenient three-hour drive from Disney World. Of course the loose screws had come rattling out of the woodwork.

"Damn you, Chanterelles," Robin told herself. "Don't you ever learn? It doesn't matter what you say, it's what people want to hear." And she'd given them all just what they wanted. She, and whomever had staged the Goose Creek Cove attack. It had been reasonably well done, in an amateurish way, but Robin wasn't fooled for a minute. She didn't know how someone had reached the Willingham's boat without being seen, or where they'd gone after Arthur struck back, but she was pretty damn sure sea monsters didn't come with coats of paint.

She hadn't bothered to try and slip that significant fact past Maximillian Pyre, and nobody she'd told about it here in Cedar Key seemed to give it much thought. They didn't seem to be giving much thought to the referendum on the Cedar Casino either, though that was coming up in less than a week. Instead, they were all wrapped up in talks about the beast and what it might mean for their town and their businesses. Well, now they knew—it meant lots of tourists and lots of money, and all it would cost them was their souls.

Robin glared down at the bottom of her empty glass, telling herself she really should order something to eat. Instead she caught the eye of her bartender and held the empty glass aloft; he shook his head ruefully but set about fixing her another. Robin turned and looked out the window at the fog-shrouded sea, wishing he would hurry it up.

The trouble with drinking alone, she'd long ago learned, was that if you didn't watch yourself you'd get to thinking about things better left unthought. She'd managed to mostly avoid that over the past half-dozen years, usually by rushing from intoxicated to oblivious as quickly as possible any time the memories began to surface. But in the last few days, that trick had gotten harder and harder to pull off.

Damn Tee Nichols anyway, Robin thought, *and damn his beanpole friend Turtle. And damn her own self too, for ever having been naive enough to believe she could change things by the power of the written word.* Okay, she'd won a few small battles, maybe she'd saved a few trees and frustrated a few bad politicians in her straight-journalist days. But when it came to the really big fights, to the things the *real* monsters cared about—forget it. They just trotted out their own media machine and their purchased politicians and their stacked decks and stacks of cash and overwhelmed anything or anyone in their way. Being a lone voice in the wilderness had a certain romanticism to it, in a Don Quixote kind of way, but continually fighting to be heard over a 300-piece orchestra while fireworks exploded overhead was just too damn much work.

Robin remembered election night in 1994, sitting on her second-hand couch in her funky Apalachicola cottage, glued to the TV. She knew the polls said the net ban would pass, but still part of her couldn't believe that would happen. It was so clearly wrong, so clearly destructive to the good but powerless people she'd been talking to for months and months. She kept thinking of that scene in *Peter Pan*, where if only enough people believed in fairies, then poor poisoned Tinkerbell would recover. And she'd sat there watching in horror as the votes for the ban racked up like the score on a runaway pinball machine. She vaguely remembered going to the freezer for chocolate ice cream, thinking that might ease the ache in her heart, and finding a chilled bottle of gin from some long-forgotten party. She'd taken that discovery as a sign. Before long, it was a way of life. A way of life that helped her hide just a little from the sad, accusing eyes of the Panhandle fishermen she'd failed to save, a way of life that eventually got her fired from the *Sun*.

So what the fuck—PR paid better than journalism, and the *Alarm* paid even better than that. If she was going to be a prostitute, Robin figured, she might as well be a well-paid one.

"Don't you want something to eat with that, ma'am?" Robin looked up to find her waitress beside her, fresh frogarita in hand and a troubled look on her face. A Cedar Key lifer, from the looks of her, not much out of high school, brown as a coconut, sweet-faced and young. Something about the innocent concern in that girl's face reminded Robin of herself at that age, and it pissed her off.

"No," she snapped. "No goddamned food, and tell that shit-for-brains bartender I'll want another of these in about five minutes. Got that?"

"Yes m'am, but . . . are you sure? That's your fourth one, ain't it, and you such a small thing, and—oh my God."

"Don't go getting religion on me, child, or you'll blow your damn tip. Just put that on my tab, and . . ." Robin stopped her rant when she realized the waitress wasn't listening to her. She was staring slack-jawed out the window, awe and fear and excitement on her face, forgotten frozen frogarita still in hand. The people at the bar were coming to their feet too, abandoning their drinks and rushing to the window. Robin twisted around to see what the fuss was about, already knowing somehow that it couldn't be good.

It wasn't. The fog on the bay was still thick and the night still dark, but a few hundred yards out an oddly dense patch of fog had taken on a strange greenish glow. And there was something moving there, something shadowy at first that quickly took on the clear silhouette of a sailing ship—a two-masted schooner, 80 feet long or more, running eerily silent under full sail through waters too shallow to support her. There was no crew on deck, no signs of life anywhere, but on her main mast, glowing with a light of its own and standing as stiff as starch, flew the unmistakable skull-and-crossbones of the Jolly Roger.

"It's the *Lara Lu*," the waitress breathed. "It's Red Luck himself, come back from the dead."

Robin looked up at the girl's awe-stricken face, back out to where the ghostly ship was fading and then re-appearing at the leading edge of the fog, and then back to the waitress. She reached up and pried the frogarita from the girl's unfeeling fingers, inhaled deeply, and drained half the glass in a single icy gulp.

Then she pulled her reporter's notebook from her back pocket and crisply snapped it open.

Chapter Seventeen

Howie McCracken thought it natural and fitting that his niece Sarah's favorite bird was the magnificent frigate. Not the gray-beaked pelicans with their fat-man waddle, or the great blue herons strolling dignified as princes through the shallows, or the wood ducks poking their feathery butts straight up at the sky to pick snails and slime off the marine bottom. *Those birds and their funny ways were for ordinary children*, Howie thought. *Sarah only had eyes for the frigates.*

And why not? They were special birds, so special that "magnificent" actually was part of their name. Big birds, sometimes seven feet at the wingspan, and built for the sky. Sleek muscular bodies, strong sharp wings precise as a star chart, long split tails in perfect black V's. They could soar on air currents for an hour or more without ever flapping their wings, Howie knew, and had been known to fly without landing for four days at a time. Howie liked it, too, that they were also known as pirate birds, and that they got their names from their great speed and daring hunting style. Special birds.

And Sarah too was special. Howie smiled down at her and placed his hand lightly on her downy-soft blond hair. Sarah reached up and took his hand—she loved touching—but she didn't take her delighted eyes off the frigate bird, darting this way and that over the Gulf in front of her. The bird was looking for fish, and Sarah was looking for—well. Howie couldn't even begin to guess.

It was Sunday afternoon, so Howie and Sarah were on the fishing pier jutting into the Gulf perpendicular to Dock Street. They were always here on Sunday afternoons; Sarah knew that, Howie looked forward to it, and Stevie reluctantly accepted it. The recently arrived crowds of obnoxious tourists packing the pier and the rest of town had actually increased since the Red Luck sighting, but Howie wouldn't let even that stand in the way of his day out with Sarah. The Cedar Key police—both of them—had run the junk vendors off the pier, but it was still so crowded with binocular-wielding monster-hunters that the regulars casting frozen shrimp and live baitfish out into the Gulf had to be careful not to hook a tourist on their back swing. Though that, Howie thought, might not be a bad idea. Maybe thin 'em out a little if a few went home with fishhooks in their eyelids.

He and Sarah had won their usual spot on the pier—halfway out on the left, looking towards the row of restaurants fronting the Gulf—without too much trouble. Most of these damn tourists seemed to have a natural regard for the obvious locals, like they were indigenous wildlife or something. And the few who didn't defer to Howie's obvious seniority—well, Howie was a big man, and still had the hefty biceps and dockside swagger he'd earned working the boats growing up.

The ones who were slowest to move aside, and who bothered Howie the most, were the grandmotherly types who gravitated so quickly to little Sarah. He couldn't blame them, she was a beautiful kid. Six years old, blond hair so pale it was almost white, eyes the soft blue of the Cedar Key sky. They all wanted to compliment her, to touch her, to ask her what her name was and how old she was. But when Sarah answered them . . .

There was still nobody who could say why Sarah was the way she was, even though Stevie had spent a fortune taking her to the best doctors in Florida, up to Emory University in Atlanta, even to specialists in New York and Boston. Some of them said it might be mercury poisoning from medicine she took as a baby, or maybe something genetic. Most of them pointed to her traumatic premature birth, the birth that had killed her mother. It always hurt Howie to think about that night, to imagine poor kind-hearted Lillian bleeding to death in the ambulance hurtling towards Gainesville, newborn Sarah in her arms and Stevie sobbing at her side.

And Stevie. He blamed Cedar Key for it all, for Lillian's death and Sarah's disability. Poor medical care, something in her diet, something in the water. Stevie never narrowed it down much, and it never made any sense to Howie, but still he blamed Cedar Key. The McCrakens could trace their time in Cedar Key back to the Confederate gunrunners who smuggled weapons and salt through the Union blockade—and now Stevie despised the place.

Sarah tugged at Howie's hand just then, and he looked down to see what she wanted. She pointed skyward, to where the frigate bird was soaring away with swift stiff-winged strokes. And Sarah, with all the obvious excitement of any six-year-old watching a favorite animal, said, "Uhhnuuhhuhhhh!"

Howie could understand Sarah's nonsensical wailing better than anyone alive, better even than Stevie. And he knew that there was meaning and intent behind her indecipherable personal language. She wasn't retarded, she wasn't stupid, anyone could see the bright intelligence burning behind those eyes. It was just that somewhere between her mind and her mouth the words got lost, got tangled up. It frightened some people, turned those isn't-she-sweet words into looks of shock and pity. And it frustrated Sarah, frustrated her into occasional temper tantrums and late-night crying fits. Why wouldn't it? To have so much to say, so many things to ask, and not be able to make anyone understand. Howie thought sometimes that he knew exactly how she must feel, and for that he loved her even more.

This time, happily, Sarah's meaning was as clear as cut glass, and Howie smiled. He knelt down beside Sarah, put one arm around her shoulder, and followed her pointing finger toward the disappearing magnificent frigate. "Yeah, I see," Howie said. "Frigate bird. Special bird."

Sarah smiled back at him, and nodded.

"'Scuse me. Sir?"

It took Howie a moment to realize somebody was talking to him. It was one of the tourists, of course, not one of his Cedar Key neighbors. She was college age, slender and stunning. Black hair tinted with a highlight or two of red, big soft eyes, fat pouty lips. She wore a blue-jean skirt that was just tight enough and a mid-riff shirt that showed off her great body without looking like she was trying to show off her great body. Howie was so immediately befuddled that he hardly noticed she was trying to hand him something.

"I'm trying to find this girl?" she said, her voice rising in a soft Midwestern accent. "She's my sister, and she's gone missing, and . . . anyway, have you seen her?"

It took all his willpower for Howie to pry his eyes off this vision in denim and look at the picture she was holding. When he did, and when his mind registered what he was looking at, Howie's mind froze up. He never knew what to say to pretty women, and this one was really pretty, and the picture she had. . . .

"Well," he managed at last. "That's Desiree."

"You've seen her? Oh that's super, that's great!" Before Howie could explain that yes he'd seen Desiree, but not in weeks, the girl spun around and starting waving toward somebody off in the crowd. "Daddy!" she shouted. "Over here!"

Daddy, Howie saw, was a fiftyish man with steely gray hair, wearing slacks and a sport jacket. He didn't have a tie on, but Howie knew instinctively that it hadn't been off long and was probably folded up neatly in a coat pocket. A suit, on Cedar Key's fishing pier? Howie didn't think he'd seen one of those since the Mormons had their convention in Gainesville five or six years back. And they'd had an excuse—God made them dress up.

It didn't take Daddy long to push his way through the crowd. He charged up to Howie, eyes filled with probing concern and jaw set hard, and thrust out a hand to be shook. "Ronald Dean," he said, taking Howie's hand in a good solid grip. "You've seen my daughter?"

"Yessir," Howie said, adding the "sir" without even thinking. "But like I was trying to tell, uh. . . ."

"Kathy," the girl said.

"Trying to tell Kathy, I haven't seen Desiree in a while. Not since before she, um, before the accident."

"I see," Mr. Dean said, and if he was disappointed, he didn't let a trace of it show. "May I ask how you know my daughter?"

"Sure," Howie said. "She worked for me, over to Mamasan's. She was our hostess."

"Mamasan's," Mr. Dean said. He produced a fine leather notebook from his coat's inner pocket and flipped it open. Howie took that opportunity to glance over at Kathy; she had squatted down on her oh-so-perfect haunches and was talking eye-to-eye with Sarah. Howie couldn't tell if Sarah had said anything yet when Mr. Dean started up again.

"Mamasan's," he said. "That would make you Howard McCracken?"

"Howie. Yessir."

"And did you see my daughter the night of her disappearance?"

"Yessir," Howie said, wondering just a little if Mr. Dean had forgotten he had two daughters, including one who was standing right there with them. "Yessir, but like I told the police, I saw her early in the evening, but I didn't even know she was missing till long after they'd put the fire out."

"I've seen the police report," Mr. Dean said, with just a hint of disapproval. "You also said that Desiree had been working for you for about two months, but that you didn't know her well."

"Yeah. She'd hang out after work with us sometimes, drinking, but mostly she kept to herself. Kinda quiet, ya know."

"Drinking." The way Mr. Dean said it put ice on the word, but he carefully wrote it down in his little notebook. "Mr. McCracken, can you think of anyone who may have wished my daughter ill?"

"What?"

"Did she have any enemies?"

"Desiree? Nah, of course not. Unless," Howie said with a quick laugh, "unless you count this Baptist minister who went back up north with soup stains on his shirt. See, there was this one time. . . ." Howie saw the chill in Mr. Dean's eyes and let the story trail off.

He licked his lips and swallowed hard, feeling like he really should give this guy something, and then he brightened. "You know who might know? Tee Nichols, that's who."

"Tee Nichols." Mr. Dean flipped back through his notebook again. "Ah. Desiree's landlord."

"Yeah, and her friend too," Howie said. "They hung out a lot, probably even—ah, yeah, her landlord. He lives over off D Street, three-four blocks from here."

"I have the location," Mr. Dean said. He snapped his notebook closed dismissively. "Kathleen," he said, "Come along. We're off to see the landlord."

"Daddy, don't you think it would be better if we split up?" Kathy was standing beside him again, and Howie was surprised to see she was holding little Sarah's hand. "We can cover a lot more ground that way. Besides, I've promised this sweet little girl I'd take her for ice cream."

"Ice cream?"

"Yes. If that's all right with her father?" Kathy turned to Howie and he nodded, feeling overwhelmed.

"Her uncle," he said.

"Uncle. Even better. Daddy, I'll catch up with you at the condo later, okay?"

"Well . . ."

"Thanks, Daddy!" Kathy pranced up to her father and stood on her tiptoes to kiss him on one cheek. Her skirt rode up in the back when she did so, and Howie made himself look away before

Mr. Dean saw him staring. When he turned back, Mr. Dean was walking away through the crowd.

"Well thank God," Kathy said. "I thought he'd never leave." She put one arm over Sarah's shoulder and hooked the other through Howie's crooked elbow, giving his taunt bicep an appreciative squeeze.

"Now then, handsome," Kathy said. "Let's go have some fun."

Chapter Eighteen

"More," the voice on the other end of the telephone said. "Lots more, right now."

Robin Chanterelles groaned, recognizing the voice of Maximillian Pyre even in her half hung-over, half-asleep state. She focused bleary-eyed on the clock beside her bed—11 A.M. No wonder she was still asleep, and no wonder she'd been groggy enough to answer that damn telephone. She hadn't had any coffee yet, and so was not yet legally sane.

"Pyre," she whispered, wincing at the sound of her own voice. "Call you right back."

"Don't you hang up, goddamn it, or I swear I'll revoke your expense account and you'll have to buy your own drinks," Pyre shouted. "You hear me?"

"I hear," Robin said. She let her head flop back down on the pillow, resting the receiver far enough away that Pyre's voice became an insistent but quiet squeak.

"Good," he said. "Like I said, I want more, and I want it now."

"More," Robin said. "More height, more intelligence, more penis length?"

"More Cedar Key stories, smart ass. Our last two issues flew off the stands, and the web site is getting four million hits a day. Four million! We haven't had juice like this since O.J. was convicted."

"Simpson was acquitted, Max."

"Oh? Wow, imagine how much we'd have sold if he'd been guilty." Robin could almost hear the numbers turning over in her editor's head. She reached blindly for the bedside table and fumbled about until her hands closed on her cigarettes. "Anyway, I want a story a day from you, including a big update for the print issue."

"A story a day. On what?"

"On the Cedar Key Beast! On the terrified townspeople, on the brave monster-hunters there to save the day, on the twenty thousand dollar reward the *Alarm* is posting for the capture of the creature."

"Twenty thousand dollar reward?"

"Yeah. Too much?"

"Max, there *is* no Cedar Key sea beast."

"No monster? You sure?"

"I'm sure."

"In that case, we'll make it fifty thousand!"

"Jesus, Max."

"Okay then—what's today's story?"

"Today?"

"Yes, yes, what's happening there this very moment?"

"Happening . . ." Robin lit up a Doral Light, trying

to ignore how her hands shook. "Well," she said slowly, "Somebody's been bombarding street venders with golf balls."

"Golf balls?"

"Yep. Rains them down from above. Pretty good shot, too. So far she's nailed two trinket dealers and shattered the windshield of a T-shirt truck. People are getting scared to buy anything."

"Golf balls. Sure they're not monster eggs?"

"Golf balls, Max. Titleists."

"Titleists?"

"I've seen 'em."

"Pass. What else you got?"

"What else. . . ." Robin hit hard on her cigarette, trying to force her way through the haze surrounding conversations at the numerous watering holes she'd visited the night before. "Oh, right," she said. "The referendum."

"Referendum?"

"Yeah. Cedar Key residents vote in three days on whether or not to allow a re-zoning for the casino."

"Boring. You know we don't do politics."

"Max, this particular vote may decide the future of the entire Nature Coast. And they say the vote is going to be damned close."

"Tell it to the *Times*. Pass."

Robin pinched the bridge of her nose, trying to rub away the frustration, and then reluctantly played her ace card. "And people say the ghost of Red Luck is telling them to vote no."

"The ghost of . . . ?"

"Red Luck. The pirate."

"Now you're talking! 'Phantom Pirate Pushes Panicked Public to Polls'—not bad, not bad at all. When's he going to show up again?"

"I'm not sure he showed up the first time."

"What? You said you saw him, there at that Toad place."

"Frog's Landing, and yeah, I saw something. I saw what looked like a pirate ship for a few seconds through the fog on a moonless night."

"Good enough for me," Pyre said. "I want you to see him again tonight."

"It doesn't work like that, boss. I can't see him if he's not there."

"You did the last time."

"Max, it's early in the morning. Please don't fuck with me."

"All right, all right. Just get me something on the pirate and the polls. And tell Pincushion to get me pictures of frightened chicks in bathing suits on the haunted beaches."

"There are no beaches here, Max."

"So?" And he hung up.

Robin clicked off the receiver and lay there for a moment, wondering if she could get back to sleep. No way, and she knew it. She didn't give a rat's ass about Max or his stories, but he had gotten her thinking again, and she could never rest once the wheels in her head started turning. She sighed and sat up, slowly, swinging her legs over the edge of the bed.

Robin still had on her clothes from the night before, which didn't surprise her much, but she was surprised to find a sheet of wax paper holding a halfdozen pieces of fudge on the bedside table. Not surprised she had bought and forgotten them, but surprised she hadn't eaten it all before she passed out. She picked up a piece and eased it into her mouth. It was—okay.

Okay. That was all. Not fantastic, not unique, not special. It started coming back to her then—she'd stumbled by Johnny Fudge's place sometime past midnight and found him not only still open but doing a booming business. He was so busy that he almost didn't recognize her, but not too busy to bitch while he rang up her purchase. "So many people," he'd said. "I just don't have time to whip up the good stuff."

Robin leaned over the bed and spit what remained of the fudge into a wastebasket. Not special is right. Not bad, but not anything you couldn't find in any shopping mall food court. It tasted okay, but it didn't taste like Cedar Key.

There was a lot of that going around. The crowds packing the streets over the past few days had overwhelmed the village's ability to provide for them properly. Some of the restaurants had resorted to using frozen shrimp, motels were hiking up their fees outrageously, there wasn't a tube of suntan lotion or a pair of cheap flip-flops to be found anywhere. There was even a nasty rumor going around that one restaurant had resorted to the old Florida tourist trick of stamping fleshy cylinders out of sting ray flesh and selling them as scallops. The money was pouring in, that was for sure, but from the grumpy expressions on the suddenly overworked and overcrowded residents, nobody was entirely happy about that.

Robin sighed and wiped her fudgy fingers on her pillowcase, recalling the first time she'd had Johnny Fudge's treats, at Tee Nichols' house. Tee Nichols ... she hadn't seen him since the day his friend Turtle freaked her out so. Been avoiding him, really, not anxious to talk about Turtle and maybe a little worried Tee would blame her for the mess Cedar Key had become. But she remembered their first playful conversation, and that first bite of really good fudge, and smiled despite it all. Maybe, she thought, maybe I should drop by there today, maybe talk to Tee.

Maybe there's still some of the good stuff over there.

Florida State Park Ranger Jennifer Aly was also thinking of Tee Nichols. She didn't have much choice—he was, after all, scrounging around in the back of her patrol boat when she happened to glance out the window of her office/home and noticed his old purple Schwinn leaning against a cabbage palm. She sighed heavily, then went to the refrigerator and poured two large glasses of tea, extra ice.

Tee looked up from the storage bin at the stern of the *Manatee II* when Jennifer approached. He saw the glasses in her hands and nodded appreciatively. "Yaupon?" he asked hopefully.

"Lord no," Jen said. "It's Lipton." She had never managed to acquire the taste for tea brewed down from yaupon stems. The Seminole Indians used to use it in some of their ceremonies, and some old-timers like Tee swore by it, but she couldn't get past the bitter taste. Blackberry tea was about as far as she could go when it came to indigenous plants, and even that was at least part for Tee's benefit. Left to herself, Jennifer would just as soon have a glass of instant.

"So—nice boat," Tee said.

"You've seen it before."

"Oh yeah, sure, but not in a while. Ol' Chigger was talking about it just the other night, and got me thinking some."

"Chigger got you thinking?"

Tee grinned at that, and let out one of his short sharp laughs. "Hard to believe, ain't it?" he said. "But Chigger, he was saying that Ramsey Waller had the fastest boat in Levy County, and I got to thinking about this boat and knew that wasn't true."

"It's not exactly my boat, you know. The state of Florida. . . ."

"Yeah," Tee interrupted. "Anyway, Chigger was saying that the morning after people saw Red Luc and the *Lara Lu* go sailing by. They say Ramsey Waller jumped in that Skyliner of his and took off after the *Lara Lu*, but there was nothing there. People say nothing but a ghost boat could outrun that Skyliner."

Jennifer didn't say anything. She leaned back

against a dock piling and poked one slender finger into her tea to send the ice cubes swirling around. Tee eased himself up on *Manatee II's* railing and took an appreciative chug on his drink. They sat quietly for a bit, looking toward where the salt estuary they were on emptied out into the Gulf.

"I see you made some modifications to her too," Tee said after a bit. Jen just nodded miserably, avoiding his gaze. "Like this here." Tee reached down and half-pulled the waterproof tarp off a two-foot square mechanical contraption resting in the boat's stern. "That's a dry ice machine, isn't it? Maybe the one Willoby Crum used to make fog in that disco of his up to Chiefland?"

Jen nodded again, started to say something, and then burst out crying. Tee was out of the boat and had his arm around her before she could catch her breath enough to talk.

"I had to do something," she said. "They killed Bambi, and that casino will ruin Cedar Key, and all the extra boat traffic and tourists and crap . . ." She sniffed loudly, and Tee pulled her closer to him.

"Damn," he said. "They killed Bambi?"

"Uh-huh," Jen snuffled. She nodded her head against Tee's funky tee shirt, drawing comfort from the mixed odors of mango, sweat and stale beer.

"So that's why you painted up a wet suit and played sea monster?"

"How'd you know that was me?"

"Who else around here could swim that far under water? And be crazy enough to try?"

Jen managed a half-smile at that. "I thought maybe if I scared a few tourists. . . . but it just backfired, Tee, now there's more of them than ever! And damn Stevie McCracken, if he gets that casino in . . . I just couldn't stand that, I just couldn't."

"So you rigged up a fog-making machine and resurrected Red Luck?"

Jen nodded again, her face still pressed against Tee's chest. "I got some slides from the university historical collection at Gainesville, of old ships, and used the *Manatee*'s bow light to project them on the fog."

Tee smiled, and Jen could hear the warm appreciation in his voice. "Such a clever girl," he said.

"But that backfired too!" Jen wailed. "That damned reporter put it in the *Alarm*, and it just brought in more tourists, and now everybody in town is making money off them, and they'll all vote for the referendum to let Howard build his damned casino."

"Maybe," Tee said. "Maybe not."

Jen pulled away from Tee's chest enough to look up at his face. "You've got a plan?" she asked hopefully.

"The start of one, maybe." Tee sucked a chuck of ice out of his glass and crunched on it meditatively for a bit. Then—"You got any more dry ice for that machine of yours, you crazy child?" he said.

Jen turned her head to one side, studying Tee like a crow watching something bright and promising. His face was impassive, but that devilish twinkle was in his eye. That twinkle had always cheered Jen up, no matter how grim things had seemed, ever since she was a little girl. She dropped her head back on Tee's chest, reveling in his familiar scent, and sighed.

"Oh, Daddy," she said happily. "Of course I'm a little crazy. It's in my blood."

Chapter Nineteen

Howie McCracken pushed his paddle steadily through the calm waters of Back Bayou, paying little attention to his rowing and one hell of a lot to the nearly bare back of Kathleen Dean. She was on the canoe's bow seat just a few feet in front of him, wearing a bikini top, cutoff shorts and a McCracken Brothers Seafood cap. She took maybe one canoe stroke for every ten of Howie's, but even so, every few minutes the hot sun sent a delicate little bead of perspiration sliding down the silken skin of her back—and those drops had Howie mesmerized.

Most often, those little splashes of liquid sunshine would appear right where Kathy's gorgeous hair kissed her shoulders. They would hang suspended there for just a minute, like a snow skier hesitating at the edge of a run, and then suddenly slip down the nape of her neck, pick up speed at the slight rise of her shoulder, and hurtle downward to disappear into the cotton tie of her bathing suit top. But every now and then, if Kathy bent her shoulders or leaned to one side just the right way at just the right time, a spot of lucky liquid might find its way under that thin cloth line, hesitate at the tie like a rabbit cautiously emerging from under a garden fence, then dart onward and downward along the gentle swell of Kathy's spine, through the barely visible, downy-soft patch of blonde fuzz in the crook of her perfect back, and vanish forever into the obliging upper edge of her shorts. It was the first and only time Howie could recall ever being jealous of a drop of water.

"Howie?" Kathy said. "I said, 'What about that one?' Is that another hawk?"

Howie blinked his eyes double-fast and forced his mind out of Kathy's waistline and back into the world. She was pointing toward a small island off to starboard, to where a handsome foot-high bird sat proudly on the sun-whitened bare branch of a dead pine tree.

"No," he said. "Well, sort of. That's an osprey, but he's like a hawk. In fact, sometimes they call them seahawks, even though they really aren't."

"An osprey," Kathy repeated, nodding her head. She spun around in her seat to face Howie, not even noticing how badly the boat rocked when she did so. "Jesus, Howie," she said. "You are *so* smart!"

Howie had to fight the urge to look around and see who Kathy was talking to. He wasn't stupid, and he was a hard worker and strong as a bull, but Howie knew he wasn't the sharpest pencil in the box. He was pretty sure everybody else knew that too, but still he liked hearing different, especially hearing it from Kathy. He didn't even mind that she was staring at him again, staring like she had when he'd pulled his shirt off right before launching the canoe. He'd thought for a second there that he had done something wrong, that maybe people who didn't live in Cedar Key didn't take their shirts off like country hicks when they went out on the water, and he'd started to put his shirt back on. But Kathy stopped him, even insisted on rubbing suntan lotion on his back and shoulders and arms (she'd put a *lot* of lotion on his biceps, even though they were already dark as weathered oak). Then she'd pulled her own shirt off and asked him to put lotion on her, and Howie had forgotten all about being embarrassed. At least until now.

"Awww, I'm not so smart," Howie protested, hoping it would cover the warmth he felt in his cheeks. "It's just stuff I know 'cause I been around it all my life."

"But that's just what I'm talking about," Kathy said. "You know so much about this place, about just where to go, what all the birds and animals are, and what all the tides and the clouds mean. There's just lots and lots of people out there who would gladly pay you to take them on trips back through here."

"You mean like a fishing guide?"

"Fishing, sure, but also just bird watching, or wildlife photography, or shell collecting, or—well, just being out here in nature. I mean, Howie, stop paddling for a second and just look at this place. It's all so beautiful!"

"Beautiful . . ." Howie said. He did what he was told, stopped rowing and swung the dripping paddle across his knees. He couldn't count the times he'd been on the bayous and inlets that separated Way Key from the mainland—fishing with friends, netting blue crabs to sell to the fish houses for a dime each, or just having fun with Stevie back when Stevie liked having fun. So maybe he didn't always notice how great it all was—but he did love it. He loved the way the blue-brown waters meandered among the dozens of little keys that dotted the bayou, he loved the thick tangles of mangrove bushes and the way they sheltered shrimp and grouper and a hundred other kinds of fish. He loved coming up on an unsuspecting raccoon washing its catch at the water's edge, or a deer come out to nibble on fresh-blooming berries. And maybe most of all, he loved the clean wide-open sky, so big and bright and blue that it made your eyes burn and your heart ache if you looked at it too long. Of course it was all beautiful, and of course he loved it all—but hell, didn't everybody?

"Howie."

Howie lowered his gaze from the far horizon, blinking salt from his eyes. Kathy was leaning forward towards him, staring at him again, but in a different way than she had before. Somehow, he hadn't noticed that her hands were resting on top of his.

"Howie," she said. "Do you know . . . I'll bet you know some place near here, some little island or something, where we could swim for a bit and then maybe stretch out our towels and lie in the sun?"

"Stretch out our towels?"

"Yeah, and lie in the sun. You know—someplace private."

Howie did know, and once he got Kathy turned around and settled in he drove his paddle hard in the water and sent the canoe zipping along like a skipped stone. He worked hard, driving that canoe onward like a fiberglass torpedo, and when Kathy half-turned and winked at him over one shoulder, he worked even harder.

Because Howie McCracken may not have been the sharpest pencil in the box—but he wasn't stupid.

Chapter Twenty

T he young woman walked the streets of her adopted home, overcome with shock and dismay. There were so many people! So much noise, so much trash. Tourists everywhere, many of them lined up at tacky little junk stands dotting Second Street like metal mushrooms after an acid rain. She'd been away, sure, but things didn't just change like this overnight. Not here, not in the village that time forgot.

The woman pushed her way gently along the crowded sidewalks, mumbling excuse me's and apologies, receiving more glares than smiles in return. A teenage boy with blue hair glopped into five-inch spikes thrust something towards her, told her she needed to buy a T-shirt, and turned away in disgust when she couldn't work up the words to answer. Something green and lurid leered at her from a shopfront window; nearby a storeowner she half recognized was shouting at someone to get the damn thing off his window. The woman recoiled from the conflict, turned and stepped without looking. Her bare foot drove hard into something that might have been a shoe, someone cursed and pushed her in the back, and she tumbled off the sidewalk and to the ground.

She sat there on the damp ground, trying to get her breath and her bearings. She was in the normally quiet little courtyard beside The Yellow Door Coffee Shop, which had somehow become packed with tables and customers. A man sat alone at the table nearest her, a big man dressed all in white. He looked like Marlon Brando in a Peter Lorre suit, hoping for peace but expecting trouble, gazing down at her from under a broad-brimmed white hat. The man stared for a second, then slowly reached up to remove the dark glasses covering his eyes. The woman saw his revealed face and gasped, feeling more and more like she'd stumbled into someone else's nightmare.

"They . . . they said you were dead," she stammered.

"Precisely what they said about you, my dear."

The woman stared up at the man staring down at her. The world unfroze around her, sound and color and noise bursting back into her consciousness, and she was suddenly very aware she was sitting on the wet ground in the middle of a crowded cafe. She looked around desperately, looking for something, *anything*, familiar and right—and then the man in the white hat reached out his hand to help her up.

"Perhaps you should join me," he said graciously. "It seems we have some things to discuss."

Chigger grinned his gap-tooth smile at the three young ladies standing beside him at the bar, enjoying the attention, and pointed without looking one by one at the trinkets attached to his camouflage hat. "This one's a shark tooth from a mako, this one's a bear claw, this metal one's the U.S. Marine Corps Seventh Calvary," he chanted. "This one's the bone from a raccoon's penis, this one—"

"A *raccoon penis?*" the tallest of the three girls said. Her voice went way up when she said it, like she thought he was bullshitting or something, and the two behind her sorta twittered at each other. Chigger frowned at the interruption, mentally went through his progression again and picked up the litany when he got back to the right place.

"This one's another shark tooth from a hammerhead, this one's a wild boar tooth, this here's—"

"You wear a *raccoon penis* on your head?" the skinny girl said again, her voice even higher this time. The other two girls were squirming like they might explode, and it threw Chigger off.

"This here's from a gopher tortoise shell," he said, putting his finger squarely on the t-shaped backbone of a sailcat. "And, um—" He stopped, confused, the rhythm of his chant hopelessly broken. It didn't matter. The three girls had burst into laughter and gone rushing towards the door, waving phony apologies as they went. Chigger couldn't believe it—they were laughing at his magic hat. People always *loved* his hat. They loved his collection of mementos, they loved the stories he could tell about each one. No one had ever laughed at his hat before, and Chigger didn't like it one bit.

Chigger took the hat off and twirled it in his nicotine-and-sunshine yellowed hands. He dropped a bit of spit on the meat of his left thumb and set to polishing the weed-guard on the wooden bass plug his granddaddy had carved for his tenth birthday, not sure what to do with this odd feeling. Then an idea struck him that troubled him even more. *Maybe*, Chigger thought, *maybe they weren't laughing at the hat. Maybe they were laughing at 'him'*. Chigger didn't think anybody had ever done that before. At least not in Cedar Key.

At least not till now.

Rodney Sewell stared down at his bruised and throbbing right fist, not quite believing what he had just done. Caddy Wier, who was stretched out on the sand in front of Rodney with one hand pressed tight over his bloody nose, had pretty much the same expression on his battered face.

"What the hell you do that for?" Caddy wailed. "You said yourself that referendum is gonna pass tomorrow."

"You said it was a good thing the McCrackens are gonna build that casino. You said it would be good to have something to do other than hunt deer and ride circles around manatees."

"Yeah. So?"

"Jeez, Caddy, don't you understand how fucked up that is?"

Caddy scowled and rubbed his nose, clueless. He started to get up, and when Rodney reached out a hand to help him, Caddy skittered away, holding his free hand before him protectively. "Okay, okay, you're right!" he said. "Just don't hit me again, okay?"

Rodney stopped, and watched in disbelief as Caddy cautiously got to his feet and then hurried off towards the state park truck. Caddy had bullied him since they were both little kids, and Rodney never thought he could do anything about it, never thought he could possibly stand up to the bigger, stronger, meaner Caddy, even when he did something as shitty as carving a flank off of poor Miss Aly's dead deer. And all the time, Rodney thought, all he had to do was get mad enough to finally fight back.

Rodney stared at his throbbing fist, reveling in the pain, and wondered what else he might be able to do if he just got mad enough.

Beelzebubba sat in the bow of the *Sailcat's Revenge*, listlessly strumming a battered pawn shop guitar. He'd meant to practice his fiddle tunes, or even just chill out with some Jimmy Buffett, but somehow every song he started ended up as a blues tune.

"Cedar Key blues," Dr. B said. "Manatee blues. How 'bout that, Miss Molly? You got the manatee blues?" The old sea cow, who had been slowly drifting away from the *Sailcat* once it became clear Beelzebubba was not going to give her water, said nothing. B plucked another minor-seventh and scrunched his eyes against the afternoon sunlight, following the fishing line suspended from the rod perched near his bare feet. The line was as still and flaccid as the hot afternoon. Nothing biting, not even crabs. "Signs and portents," the defrocked biologist said to the still air. He believed in omens, couldn't always interpret them but knew they always meant something, and every fish in the channel turning their nose up at fresh shrimp was clearly a bad sign.

Beelzebubba turned to study the thickly forested shoreline of Atsena Otie Key—he was anchored about 50 yards out, in the channel between Atsena Otie and Way Key—scanning the shore and the bushes for ibis. He hadn't seen an ibis in three days. That was *very* unusual, and it worried him both as a biologist and as a believer in portents. People said the crane-like ibis had a special sense, that when a hurricane was coming they were the last birds to take off and the first to re-appear. There were no hurricanes coming, nothing but clear weather forecast for days to come—so where were the ibis?

Beelzebubba turned back toward Way Key and the town of Cedar Key. The distant whine of a power saw and sporadic hammering carried over the water from where the Cedar Casino was rising from the east end of Dock Street. "Hasn't even been approved yet, and they're already starting to build," B said. "Arrogant bastids." He thought back to the idea Pambellina had hatched that morning, when he was taking her home after they dropped off Desiree. Crazy scheme, he thought, crazy little Elf. Still. . . .

Beelzebubba opened the cooler at his feet, reached first for a beer, then hesitantly settled instead on the long silver decanter. He took a deep breath and drew a mouthful of his latest marine margarita right out of the mixer. B swished the cool, salty concoction around in his mouth, unable to make himself swallow, then finally gave up and spit it over the side. Several two-inch minnows rushed up to investigate the disturbance, tasted the faux-margarita in the water, and just as hurriedly swam off.

B sighed heavily and screwed the cap back on the decanter. "Signs and portents," he said glumly. "Signs and portents."

Stephen McCracken stood watching his brother and child play in the back yard, studiously ignoring the whir and buzz of the fax machine behind him. He knew what it said—that Jacob Black's latest report had satisfied his employees, that Stephen's fortune was all but assured. He wondered idly why that didn't please him more than it did.

Howie and Sarah were crouching over an upturned rock at the edge of the garden—Howie had unearthed some sort of backyard bug, no doubt, and little Sarah was obviously delighted. Normally seeing her happy made Stephen's heart swell, but today his happiness was tempered by the niggling, gnawing presence of doubt. He had no choice, Stephen told himself for the

ten thousandth time. He was doing the right thing—
wasn't he?

Behind him, the fax machine droned on.

Amelia the emu slowly eased her long hairy neck out
from between two protective scrub pine trunks, surveying the area ahead of her with eyes and nose. This
seemed to be a safe enough place—the scents were
unfamiliar but not threatening, nothing moved but a
few lesser birds and a squirrel or two. Still, Amelia was
uneasy.

Emus are quite intelligent, as birds go, but even so
there wasn't a lot of room for memory in Amelia's
feathery head. She felt no real nostalgia for her safe
and well-fed early days with her brood-mates on the
Jefferson County emu ranch, and if the post-ranch
memories of excited people running from and at her
troubled her at all, she concealed it well.

But what Amelia lacked in memory, she made up
in instinct. She had no conception of geography, but
something had driven her unerringly south ever since
she'd accepted that the food bins at the ranch were
never going to be full again. And that had paid off—
she'd never been here before, but the constant sun
felt natural and right on her dark feathers and
chicken-yellow legs. She hadn't seen any other emu
in a long, long time, but that was all right. South felt
right.

At least, it had until now.

Amelia cautiously stepped out from her shady shelter, moving her nostrils away from the pleasant but overpowering pine scent. A deep breath brought her the smells of water and salt, which called up a hazy image of the warm sand she'd like to bury her eggs in. But there was something else here too, something indistinct but undeniable. Like ozone before a storm, the still moist air was filled with the scent of expectancy, the scent of something about to happen. The promise in that humid air drew Amelia on but frightened her at the same time. She couldn't begin to reason it out, and her instincts were as uncertain as she was.

So Amelia the emu stood unmoving in the Levy County pine forest, facing the not-so-distant Cedar Key, waiting to see which way the wind would blow.

Chapter Twenty-one

Tee was sitting at his kitchen table, clearly visible from the street through his wide-open front door, when Robin walked up. She knocked anyway, timidly, keeping one eye open for that damned skink. Tee looked up from the morass of papers on the table before him, grinned that lopsided grin of his, and waved her in. Robin smiled gratefully and entered, feeling no less responsible but maybe a little less guilty. Then she remembered the sheaf of papers tucked under one arm, and the guilt came rushing back.

Tee wore nothing but cutoffs, as usual, despite the handful of hungry mosquitoes drifting hopefully around the room. He held a gnawed-up yellow pencil in his teeth and a coffee mug commemorating the 1986 Olympics in one hand. A long yellow steno pad was on the table in front of him, covered with lists of names, many of which had been crossed out or written in again. Robin looked at Tee and saw the fatigue behind his smile, and her heart sunk.

"Tee . . ." she started.

"Sure," Tee said. He rocked his chair back on two legs so he could reach the refrigerator door, opened it, and pulled out a plastic milk jug filled with a sludgy yellow liquid. Tee peered into each of the several glasses sitting on the table top till he found one that met his approval, then splashed it full of juice and passed it to Robin. "Honey, honey?" he said.

Robin took the glass, tried and failed to force a little smile. "I just walked over from city hall," she said. "Five blocks, and it took me twenty minutes. Oh God, Tee, I am so sorry."

"Me too. Fuckers keep trying to park in my front yard, seem to think it's a vacant lot." Tee took a sip of his drink and gazed at Robin mischievously over the rim of the glass. "Couple of 'em even ran over the board full of nails I keep out there to discourage salesmen."

Robin let herself smile a bit at that, and took a drink of her tea. The smile vanished.

"Oh my God, Tee, what is this?" she said, struggling to keep from retching. "Christ, that's foul!"

"That's yaupon," Tee said. "Made from that tree you see in my side yard there, the one that looks like holly. Seminoles used to say it gave them religious visions, and I know it's good for people who had too much to drink the night before."

"Well . . ." Robin said dubiously, "If it'll cure this hangover . . ." She raised the glass and drank as fast as she could, gagging it down before the taste hit.

"Didn't say it cured hangovers, said it was good for people who'd had too much to drink," Tee said. "It's a purgative." He said that last part to an empty chair; Robin was already up and rushing towards the bathroom, one hand locked tight over her mouth.

She was a little ticked but did feel much better when she emerged a few minutes later. Clearer headed, somehow. The nasty taste of the yaupon was gone, thanks to the glob of Tee's toothpaste she'd smeared on a finger and then rubbed across her teeth, but she was still pleased to see the tea was gone from the table and in its place sat a can of Diet Coke and a stack of saltines. She eased back into her chair and started on the crackers without saying a word.

"Been looking at this paper of yours," Tee said. More than looking, Robin saw, the computer printout of registered Cedar Key voters she'd brought with her was now marked with a tiger-stripe pattern of highlighted names. "The blue ones," Tee explained, "Those are the ones we can count on to vote against this referendum. Red ones are people who'll probably vote for it. I played it real conservative here; anybody I'm not sure about I marked red."

Robin nodded, feeling a little surge of hope. There were clearly more blue lines than red ones. That feeling didn't last long.

"Now you tell me about these others," Tee said. He pointed to the first of the many names Robin had highlighted in yellow before she came over, and Robin felt despair slinking in again.

"There's one hundred of them, exactly," she said. "Notice anything unusual?"

"I notice that I don't know a damn one of them."

"Look at the dates they registered to vote, and the dates they gave for when they moved here."

Tee did so, running his finger along the first few yellow lines from name to dates. He moved more quickly once he'd spotted the pattern, finally flipping to the last sheet for a quick glance at the last yellow lines.

"They're all the same date," he said.

"Right. Exactly one year ago tomorrow."

"Which means that they'll be eligible to vote in the referendum. Eligible by one day."

"Uh-huh."

"Damn."

"Uh-huh." Robin took a sip of her Coke, watching Tee do the mental calculations. There were more than enough of those yellow lines to swing the election one way or the other, and she had a pretty good idea which way they'd be voting. "Any idea who they are?" she asked.

"They're Stevie McCracken's men," Tee said flatly. "Most of these addresses are in a trailer park he owns out off Route 345."

"One hundred men?"

"Construction workers, mostly. He brought them all in about—well, about a year ago. They remodeled an old warehouse into Mamasan's, fixed up some of his boat facilities, do some other odd jobs for him. Mostly though they get drunk in Chiefland and race their trucks through the wildlife preserve. Never could figure out why they were still here."

"Now we know."

"Now we know. They're Stevie's secret weapon."

Robin nodded miserably. She started to take another bite of cracker, changed her mind and dropped it wearily back onto the stack. "God Tee, I am *so* fucking sorry."

Tee nodded thoughtfully, then glanced up at Robin and frowned. "I'm sorry too, girl, but you say that like this is all your fault."

"Well it is, at least partly. I mean, it's all McCracken's doing, but I sure didn't help things with those stories I wrote."

"How you figure?"

Robin stared at Tee, unsure if he was being sympathetic or just dense. "Look at that voting role, Tee. How many of those red lines would be blue if I hadn't brought the tourists and their money pouring in here with my monster stories?"

Tee nodded, picked up the voter sheet and studied it for a minute. "Well, let's see," he said slowly. "By my calculations, that would be—none."

"None?"

"Damn few anyway."

"You're kidding, right?"

"About this? Never." He reached across the table; Robin thought he was going to take her hand, but instead, he picked up her Coke and helped himself to a swig. "You underestimate us, girl. Sure, people around here like money. Who doesn't? But that's not what Cedar Key is about. Nobody who really wants money is going to come here in the first place."

"Stevie McCracken wants money."

"Stevie McCracken was born here. And you know why he wants money?"

Robin opened her mouth to answer, then closed it and shook her head.

"He wants money so he can get *out* of Cedar Key."

"But he's already rich, isn't he? Like the richest man in town?"

"Sure, but mostly what he's got is property. Boats and buildings, that sort of thing. He may own more than anybody else around here, and he and Howie make a nice little income off it, but it won't get him the really big money unless he can sell it."

"Or turn it into a money machine, like a casino."

"Right." Tee tapped the table absently with his chawed-up pencil. "And to be fair to ol' Stevie, he's got some pretty heavy expenses too."

"Expenses?"

"Medical expenses."

"Oh." Robin pondered that a bit, then started in again. "Okay, so Stevie's the exception, but you can't tell me the people who own those restaurants and hotels, and the little shops and art galleries, you can't tell me they're going to vote against something that will line their pockets for years to come."

Tee looked at Robin with something like pity in his eyes. Then he bounced up and went directly to a particular stack of papers in his living room bookcase. He came back with an eight by ten black-and-white photo of two giggly young women in bikinis flanking what looked like a big black hot tub.

"There," Tee said. "You know what that is?"

"A promising start to a Saturday night?"

Tee grinned wolfishly and nodded. "A Tuesday night, if I recall correctly. Thank god for Spring Break. But that's not the point here. Do you know what *that* is?" He jabbed one lanky finger at the black object in the center, and Robin studied it more carefully. It was about as big as a hot tub, but a perfect half-globe, and looked to be made of iron, like one of those skillets you find in old Southern kitchens. It was pitted with age, and rough around the edges.

"One half of the world's largest cannon ball?" she said, half-seriously.

"Not even close," Tee said. "That is a salt kettle."

"A what?"

"A salt kettle. People around here used to fill them with seawater, then light big fires under them. When the water evaporated, what you had left was lots and lots of salt."

"Salt," Robin said. "Right."

"Don't laugh; salt used to be very valuable. Back before refrigeration, salting meat was about the only way to keep it fresh. At the start of the War Between the States, the Cedar Keys supplied 150 bushels a day to the Confederacy, to preserve pork and beef for the soldiers. So important to the war effort the damn Yankees sent in a fleet to capture the Keys and shut down the operation. And even then we were smuggling it out through the Union blockade, along with guns and ammunition."

"Oh. So?"

"So," Tee said. "We used what we had plenty of to

fill a need and keep people here working. After the war, when the demand went way down, then we turned to supplying wood for pencils."

"And we all know how well that turned out."

"I didn't say we always did this right," Tee grinned. "Anyway, when the cedar was all used up, some people around here actually made a living harvesting Spanish moss."

"Really?" Robin thought of the stringy gray clumps that hung from every hardwood tree of any age in most of Florida. "What in God's name for?"

"Henry Ford used it to stuff the seats in his new automobiles. For awhile, anyway, till people started complaining that his cars made them itch."

"Itch?"

"Sure. Lotsa bugs live in Spanish moss, you know. Ticks, chiggers . . ."

"Got it. So, after the Spanish moss . . . ?"

"After that, some local genius discovered you could make a pretty darn good whisk broom out of the palmetto fronds that grow all over around here. We had a booming brush-and-broom industry here till World War Two brought plastics and wiped it out."

"Tee, this is all very interesting, but I don't see—"

"After that we had a red-hot oyster business for a spell, but we got carried away and pretty much wiped that out. So people turned to fishing, and shrimp, and were doing just fine with that till the net ban. Now we got clams."

"Right. Long live the clams."

Tee frowned, and Robin felt like a schoolgirl who'd

smarted off once too often in a favorite teacher's class. "You ain't *listening*, girl," he said. "What we do here, what we've always done here, is we survive off what surrounds us. We make do with what we got, and we don't worry too much about what we ain't. That's why there's no movie theater here, no shopping mall, no McDonald's or Burger King. Sure, it'd be nice to see a movie now and then, but not nice enough to sacrifice the space it would take to put up a theater, or to work the extra hours it would take to buy tickets."

Robin nodded, knowing all that was true, but thinking too that Tee was over-rating human nature in general and his neighbors in particular. "That's great, Tee, really. But do you really think people will think about all that when they're voting?"

"People around here will. People here know their history, they've learned what happens to us when we forget what's important. Some of 'em need to be reminded, that's all. And we've got two days to remind 'em, to change enough of these signatures from red to blue."

Robin looked at the list and nodded dubiously. "I dunno, Tee. What about Stevie's secret weapon?"

"Well hell girl, that don't worry me none. We got us a secret weapon of our own." Tee flashed that devilish grin again, looking not at Robin but over her shoulder. She followed his gaze and turned just in time to see someone coming in through the house's side door. It was a woman, obviously enough, fresh out of the shower, one white towel draped around her torso and another wrapped turban-style around her wet hair.

The woman had curvy legs brown as beach nuts, a supple figure that made the towel bulge right where it was supposed to, and a pretty round face that danced right at the edge of Robin's memory. But it wasn't until she pulled the turban free and her lustrous black hair came spilling out that Robin realized who she was looking at.

"Omigod," Robin said, soft at first and then loud and insistent. "Omigod, you're supposed to be dead!"

The ghost of Desiree Dean glanced up at Robin and smiled hesitantly. Tee reached across the table again; this time he took Robin's hand and patted it as if he were consoling a not-very-bright child.

"You know, Miss Chanterelles," Tee said patiently. "You really shouldn't believe everything you read in the papers."

Chapter Twenty-two

"With all due respect, Ms. Dean," Robin Chanterelles said, "You really are a lousy liar."

"Oh, but it's all true," the young woman seated across from her answered, in a tone that clearly said it was all bullshit. "And please, call me Desiree."

"Okay, Desiree. So, you're saying that after the explosion you and Pimlico Phil just took off for New Orleans? Without telling anyone?"

"Sure. I mean, it was pretty clear we were both out of work, and neither of us wanted to deal with the questions from police and newspapers and such that we knew were sure to come, so, you know, what the hey. We didn't mean to scare anyone, and we *did* tell someone, we told Tee. But I guess he'd had a few beers that night. . . ."

"This old memory of mine, you know, sometimes it works. . . ." Tee left the sentence hanging and went back to work on his heart-of-palm salad with pistachio ice cream. ("It really is heart of palm," he told Robin when he ordered it. "They have to cut down the whole damn tree to get at the cabbage inside the trunk. Don't know where the ice cream comes from.")

"Sure," Robin said. "What the hey." She took a long pull on her Corona and lime, fighting the urge to order something stiffer. She was being lied to, of course, but Tee and Desiree were so damned affable about it she didn't mind. Maxmillian Pyre was going to shit bricks, though—not only had his sea beast not shown its scaly head in nearly a week, its most famous victim was back in the land of the living, unharmed and happy. Max would no doubt put some twisted spin on it, but Robin could practically hear *The Alarm*'s sales dropping. She smiled and dug into another forkful of fresh crabcake.

The three of them were having a late supper at The Seabreeze, the last and largest of the restaurants on Dock Street's waterfront. The Seabreeze's business had actually dropped off in recent days, despite the influx of out-of-towners, because its spectacular view of the Gulf was being noisily disrupted by the rising tower of the neighboring Cedar Casino. During the day the whine of saws and banging of hammers made lunchtime conversation a chore, and at night the needle silhouette of the casino's faux crow's nest towered like Dracula's castle over an unsuspecting village. Still, Tee had insisted they come there. The beer was cold and the food was fine, so Robin had no complaints.

"Pretty clear night out tonight," Desiree said. Robin nodded, and Tee grinned around a mouthful of salad.

"Yep," he said. "But I 'spect that'll change."

"I should hope so," Desiree said. "And pretty soon, too. Ms. Chanterelles, do you know what time it—oh my gosh."

Robin looked up from her meal and immediately wondered if Desiree had seen a ghost. Her copper-tone-tanned face had gone white, and she was staring open-mouthed over Robin's shoulder towards the entrance to the restaurant. There were three people standing there talking to the hostess—Howie Mc-Cracken, a very pretty girl who looked to be about Desiree's age, and an overdressed and sour-faced middle-aged man. The men hadn't noticed them yet, but the woman was staring at Desiree with an expression of devilish glee on her face.

"Ohmigosh," Desiree said again. "What is *he* doing here?"

"Oops," Tee said. "Knew I forgot to tell you something." He wiped an errant bit of green ice cream off his beard, glanced toward Robin and added, "That's her father."

"Daddy," Desiree whispered. She pushed her half-finished shrimp cocktail away, sat up very straight and carefully folded her hands in her lap. Despite the girl's suddenly rigid posture, it seemed to Robin that Desiree had suddenly shrunken to about half her normal size.

The young girl at the door—Desiree's sister, Kathy, no doubt—clapped her hands in delight and came darting over to their table. She threw her arms around Desiree's neck, laughing, and Desiree relaxed a bit—

but only a bit. She hugged her sister warmly, but her eyes were locked on her father. He'd spotted her too, and was striding across the room, face expressionless but eyes ablaze.

"God Desiree, you had us so worried," Kathy squealed. She pulled back from Desiree far enough to give her a quick appraisal. "You look great, though. Where's your glasses—are you wearing contacts?" And then, as her eyes dropped to the top of Desiree's low cut T-shirt, "And you got a tattoo!", her eyes widening as if Desiree had sprouted wings. Desiree smiled at that, and nodded.

"Just today, and yes, I got contacts," she said. "I'll show you later, okay?" Kathy started to protest, but the shadow of their father fell over the two girls, and she nodded and stood up.

"Look Daddy," Kathy said. "She's all right."

"I see that," Mr. Dean said. "Desiree, are you all right?"

"I'm fine, Daddy," Desiree said. To Robin, it seemed Desiree was more interested in the Sea-breeze's hardwood floor than in Mr. Dean—but then Desiree abruptly stood up and threw her arms around her surprised father. "I'm sorry I worried you, Daddy," she said. "But I really am just fine."

Mr. Dean slowly wrapped his arms around his daughter, patting her awkwardly on the back. "There there," he said, his voice momentarily softening. "There, there." Howie McCracken arrived at that moment, and Kathy crushed herself up against his side. Robin noted the immediate and obvious surge of pride that gave Howie. She glanced at Tee to see how he was taking all this, and was not at all surprised to see him grinning as if it were all some great private joke.

"Fog's coming in," he said, and gestured at the window behind him. Robin wondered when he had ordered a second beer, then realized the Corona he was sipping from was hers.

"Now then," Mr. Dean said. He placed both arms on Desiree's shoulders and firmly pushed her back a step. "I trust you have an explanation for all this, young lady."

"I do, Daddy," Desiree said. She glanced over at Tee and a quick smile darted across her lips. "But it's kind of complicated."

"I'm sure," Mr. Dean said. "Fortunately, we'll have plenty of time to discuss it on the way home."

"Home?" Desiree said, her voice cracking just a little.

"Home, yes, of course. It's too late to get started tonight, but we should be able to find an early flight out of Tampa tomorrow morning. For now, let's just get back to our hotel room and get some decent clothes on you." Mr. Dean sidestepped the immobile Desiree, who was gazing down at her Buccaneer's T-shirt and worn-thin cutoffs. He produced a thick gold money clip from his pocket and extended a twenty-dollar bill toward Tee. "For my daughter's dinner," he said.

"Why, thank you," Tee said. He reached for the twenty, but Robin swatted his hand away.

"That's not necessary," she said. "This meal is being compted by my newspaper."

"Newspaper?" Dean said as if someone had just force-fed him month-old lemons. "Desiree, just what have you gotten involved with here?"

"My my," Tee said loudly, to no one in particular. "Would you look at that."

"I've gotten involved in something important, Daddy. We're trying to save this wonderful town."

"Save this town?" Mr. Dean took a long look around the room, at the casual decor, at the platters of steaming fresh seafood, at the action-hungry eyes of the tourist diners and the quiet amusement on the faces of the employees and local customers, all of whom were watching the scene before them. "What on earth for?" he said.

"Oh, Daddy," Desiree said, and the despair in her voice was as palpable as the sudden anger in the room. Robin watched her search desperately for support—she looked first at her sister, then at the many Cedar Key locals sitting at the bar, and finally at Tee. Robin couldn't decide if the girl was going to take off running or just bust out in tears—but Desiree suddenly stood up a little straighter, raised her head high and did the exact last thing Robin would have expected.

"Daddy," Desiree said. "Fuck you."

Robin couldn't help herself—she let out a quick sharp laugh, then snatched up a napkin and tried to disguise it as a cough. She wasn't the only one who wanted to cheer Desiree on; snickers and "You go, girl," whispered from the edges of the room. Even Kathy let out a quiet giggle, which brought her a furious stare from her father. When he turned back to Desiree, Robin saw a barely controlled outrage in him that frightened even her.

"What did you say?" Dean said, his voice full of knives.

"I'm glad you asked that," Tee said. "What I said was, 'Well, well, would you look at that.'" Robin glared at Tee; she kicked him hard under the table and was rewarded by a loud "ouch!"

"Young lady," Mr. Dean started again, "I don't know where you picked up such language, nor do I care to, but—what is *that?*" He raised his arm and, like some ghastly vision of doom from beyond the grave, pointed one accusing forefinger at Desiree's chest.

"Oh," Desiree said. "That's a tattoo, Daddy." She raised her hands towards her breast in what Robin thought was a protective gesture, but at the last instant hooked her fingers through the shirt collar, raised her arms as if she planned to rip it loose, and looked up at her father with a maniacal gleam in her eyes. "Would you like to see?" she asked.

"Desiree! Don't you dare!" Mr. Dean took a hesitant step toward his daughter, his voice shifting from accusation to desperation. Every eye in the place— particularly, Robin noted, the male eyes—were locked on Desiree and her shirt. And Desiree knew it, and seemed to revel in it. She held her position, staring down her father while no one in the room did so much as breathe. And then, when it seemed the whole world had frozen, she smiled just a little wider, tensed her arms and—

"Oh hell," Tee said. He stood up, pointed dramatically out towards the Gulf, and shouted, "Everybody look out the fucking window!"

For a moment, no one moved. And then, as if fighting their way out of some sorcerer's spell, one head and then another turned to where Tee was pointing. A low murmur of voices quickly became an excited buzz, and suddenly everyone in the restaurant was on their feet and rushing towards the windows overlooking the Gulf. Even Desiree and her father, caught as they were in their public personal showdown, turned to see what all the fuss was about.

It was about this: The night was clear and moonlit, and the channel between Cedar Key and Atsena Otie was quiet and calm—except for a strange round cloud of thick fog, clinging to the water about two hundred yards out like a Godzilla-sized cotton ball. Red and yellow lights flashed within the fog, like summer lightning in a distant sky, and each time they did so a slender form became more and more distinct—long and low across the beams, two proud masts reaching upwards towards the stars, an ominous dark flag flapping from the main mast.

"Oh, my God," someone whispered. "It's the *Lara Lu.*"

And it was.

Chapter Twenty-three

It had been possibly the weirdest day of Howie McCracken entire life, even before the specter of a local legend came cruising along in a cloud of supernatural smoke. He'd spent most of the afternoon in the company of the most beautiful woman he'd ever seen, taking her on a boat tour of the backwaters and bayous of his hometown. And she'd enjoyed it! This woman-child who outshone every girl he'd ever dated in his miserable life had clapped her hands and embraced every little bit of Cedar Key he'd shown her, from the great blue herons hunting the mud flats of Back Bayou right up to the sky-blasting sunset over Goose Cove. When he'd taken her back to her hotel she'd kissed him—kissed him!—and insisted he join her and her father for supper. They'd even agreed to eat late, so Howie could sit through another long and boring planning session with Stevie and that greasy lawyer, Mr. Black. Howie hadn't been able to decide if was going to die of boredom, hunger or anticipation when Stevie finally let him cut out.

Supper had been postponed again, though, by the

apparition of Howie's former hostess, a woman who he would've sworn (though not to Kathy) was resting comfortably and permanently on the sandy bottom of the Gulf of Mexico. But there she was, bold as life and twice as lively, sipping beer at the Seabreeze with that old fox Tee Nichols and the tabloid reporter who'd been making Cedar Key look like some sort of coastal madhouse.

And *then*, while Howie was trying to decide if he should step in and grab Desiree or let her go ahead and strip down right there in front of God and her father, *then* Red Luck himself had come sailing down the main channel, quiet as a cat but lit up like a Christmas tree. So much for trying to win over Kathy's gloomy old man over fresh red snapper, Howie thought. What next?

Well, this: The *Lara Lu* had pretty much cleared the Seabreeze and was rounding the point of Cedar Key's east end, apparently intent on following the main ship channel through Rocky Gap in Corrigan's Reef and heading out to deeper water. That put her directly east of the rapidly rising Cedar Casino, but still in clear view of everyone in every restaurant and bar on Dock Street, not to mention the growing crowd assembled on the fishing pier. And suddenly, the lights darting here and there within the *Lara Lu*'s personal fog bank ceased their flickering. With the moon full and bright as it was, and the internal lights suddenly vanished, the fog stood out white and ominous as the last tooth in a sun-bleached skull.

And then she struck. A brilliant ruby red light

stabbed out of the fog right at the heart of the Cedar Casino. For one superstitious instant Howie thought the casino would explode, or maybe burst into hell-spawned flames. Instead, the light flashed a blurry red smear on the casino's seaward wall, a blur that bounced up and down for a second, then quieted and suddenly coalesced into a sharp and unwavering brand. It was bright as blood and clear as sunshine, twenty feet around and familiar as a fairy tale.

It was a skull and crossbones.

"Well," Tee Nichols said just before the room exploded into shouting and cheers, "That looks like a pretty darn clear message to me."

"It is not a message, it's a trick!" Howie turned to see his brother Stevie at the rear of the crowd packing the Seabreeze's window, with the impassive Mr. Black beside him. "It's a damned obvious trick, Taylor Nichols, and I know you've got something to do with it!" Tee put one hand over his chest and raised his eyebrows in a hurt "who me?" expression; Stevie snorted angrily and turned to look wildly around the room. "Ramsey!" he shouted above the excited rumble of the crowd, "Ramsey Waller, you get your ass out to your boat and you get out there to that damned phony ship!" Ramsey hesitated just a moment, maybe deciding between his fear of ghosts and his fear of Stevie McCracken, then broke and ran for the exit. Howie turned back to Tee just in time to see the old beach dog wink at Desiree Dean and pat his hand reassuringly on a front pocket. Howie wasn't entirely sure, given the noise in the room, but he thought he heard a metallic clink when Tee did that.

Howie suddenly realized he'd lost track of Kathy in all the commotion. He searched the room frantically, standing on his tiptoes so he could see over the crowd, and finally spotted her near the bar, talking earnestly with her father. Howie pushed through the crowd, making steady but slow progress through the tight-packed bodies. Focused as he was on Kathy, Howie still couldn't avoid hearing the many excited conversations among the Cedar Key residents there. By the time he finally forced his way into the open on the far side of the crowd, he knew the casino referendum had been lost.

"—her go, Daddy," Kathy was saying when Howie finally reached her. She was holding Mr. Dean's hands and looking at him tenderly, talking calm and quiet. Mr. Dean was searching the room with confusion in his eyes, barely aware that Kathy was even there. Desiree was nowhere in sight.

"But—a tattoo!" Mr. Dean mumbled. "And drinking, running around half-naked. Her mother—"

"Her mother," Kathy said sharply, and then repeated in that same gentle tone. "Our mother left us a long time ago. She left you a long time ago. Mom's not here any more, Daddy. And Desiree is not Mom."

That got Mr. Dean's attention. He stopped his mumbling and stared down at Kathy, jaw gone slack. "Of course she's not. I never—"

"Yes you did, Daddy. You did it all the time, every damn day. Maybe you figured it was too late for me, but you pushed poor Desiree to be just like Mom, or what Mom used to be, and every time she fell short of that you just dismissed her like a disobedient puppy. No wonder she's always been so afraid of doing anything. She was always trying to please you, and she knew she never could."

"I didn't," Mr. Dean said, but his voice had gone weak, and he looked completely deflated. "I never meant . . . I love Desiree, Kathy. And I love you too."

"I know, Daddy, I know." Kathy slipped into her father's arms. He held her tightly for a moment, and Howie could've sworn he saw just a little bit of moisture in the old grump's eyes.

"But," Mr. Dean added after a moment, "A *tattoo* . . ."

Kathy sighed and nuzzled tighter against her father's chest, a happy smile playing on her lips. "Oh Daddy," she said, "You are *such* an asshole."

Howie smiled, too, and quietly turned away. Much as he wanted to be with Kathy, he could see they needed a little time on their own right now. Fortunately, there was still plenty going on to keep him occupied.

No one had left the restaurant as far as Howie could tell, but people had gone back to their seats or charged the bar to clamor for drinks, so Howie had a clear view of the entire room again. The *Lara Lu* was gone, though whether it had sailed out of sight or simply ascended to heaven, Howie couldn't begin to guess. Stevie was still there though, glaring over at Tee Nichols while Ramsey Waller tried to tell him something about his Skyliner being sabotaged. Finally Stevie brushed Ramsey aside and stalked over to stand towering above the calmly sitting Tee.

"You think this will stop me?" Stevie said. Howie recognized the razor tone in his voice and hurried over to join them.

"Naw," Tee said in that maddening lazy way of his. "But I figure it's like the barbed wire they wrapped around the banister to keep grandma from sliding on it—don't stop her, but it sure as hell slows her down."

"You think this is all a joke, don't you?" Stevie hissed. "The referendum—"

"You've lost the referendum, Stevie. You gotta know that." Tee glanced at the empty bottle in his hand, frowned, and reached over to a nearby table for a near-full longneck someone had left behind in all the excitement.

"I'll have another referendum. I can do that."

"Not for a year. That's what the city charter says." That was the reporter girl, that Robin Chanterelles. She had her reporter pad out, Howie saw, but she wasn't writing in it just yet.

"A whole year, Stevie," Tee chimed in. "Even you can't afford to keep all those ringers on your payroll for another year."

"It's Stephen, damn it. And my partners can afford it." Stevie threw a quick glance to where Mr. Black was standing behind him, and Howie wondered if "partners" was really the right word to use here.

"They can afford the money," the reporter girl, that Robin Chanterelles, said. "But can they handle the press? Amalgamated Omnivore has never been too fond of publicity."

Howie had never heard that name before, but it was clear Stevie had. And Mr. Black too—he shifted his gaze from Stevie to Robin, watching her like he was trying to read a poker player he'd never seen before. The reporter met his eyes and stared right back. Mr. Black was the one who looked away first, and Howie could have swore he backed up a step.

"Publicity hasn't hurt us yet," Stevie said.

"I'm not talking about bullshit monster stories in a bullshit tabloid," Chanterelles said. "I'm talking about a deliberate attempt to circumvent the election laws of a city and county. I'm talking about recklessly saturating the floors and walls of a leased building with accelerants to ensure it would burn like matchsticks. I'm talking about"—her eyes flickered from Stevie to Mr. Black and back—"I'm talking about a major multi-national corporation conspiring to circumvent the environmental and electoral laws of the state of Florida, in pursuit of a few quick bucks."

Stevie glared wild-eyed from Chanterelles to Black and back again. "You're bluffing," he said. "You're crazy. You're a disgraced, drunken whore shilling for a disreputable supermarket tabloid. Who's going to print anything you write?"

"The *Apalachicola Sun*," Chanterelles said proudly. "And after they see the *Sun*, the Associated Press. After that, every newspaper in Florida. Who knows? With Omnivore involved, it might just go national."

Stevie glared down at Chanterelles like he might

blow an artery, his mouth flapping open and closed like a grounded grouper. Finally he turned to get support from Mr. Black—but Mr. Black was gone.

"Aw hell, Stevie," Tee Nichols said, in what seemed to be sympathy more than mockery. "It's only money."

That was it for Stevie. He let out an animal scream, picked up a heavy wooden chair from the nearest table, and spun around, ready to bring it crashing down on his enemies. The reporter lady hit the floor, Tee didn't even flinch—and Howie McCracken stepped in, grabbed his brother by both wrists and held him there.

"Enough now, Stevie," Howie said, surprised by the determination in his own voice. "That's enough."

It seemed like they stood like that for a long, long time, arms locked, Stevie growling at him practically nose to nose. Howie was surprised how much stronger he was than Stevie—stupid, really, since he outweighed his brother by a good thirty pounds and stood two inches taller. Eventually, Howie felt the tension in Stevie's arms relax, and saw sanity return to his eyes. He took the chair from his brother and put it back down, watching Stevie all the time to see if he was going to go nuts again. Howie didn't think he would. All of the anger had leaked out of Stevie, and maybe all the fire too. He looked just about as deflated as Howie had ever seen him.

Seeing Stevie like that, vulnerable and, hell, *needy*, that was probably why it took Howie a moment to understand what happened next. There was a sudden bright flash, and Howie thought somebody had taken a picture. When the loud rumble came right after it, he thought instead that it was thunder, real close and real loud. But when he saw the look on the faces of Tee and the reporter lady, he knew it was something other than that. And when he saw the blood drain right out of Stevie's face, he suddenly had a pretty good idea what was going on. Something had exploded, something big, right outside.

And the Cedar Casino was on fire.

Chapter Twenty-four

Robin Chanterelles watched the blasted wreckage of the Cedar Casino burn and wondered whether she should be pissed off. She'd wanted the damn thing stopped, of course, but it seemed Red Luck and his dramatic lightshow had already accomplished that. This felt like overkill.

"You do this?" she asked Tee Nichols, knowing as she said it that this wasn't his style.

"Me? No." Tee shielded his eyes against the blaze with one hand and scratched at his beard with the other. "Nice touch, though."

Tee and Robin were among the hundred or so people watching Stevie McCracken's dream go up in flames from the opposite side of A Street. More people watched through the windows of the Seabreeze, but those seemed to be mostly tourists. As far as Robin could tell, the people who dared to get this close to the fire were mostly locals. Tee and Stevie, of course, but also Turtle, and Chigger, The Chipmunk, Anna from the L&M, Madonna from Neptune's Lounge, Johnny Fudge and lots of other shopkeepers she knew by sight if not name, plus plenty of folks she'd never seen but recognized as local by their sun-and-wind worn faces. Desiree Dean and her sister were there, too, their father standing between them with an arm draped protectively over each girl.

Stevie McCracken stood beside Tee, his murderous intentions of a few minutes before apparently forgotten by both men. He looked like he was in shock—moving slow, saying nothing. It was brother Howie who'd taken command in Stevie's mental absence, Howie who'd led the charge out of the Seabreeze and out onto Dock Street. Now Howie was loudly haranguing Turtle Thomas, who stood just the other side of Stevie.

"But you've gotta put it out!" Howie was shouting. "You're the goddamn chief of the goddamn fire department!"

"Yep," Turtle said calmly. "The *voluntary* fire department." Turtle rocked forward on the balls of his feet and spit something dark and juicy towards the flames. "Ain't volunteering to save a building that can't be saved."

Robin had to agree. Stevie's crew hadn't started putting up the casino walls yet, but they had built a spidery framework encompassing what was left of Mamasan's and the empty spots where Pimlico Phil's and the warehouse between the two had stood. That structure now glowed angry red against the night sky, a spider-web of flaming framing. If it wasn't a total loss yet, Robin figured, it would be soon.

The first segment to go, it appeared, had been the

towering crow's nest Stevie had vowed would guide boatloads of gamblers right to the casino's side. That didn't fit with the theory already circulating through the on-lookers that the *Lara Lu*'s scarlet spotlight had caused the blast, but Robin had covered enough fires to read the story in this wreckage. The tower had gone first, tumbled sideways, falling east to smash the casino's waterside framing and throw flaming debris all across the construction site, and then splash down in the dark Gulf. That was damned fortunate, Robin thought, or maybe damned good planning. If the tower had fallen westward, it would have crashed through the roof of the Seabreeze where she and so many others had been watching the Dean drama and the arrival of the *Lara Lu*. The fact the tower had tumbled in the safest direction possible said something about the sensibilities—and the skill—of whomever had set the charges.

Turtle spit flame-ward once again, and Tee sidled nonchalantly up beside him. "She's done, all right," he said thoughtfully. "Course, hate to see that fire spread to any of these other buildings."

Turtle looked down at Tee from his six-foot-several viewpoint and nodded. He stuck two fingers in his mouth, let out a piercing whistle, and loped off towards the fire department. Robin saw half a dozen other people take off after him.

Stevie saw them too, but it didn't cheer him any. "Doesn't matter," he said bitterly. "It's too late."

"Aw Stevie," Tee said, "Don't look at it that way. Look at it as a new beginning."

"A new beginning."

"A clean slate, a chance to start up something new and better."

"Sure," Robin chimed in. "Surely you've got that place insured all to hell. You've got a nice fat check coming to you."

"She's right, Stevie," Howie added. "We still got some of the money from the first fire, and now we got all this coming. Once the check comes in, you can do any damn thing you want to."

Stevie looked up at Howie, slowly coming out of his deep dark funk. The three of them had him all but surrounded, Robin thought, as if they were trying to protect him from the sight of his building burning. Odd, she thought, but what the hell. As villains go, Stevie McCracken didn't really seem to be that bad a guy.

"Anything I want . . ." Stevie whispered.

"Sure," Robin said. "Build yourself a great big mansion and retire."

"Or," Tee said, "Sell the great big mansion you've already got and get the hell out of Cedar Key."

"Or," Howie said, "Stay right here where you belong and try something new." When Stevie didn't respond to that, Howie leaned in a little closer to him and said in a voice that wavered only a little, "Cause remember, Stephen, half that money is mine."

That last one got Stevie's attention. He looked up at his baby brother like he was seeing Howie for the first time. He raised his hand in a half-threat, started to say something, then stopped and let his arm drop back to his side. After a moment: "Something new?" he said.

"Something new," Howie answered. "Echo-tourism."

"Ecotourism," Robin corrected automatically.

"Yeah, right, ecotourism. Kathy's been telling me all about it. That's what she studies in college. That and developmental child care." Howie stumbled a little over "developmental" and Stevie gave him another wondering look, but Howie plunged on. "What we do, see," he said, "We rebuild the docks the way they was before we took 'em over, only with bigger slips, for the tour boats."

"Tour boats."

"Right. Echotours. We get two or three flatboats that'll hold fifteen, twenty people each, and run regular tours. Take people out to the factory ruins on Atsena Otie, to the lighthouse on Seahorse Key, or shell collecting on North Key and Rattlesnake. Maybe run dolphin and manatee feeding trips."

"Can't do that," Tee said. "Gets the dolphins thinking people are good for 'em. And it's eco-tourism."

"Okay, no dolphins," Howie conceded. "But we do dinner tours out to see the sunset, and maybe whole-day trips down to Homosassa and Crystal River. We get the Seabreeze or Frog's or any one of those places to cook up lunches, and my Mamasan's girls do the serving."

"Lots of out-of-work fishermen around here to be mates and captains," Tee added.

"Sure. Maybe even we could do some fishing charters too."

"You could rent canoes and kayaks," Robin chimed in.

"Run some bird-watching tours back to the bayous," Tee said.

"Sure, lotsa birds," Howie said. "And we do it all"—Howie waved one arm toward the burning casino, pointing out something no one else could see—"from our brand new office, right there beside the gift shop and sea museum."

"Gift shop . . ." Stevie said. He was looking at Howie dubiously, but Robin could see the wheels in his mind starting to turn.

"And sea museum," Howie finished. "We sell sharks teeth and sea shells and shit, and the museum could have like aquariums, and pictures of fish people caught around here, and sponges and stuffed fish and stuff. We could charge a dollar or two to get in." Howie paused just a beat before plunging on. "And before you know it, Sarah will be able to sit there taking tickets. She *will*, Stevie," Howie said, cutting off Stevie's protest. "She will, you wait and see."

"Be a hell of a thing, Stevie," Tee said. "A hell of a thing."

"It's Stephen," Stevie said distractedly, and then, after a moment's pause, "Maybe a snack bar. Something simple but high-volume, to sell drinks and sandwiches to the people going out on the tour boats."

"Sure, Stevie, sure, whatever you want. Now look here," Howie draped an arm over Stevie's shoulder and turned him parallel to the fire, walking away from the Gulf. "Kathy says maybe we could . . ."

Robin watched the two brothers walk slowly down A Street, flames to their side and dreams before them. "'Use what we got, without destroying anything,'" she quoted.

"Uh-huh," Tee said. "Hey, are we still on your newspaper tab? Cause I need a beer."

"Now that," Pambellina said, facing landward and speaking loud enough to be heard over the slap of waves against her repaired dingy, "That is an A-Number-One World-Class fire."

"Not bad, if I do say so myself," said the fat man in the middle seat. "The tower was a little tricky, but it worked out well enough."

"Fucking genius," Pincushion called out from the boat's stern. "Pimlico Phil is a fucking genius."

"Nothing any one with a few years of U.S. Navy demolition training couldn't do," Phil said. He used the oar in his right hand to turn the dingy broadside to the conflagration lighting the shore across the main channel, so all three could watch without twisting around. "It certainly helped that I had the proper materials to work with."

"One good thing about being a pirate," Pambellina said. "The hours are weird and the pay sucks, but you make all kinds of useful contacts."

"Indeed," Phil said, behind him Pincushion echoed with an "indeed" of his own. They watched the fire for a few moments in silence, waiting patiently for Dr. B and the *Sailcat's Revenge* to arrive and tow them home.

"Funny," Pambellina said after a bit. "But in a way, I hate to see the place go."

"Really?" Phil said. "I thought—"

"Don't get me wrong, I hated that place and what it was gonna do to Cedar Key as much as anybody. But still," she let out a long sigh before finishing. "See, Desiree told me they were gonna hire dancers. I always wanted to be a dancer." Pincushion let out a short laugh at that, and Pambellina glared at him over Phil's shoulder. "What, you don't think I can dance?"

"You too skinny," Pincushion laughed.

"Am not!"

"What our colorful friend means," Phil interrupted, "Is that you might not have, ah, exactly the qualifications for the sort of dancing they had in mind."

"You mean titties," Pambellina translated. "Hey, there's a lot more to titty dancing than having big titties."

"Is not," Pincushion said. He winced and added a "hey!" when Phil poked the butt end of an oar in his side.

"I can dance," Pambellina insisted. "I can dance damn good. Phil, you give me a little tune, give me some dancing music." She stood up and climbed to a precarious perch atop the dinghy's bow seat; after a moment's hesitation, Phil started a wordless ba-da-da-daa, ta da-da-daa rendition of the stripper's theme. Pambellina caught the tune, swinging her slender hips in time with Phil's song and the gentle sway of the dingy beneath her feet. Pincushion joined in, slapping out a steady beat against the boat's side, and after a minute Pambellina really let herself go.

The moon provided a spotlight, the prophet and the painted man kept the beat, and the smiling elf danced by firelight on the surface of the shimmering sea.

Chapter Twenty-five

Robin hardly even flinched when the third golf ball smacked into Tee's tin roof. She sat quietly beside Tee on the stoop of his front porch, tracing the ball's progress by sound. The moonlight was just bright enough for her to catch a glimpse of something small and white skipping off the edge of the roof to land in the brush beside the house.

"Got it," she said. "Right there beside the yaupon tree."

"Uh-huh," Tee answered. "That'll be an easy one to find." He tossed an empty beer can towards the yaupon tree—"To mark the spot," he said—and took another sip off the fresh one in his right hand. Robin was working on a beer of her own, several empties were stacked in a small pyramid before her. Two more lay overturned inside the porch, thrown there when Robin thought she had seen Tee's killer skink stalking about. The night's excitement had pretty much quieted down, though the rhythmic flicker of red light over the town center suggested that Turtle and his crew were still at work hosing down the smoldering ruins.

It occurred to Robin that she should be getting eaten up by mosquitoes, but she hadn't suffered a single bite. Maybe her skin had toughened up enough to discourage them, or maybe it was because she was sitting within Tee's protective aura. Tee himself was bite-free, of course, and was busying himself by scratching sand from between his toes with a small square of white paper.

"What you got there, Tee?" Robin asked.

Tee stopped his scratching and looked at the paper a moment before going back to work. "It's a business card," he said. "Desiree's daddy gave it to me. Said if we had any legal troubles with Stevie, or with that Mr. Black guy, to let him know."

"Nice of him."

"I guess, though I think mostly he did it to please Desiree. Still, I'm thinking the next time I get hit with one of those public nudity charges I'll give him a call."

"Public nudity?"

"Yeah. And of course he told me to let him know if Desiree tries to get any more tattoos."

Robin smiled a bit at that. "I guess that means she's not going back up to Ohio with him?"

"Guess not," Tee said. "She said something about moving back in here, but only if I'll get her a bigger bed."

"A bigger bed?"

"A double, she said. I figure it'll be worth it."

"You mean worth it so you can watch her shower again."

"Something like that."

"Right, something like that." Robin took a pull off her beer and listened to the scratchy serenade of the night's crickets. "You know," she said after a bit, "I was surprised she still had that tattoo. Pincushion said it had been burned right off her breast in the first fire."

"Different breast. New tattoo."

"Oh yeah? Have you seen it yet?"

"The breast?"

"The tattoo."

"Oh, yeah." Tee sipped on his beer, making Robin wait for the description he had to know she wanted. Finally, "It's a manatee," he said.

"A manatee?"

"Cute little thing, about the size of your thumb. Got a trail of bubbles coming out behind her butt."

"Bubbles? You mean Desiree has a farting manatee tattooed on her tit?"

"Yep."

"Huh."

"Yep." They drank in companionable silence for a bit. Robin finished off her beer and carefully stacked it atop the pyramid, which was more difficult than it should have been. Getting drunk, she thought.

"Hey Tee," she said after a bit. "Who's Sarah?"

"Sarah? That's Stevie's little girl. Sweet kid."

"But medical problems?"

"Sweet kid," Tee said again. "You want another?"

Tee reached into the porch behind them, where several more Buds were floating in a tin bucket of ice and cold water.

"I guess not," Robin said, though of course she did. "Gotta get up early tomorrow afternoon and write this story."

"Shit, girl, you know you could write this one in your sleep."

"Probably could. God knows I've done it before. But I want this one to be particularly good, since it's the last one *The Alarm* will ever get from me."

"Quitting journalism?" Tee said it like he didn't believe it.

"No, just quitting *The Alarm*."

"Why's that?"

"Because it's bullshit, Tee. Absolute bullshit." Robin slapped away a can at the base of the pyramid, just to see it fall. The clanking cans got a neighborhood dog barking; she waited for him to calm down before saying anything more. Finally, "There's enough bullshit in the world without me adding to it," she said.

"That boss of yours ain't gonna like you leaving."

"True," Robin said, grinning in the moonlight. "One more good reason to do it."

Tee raised his beer in tribute; Robin acknowledged it with a nod of her head. "So what you gonna do then?" Tee asked.

"I'm thinking I'll head up to Apalach and see if I can get my old job at *The Sun* back."

"Getting back in the game, eh?"

"If he'll have me."

"Thought you'd given up on saving the world."

"I have," Robin said. She took a long look around Tee's tangled yard, loving the way the moonlight added a touch of magic and mystery to the wild growth all around her. "Still," she said, "I guess maybe there's still a few places worth fighting for."

"And people. And ideas."

"And people and ideas."

Tee cracked open another beer and handed it to Robin, she took it and knocked back about a third of it before remembering she wasn't having any more. What the hell, she thought. "So, Tee," she said. "What are you going to do now?"

"Do?" Tee said, sounding confused.

"Yeah, do. The excitement's all over, the town is saved, the girl rescued. So, what will you do now?"

"Oh, right," Tee said. He rested both his bony elbows on the porch step behind him, leaned back and stretched his legs out in the grass. "Robin, honey," he said. "I don't have to *do* anything. I'm *home*."

Well, Robin thought. *Well, of course.* She raised her beer high and drained it all in one long sweet gulp. Then she twisted around on one knee to straddle Tee right at the waist, took his head in her hands and kissed him right on the mouth. She felt his surprise, but he relaxed quickly and kissed her right back, passionate but gentle. After a bit he lifted his hands and settled them on her rear end, and Robin let them stay there, because, what the hell. That moment went on for a long pleasant time before Robin pulled back, gave Tee one more quick kiss on the forehead, and rose to her feet.

"See ya, Tee," she said.

"Yep. See ya."

Robin passed out of Tee's yard and turned right, heading toward the Gulf and the moonlight. Behind her she heard the happy "choosh" of Tee opening himself one more beer. She reached towards her shirt pocket for a cigarette, then stopped and put it back. A cigarette would taste just as good the next day, or maybe even the day after that, but right now she had the taste of Tee's lips in her mouth. He tasted like cold beer and salty sea air, like whiskers and laughter and key lime fudge.

He tasted like Cedar Key, and Robin wanted that flavor to linger for a long, long time.

Bestselling murder and mayhem from Pocket Books.

The Frumious Bandersnatch
A Novel of the 87th Precinct
Ed McBain
When a rising rap star is kidnapped, can the detectives of the 87th Precinct find her before her star is extinguished forever?

Vespers
A Novel of the 87th Precinct
Ed McBain
It will take more than a leap of faith for the cops of the 87th Precinct to solve a priest's vicious murder.

Something's Down There
Mickey Spillane
You're not retired until you're dead.

The Mesa Conspiracy
A Department Thirty Novel
David Kent
A dying woman's last words reveal a secret with the power to shatter lives and change the course of the United States government.

Available wherever books are sold.